"You're pregnant, aren't you?"

All her fears concerning what would happen if Conner learned about the baby seemed to float at the forefront of Delaney's mind. The possible custody battles, the difficulty of sharing a child, her worry that he might not be the best influence, considering what she'd heard about his reputation...

She didn't want to do anything that would risk the security of her baby's future. But the truth was the truth. She couldn't get around it anymore. She'd cheated him, and her sense of justice demanded she admit it.

"Yes," she said.

He gulped air into his lungs as though she'd slugged him, then jammed his hands into his pockets and whirled toward the door. Delaney thought he was going to walk out on her without another word, but after two steps he turned back. "You did it on purpose," he said. "You *meant* to get pregnant. That's what you had in mind from the very beginning."

The loathing in his voice hurt even more than Delaney had imagined it would. "Yes."

"And what the hell do you hope to gain from it?"

"Nothing. I just want the baby. That's all I've ever wanted."

"Yeah, right," he said, and strode out. Then silence fell. But the peace was gone.

Dear Reader,

When I set out to write A Baby of Her Own, I planned to play with the "what if" concept of having my heroine do something most of us would never do, something that could change her whole life, something she might easily regret beyond any other action. I was interested in the emotions she'd face and how she'd deal with the consequences.

But as I got to know Delaney, the heroine, and Rebecca, her best friend, their opposite natures intrigued me. I found they had quite a bit to say about choices and maturation, friendship and unconditional love. Rebecca is probably one of the most imperfect "good" characters I've ever worked with—a real loose cannon—yet I love her as much as Delaney and would gladly claim either as my best friend, if I had the chance. I hope that by the time you finish this story, you'll feel the same. And I hope that you'll watch for Rebecca's story, coming from Superromance in 2003. (Watch for my Harlequin single title, too! Taking the Heat will appear on your bookseller's shelves in February 2003.)

I love to hear from readers. Please feel free to visit me online at www.brendanovak.com or send me a note— P.O. Box 3781, Citrus Heights, CA 95611.

Here's wishing you the unconditional love we all crave!

Brenda Novak

Books by Brenda Novak

HARLEQUIN SUPERROMANCE
  899—EXPECTATIONS
  939—SNOW BABY
  955—BABY BUSINESS
  987—DEAR MAGGIE
1021—WE SAW MOMMY KISSING SANTA CLAUS
1058—SHOOTING THE MOON

A Baby of Her Own
Brenda Novak

HARLEQUIN®

TORONTO • NEW YORK • LONDON
AMSTERDAM • PARIS • SYDNEY • HAMBURG
STOCKHOLM • ATHENS • TOKYO • MILAN • MADRID
PRAGUE • WARSAW • BUDAPEST • AUCKLAND

ISBN 0-373-71083-6

A BABY OF HER OWN

To my second-oldest daughter, Megan, for her strength
of spirit, her leadership ability and her constancy.
Meg, you're a light to everyone who knows you,
someone capable of great things because at twelve years
old you've already learned the power of self-discipline.
I can always depend on you to choose the right and
stay the course, and that has been an incredible blessing.
If you forget everything else I've ever taught you,
remember this: my love is everlasting.

CHAPTER ONE

"ARTIFICIAL INSEMINATION. Of course! That's the answer."

Delaney Lawson almost choked on her drink. Swallowing hard, she sent a quick glance around the redneck bar that was the center of Dundee, Idaho's weekend entertainment to see who might have overheard, then lowered her voice. "I hope you're talking about breeding horses, Beck."

Rebecca Sparks, her friend and housemate, didn't look the least bit abashed. "You know I'm not talking about horses. I'm talking about you," she responded, fiddling with her new short haircut. "Because of what you said last night."

Delaney grimaced. "Forget about last night. Buddy had just told me that the two of you are getting married, that you're going to be leaving the state in five months. *And* it was my thirtieth birthday. I had a right to be depressed."

"I was planning to tell you *after* your birthday."

"Oh, well, what are big, dumb guys for?"

"I can think of several uses for Buddy. But you weren't upset about my engagement or your birthday. You were depressed because you can't find anyone to love, and Aunt Millie and everyone else in this godforsaken town is asking when you're going to get married. And because—more than anything—you want a baby."

"I was depressed because you're marrying a man you

met on the Internet, a guy you've seen only once, and I'm turning thirty without the prospect of a family in sight. It's all those things," Delaney insisted. "Besides, Valentine's Day is in a couple of weeks, which doesn't help."

Someone started the jukebox and Rebecca looked away. Delaney knew she didn't like displays of emotion. Rebecca expressed herself with sarcasm and laughter, not words like *I love you* and *I'm going to miss you.* But Delaney understood how deeply she cared, and returned those feelings. They'd been part of each other's lives for twenty-four years.

"I'll come back and visit every chance I get, you know that," Rebecca said after a long silence.

"I know," Delaney told her. "I'll be okay. I mean, we're adults. We have lives to lead. I just hope Buddy turns out to be everything you think he is."

"Buddy will drive me crazy, like he did yesterday when he let the cat out of the bag early—but we fit, you know?"

Delaney nodded, even though she wasn't sure she agreed. Physically they were opposites—Buddy short, round and dark; Rebecca tall, thin and dishwater blond when her hair wasn't colored something more trendy—but it was the differences in their personalities that worried Delaney. From what she could gather, Buddy seemed nice, but he was also quiet, steady and ploddingly predictable. She couldn't see her volatile friend settling for a couch potato. Or maybe that was exactly what Rebecca needed. Maybe Buddy's easygoing nature would temper Rebecca's high spirits and they'd reach some common ground and live happily ever after. Delaney certainly hoped it would end that way.

"You'll find someone," Rebecca said, but her words rang hollow to Delaney, who was running out of patience.

She'd wanted to get married for several years now and she felt as if she couldn't wait another day.

"Maybe."

"There's still plenty of time to have kids," Rebecca cajoled.

"Not if the next ten years go like the last. As much as I love the people around here, I don't really *belong* to any of them. But you probably can't understand what it's like to feel so detached. You grew up in a family with three older sisters—"

"Who I want to choke most the time," she interrupted, stirring her gin and tonic with one long fingernail.

"Still, you're connected. You're blood. You get together for holidays and stuff that wouldn't be the same if any of you weren't there. My mother died shortly after we moved here. I don't know who my father is—even my mother didn't know that. And I was raised by Dundee's own Mother Teresa. Aunt Millie would've taken in and loved any child." She sighed wearily. "I've been wanting a family of my own since forever, but it looks like I'm going to die an old maid."

Rebecca licked her wet finger and leaned back to light a cigarette. "Then, do something about it," she said on a long exhalation. "Get artificially inseminated."

"Not so loud," Delaney whispered. "We live in a small town, for heaven's sake. This isn't New York or L.A. And we grew up here. Everyone knows us. I don't want word getting out that I'm considering something so...radical. It could embarrass Aunt Millie and Uncle Ralph, make them regret they ever took me in."

"I knew it!" Rebecca clapped her hands, although she did it carefully so she wouldn't crush her cigarette.

"What?" Delaney asked, exasperated.

"That you've been thinking about having a baby on your own!"

"And how did you know that?"

"I've seen you stare at the parenting magazines we pass in the grocery store. I've seen how you admire every child you come across."

"Maybe I have been thinking about it," she said. "But I don't believe that doing things the artificial way will work."

"Why not?" Rebecca squinted at her through the thin stream of smoke curling toward the ceiling.

"First of all, it's expensive and my insurance won't cover it. Librarians in a town of fifteen hundred people only make so much. And now that you're going to be moving out, my house payment will double. Aunt Millie needs a few things, too, like another coat of paint on her place. Second, I wouldn't even know where to find the right doctor. We only have a general practitioner around here, and I'm sure it would take some sort of specialist. Finally, I probably wouldn't qualify. Don't you have to be married? Or at least infertile?"

Delaney cast another furtive glance at the Honky Tonk's fellow patrons. The divorced Mary Thornton, who'd been captain of the cheer squad in high school, sat with her crowd in the corner, but the place hadn't filled up yet. Elton John was singing "Rocket Man" on the jukebox. He competed with the clack of balls coming from the direction of the pool tables, a television droning in the corner and Rusty Schultz at the bar, loudly detailing his frustration with a car engine he was trying to rebuild. "In any case," she finished, sitting back to avoid Rebecca's secondhand smoke. "I'm sure they don't give sperm away to just any woman who happens to want it."

"*They* might not, but I know a lot of men who would."

A devilish smile curled Rebecca's ~~~~ end of her cigarette on a small tin as~~~~ yourself laid and be done with it?''

"Rebecca!"

Her friend held up the hand with the ciga~~~~ nails gleaming even in the dim light. "Con~~~~ what about all those assertiveness training classes yo~~ ve been taking online? You're always telling me your instructor says to take charge of your life, decide what you want and make it happen.''

"I don't think my instructor had something like this in mind."

"Well, it applies, and getting pregnant wouldn't be that difficult. First of all, a willing partner would be free,'' she said, ticking the points off on her fingers as Delaney had just done. "So you can afford the mortgage and still get Aunt Millie's house painted this spring. Second, you wouldn't have as much trouble finding a donor as you would the right doctor. Can you imagine approaching Dr. Hatcher for a recommendation?'' She took a long drag on her cigarette, then set it aside to smolder. "And three, if you're picking up some guy at a bar, it's better if you're *not* married.''

Delaney tried to appear scandalized, but immediately gave up the charade. This was Rebecca; knowing her was the closest she'd ever come to having a sister. And as low as Delaney thought tricking a man would be, she was actually getting desperate enough to consider it. "It just seems so…dishonest. Almost like stealing.''

"It's not stealing if he *gives* you what you want,'' Rebecca said, reclaiming her cigarette.

"Maybe, but I keep coming back to—''

"Your morals. I know.'' Rebecca angled her head so she

exhale in Delaney's face. "You've always had a
too many."

Delaney propped her chin in her hand and stared glumly
at the glassy-eyed elk head hanging on the opposite wall.
"I've had a lot of people to answer to. And not only Aunt
Millie and Uncle Ralph. What about old Mrs. Shipley? She
taught me everything I know about the library, groomed
me to take her place. And Mr. Isaacs on the city council
put in a good word for me last review, which helped me
get a raise. Mrs. Minike volunteers countless hours at the
library—"

"And you've hired her daughter to help out part-time."

"Shelving books for minimum wage." She rolled her
eyes. "I'm just saying it isn't easy feeling obligated to a
whole town. And with gossips being what they are—"

"Don't worry about gossip. I don't."

"Much to your parents' mortification, I might add. Your
father is mayor of this town. I'm sure he'd appreciate a
little more discretion."

Rebecca shrugged. "He's been in office so long, it would
take a crowbar to get him out. No one even bothers to run
against him anymore. Besides, ever since I took off with
that motorcycle gang, the old ladies in this town sort of
lost interest in me. Now when people mention my name,
the most they get is a halfhearted response like, 'Oh, yeah?
What's that Sparks girl up to now? She always was a handful.' I guess I've already provided my share of the town's
entertainment. They're eager for someone else to relieve
the tedium, and I think it's your turn."

"My *turn?*" Delaney asked wryly.

"Yeah, the only controversial thing about you is your
strange name. That raised a few eyebrows when you first
came to town. I still remember old Mrs. Hitchcock shaking
her head and wanting to know what your mama could've

been thinking. But you moved here when you were six, so we've had twenty-four years to get used to it, and it's time for something new. I mean, look at you. You were a quiet, obedient child. You always got good grades. When we were teenagers, you won the baking contest at the county fair four years running, and you placed in the barrel racing, too. And now everyone stops by the house on Sundays to buy your pies, and when they walk away they say, 'That Delaney's just about the sweetest thing. I wonder when she's gonna get married.' Only there's no one here to marry.''

"Most people would say there's always Josh Hill,'' Delaney said. "Or his brother.''

Rebecca stubbed out her cigarette. "You know how I feel about Josh Hill.''

"He's not that bad. I don't understand why you hate him so much.''

"I know him better than you do. Anyway, he's seeing Mary Thornton, and his brother's met someone from out of town. The Hill brothers aren't exactly available. Which leaves Billy Joe or Bobby West or Perry Paris.''

Delaney made a face. "Marrying one of them would be like marrying my brother.''

"Exactly the reason I'm marrying someone who lives in Nebraska.'' She folded her arms and leaned back. "That and the fact that he doesn't know me very well. But my point is this—you can continue to let the town hem you into being perfect and proper and lonely your whole life. Or you can exchange one night of naughtiness for a baby. It's up to you.''

"Isn't that simply changing passive behavior for aggressive behavior? My goal is *assertive* behavior. Assertive behavior promotes 'win-win' solutions,'' Delaney said, parroting her online coach.

"What's a donor got to lose? I think most men would see hooking up with you as a win-win situation."

Delaney took another sip of her margarita, savoring the salty taste and letting the ice melt in her mouth before swallowing. Every assertiveness assessment she'd ever taken had shown her as far too passive. She lived to please others, feared losing their esteem if she acted out or made a mistake. Maybe Rebecca was right. Maybe, instead of taking what life gave her, she should take what she wanted from life.

She smiled, thinking that sounded very assertive. Her coach would be proud. "I'd get to choose the father, see what he looks like. That beats the artificial method."

"And getting pregnant the natural way is infinitely more fun than lying on your back in a sterile room where the only man within twenty yards is wearing a mask and surgical gloves, right? It's been a long time since you were with a man. Don't you miss it?"

Delaney quickly nodded. "Oh, yeah. Of course I do," she said, but what she missed was having someone to love. Someone who'd love her, too. The physical aspect was nice—frosting on the cake, so to speak—but it meant nothing without love.

"When's the last time you made love?" Rebecca asked.

"There was…you know, that one boy I told you about before," Delaney said, trying not to fidget. "The one who came to stay with Mrs. Telfer the summer we turned seventeen."

"Booker Robinson? He was a little bastard, wasn't he? His parents sent him to the country to learn about hard work and manners because he was getting into too much trouble in the city, and he turned this town on its ear in less than a month." She smiled wistfully as though she had rather liked Booker and didn't think him a bastard at all. "That was the *first* time you were with a boy, but it wasn't the *last*, was it?''

''Um, of course not. There was…um, Tim Downey, you know, on prom night.''

''And?''

''And what?''

''That's it?''

''Isn't that enough?'' Delaney asked.

''That's pretty pathetic for a thirty-year-old.''

Not for the daughter of a woman who rambled from town to town and changed men almost as often as she bought shoes. Maybe Delaney had gone to the opposite extreme, but at least she wasn't like her mother. ''I've been saving myself.''

''For spinsterhood. Great.'' Rebecca finished her gin and tonic, ordered another one, and had the grace to wait until Maxine, the bar's only waitress, headed back to the kitchen before adding, ''Now I know why an illegitimate baby coming from you is going to scandalize the whole town.''

Something in Delaney's face must have revealed her alarm at this idea because Rebecca added, ''But they'll get used to it.''

Delaney started wringing her hands. ''You think so?''

''Sure. Look at how Millie and Ralph took you in and everyone in town's adored you from day one. They'll gossip and fuss and be amazed but, bottom line, they'll secretly thank you for the juicy controversy and eagerly await the baby.''

The people of Dundee had been good to her. Delaney didn't want to repay them by setting a bad example for the town's youth, but Rebecca made getting pregnant sound so simple. *One night in exchange for a baby.* Delaney's *own* baby. Someone to care for, someone to love. Someone to teach and to guide. Surely Dundee could forgive her one small indiscretion.

She moved closer. "If I do this, and happen to find…you know, someone who's right, how do I know he won't have AIDS or some other STD?"

Rebecca laughed. "Out here? In Idaho?"

"AIDS is everywhere," Delaney said defensively.

"Well, your chances of getting an STD out here are pretty slim compared to most other places," Rebecca said. "But I guess there's no guarantee. The whole plan depends on a certain element of spontaneity, so you can't exactly drag your target down to some clinic, right? All you can do is ask if he's been tested and see whether you trust the answer."

The smell of onion rings lingered in the wake of Maxine, who smiled as she bustled past them with platters of food for Johnny Coker and his new wife, a few tables away. "Your drink's coming right up," she told Rebecca.

"No problem."

"What if he only practices safe sex?" Delaney asked when she thought Maxine was once again at a safe distance. "What good will a one-night stand do me if he uses a condom?"

"Probably more good than you think."

Delaney scowled at the sarcasm in her friend's voice. "Be serious."

"I am serious. When the time comes, you just tell the guy that you're on the pill, then get him so excited he forgets about everything else."

Right. She just had to get him excited, that was all. *A complete stranger!* "I've always considered myself a better person than to do something like this," she said so she wouldn't have to focus on the mental picture of what it might take to get a man worked up to the point of total forgetfulness.

"You *are* a good person. This isn't going to hurt anyone, Laney. It's just a one-night stand—something that happens all the time with millions of people. You'll go on your merry way, and he'll go on his. No big deal."

"What if I don't get pregnant?"

"Then you might want to consider artificial insemination or simply wait and hope for the right person. But if you time it correctly, chances are good that it'll work out."

Delaney rubbed her lip. "It's just one night. No big deal…"

"That's what I said. People do it all the time."

"It's not hurting anybody."

"What he doesn't know can't hurt him. It's not like you're ever going to go after him for child support or anything. And you'd take great care of the baby, right?"

The baby. *Her* baby. A longing so powerful she could hardly speak clamped down on Delaney's insides. "Of course I would."

"Then, that's what matters. So there's no problem."

"Right." Delaney stared at her glass, thinking maybe she'd drunk too much because this whole thing was actually starting to seem plausible. But she wasn't even finished her first margarita. "So who do I—you know?" she asked.

"Anyone with the right equipment," Rebecca responded. "Look around you. This place is filled with guys. Dexter's right over there. He's been trying to get lucky since the eighth grade."

"Dexter's been trying to get lucky since before that," Maxine announced, catching the tail end of the conversation as she appeared with Rebecca's drink. "I remember him sneaking into the girls' rest room at school and looking under the stalls at me when I was only in the fifth grade."

"Yeah, Dex has always been a little pervert," Rebecca agreed. She paid for her drink, and Maxine hurried off to collect her next order.

Delaney rolled her eyes. "Dex, Becky? That's the best you can do? He's dumber than a doornail—not the kind of genes I want to pass on to my baby. Besides, no one from around here is even a possibility. How much of a secret will it be if I sleep with Dex and then wind up pregnant?"

Rebecca frowned. "Maybe you should sleep with several guys in the next few weeks, just to create some confusion."

"No way!"

"I'm kidding," her friend said, laughing her deep smoker's laugh. "I think this is going to be hard enough for you to do the first time. Do-gooders typically don't lie well, and, let's face it, you don't have a lot of experience with the seducing end of it, either."

"Which is all the more reason we'll have to go out of town. Somewhere far away."

"How far?"

"California, at least. Isn't California the sex capital of the world?"

"That'll be expensive. What's wrong with Boise?"

"It's only a two-hour drive from here!"

"Exactly. It would save us plane fare, and it'd be just as good as going halfway across the country. Big-city valley people aren't interested in small up-country towns like ours. What are the odds of running into Joe Schmoe Donor from Boise out here in Dundee?"

Joe Schmoe Donor? Delaney liked the sound of that. Joe Schmoe created a generic, anonymous image, and *donor* carried with it the connotation of something freely given. She was only looking for a *donor*. Maybe she could do this, after all.

"We don't get Boise people up here very often," she mused.

"My point exactly. Boise is plenty far away. And even if you do run into your man later, here or anywhere else, he'll be none the wiser."

"He might suspect if I'm pregnant at the time."

"Why would he? Why would he assume he's the only one you've slept with? Heck, for all he knows you might've gotten married."

"O-ka-ay," Delaney said, drawing the word out and feeling more eager to trust Rebecca on this than she probably should. "I'll buy that."

"Good. So, are we going to do it?"

A gust of cold air and a few flakes of snow blew into the Honky Tonk along with Billy Joe and Bobby West. Although they were brothers, they didn't look much alike. Bobby was wiry and thin; Billy Joe was almost as big as a house. Like Rebecca, Delaney had known them since grade school. She'd grown up with the men in this town and doubted she'd suddenly find herself wildly attracted to one of them. If she waited for love to strike, she could spend the next fifty years alone.

"Okay," she said at last, straightening her spine. "We're going to do it."

"We are?" Rebecca's brows shot up.

"Definitely."

Her friend looked skeptical. "I don't believe you."

"Why? I can break the rules when I want to." Delaney nervously tucked her shoulder-length brown hair behind her ears. "I've just never wanted to before."

"Then, let's go." Rebecca stood, gathered her cigarettes and lighter and slung her purse over her shoulder.

"Tonight?" Delaney squeaked, terror seizing her heart and nearly sending her into cardiac arrest.

"Why not?"

"You haven't finished your drink."

"Considering our agenda, I think I'd better leave the rest, don't you?"

She started toward the door, but Delaney called her back. "Wait! I'm— I—I just need a couple of days to get used to the idea," she managed to say. "And…and…you talked about timing."

Rebecca propped one hand on her hip. "The timing is good. I know because we've been on the same cycle for the past few months."

"But—"

"That's what I thought," she said with an exaggerated sigh. Piling her things on the table, she scraped her chair across the wooden floor and sat down again.

"What?" Delaney demanded.

"You're not going to go through with this. It's just a dream."

"I'll do it!"

"No, you won't. We grew up two houses from each other. I've known you since I was seven, and you've never done anything wrong in your life. You're like…you're like Abraham Lincoln. Didn't he walk some ungodly distance to return a penny? The store clerk probably thought he was an idiot."

"I wouldn't walk very far to return a penny. I'd just leave an extra one the next time I was in."

Rebecca smacked the tabletop. "Ugh! See what I mean?"

The jukebox was playing one of Garth Brooks's older hits as Billy Joe and Bobby West ambled over. Standing at the table dressed entirely in denim and wearing a pair of silly good 'ol boy grins, they tipped their black felt cowboy hats when Delaney and Rebecca looked up, then dragged over two chairs from the next table.

"Howdy, ladies."

Delaney couldn't help it; she frowned when they sat down. She could spend the rest of her life throwing darts and playing pool with Billy Joe and Bobby, or she could go to Boise and do something about getting what she wanted most.

Summoning all her courage, she stood. "We were just leaving, boys."

They blinked at her in surprise—and so did Rebecca.

"Aw, come on," Billy Joe said. "We just got here."

"Are we going where I think we're going?" Rebecca asked uncertainly.

Delaney nodded, then prayed she wouldn't lose her nerve. One night. It would only take one man and one night, she told herself.

But there was another small problem. Delaney had stretched the truth a bit when it came to her sexual experience. When Booker Robinson had tried to get down her pants, she'd slugged him—probably the only aggressive act of her life. He'd been embarrassed about the black eye and had tried to take revenge by bragging that he'd gotten more than he had. Delaney hadn't bothered to contradict him. It helped her seem less different from the other girls at school, less alone. And on prom night, Tim Downey had gotten so drunk he'd passed out before he so much as kissed her good-night. She'd had to drive him home.

In fact, Delaney was still very much a virgin.

CHAPTER TWO

CONNER ARMSTRONG KNEW what fun was. He'd spent a good portion of his thirty-one years trying to destroy himself with good old-fashioned reckless living, but he doubted he was going to find any excitement here. That, of course, was why the old man had sent him to Boise. Clive Armstrong was trying to teach him a lesson, trying to force the illegitimate son of his adopted daughter to straighten up at last—and Conner figured the only way his grandfather thought he'd be successful was to remove all temptation.

He glanced around the small hotel bar, which was nearly empty, and frowned, figuring it just might work.

Hell, who was he kidding? It *had* to work. Conner had run out of second chances, and although he'd never admit it to Clive or anyone else, he secretly embraced the challenge his grandfather had placed before him. He was ready to grow up, deal with the past, move on. He'd been ready for some time, but old habits died hard.

A work-roughened man with big hands and a whiskery jaw came in through the street entrance. Shaking off the snow clinging to his hat and clothes, he settled at the bar next to Conner, then nodded. "You new in town?"

He was wearing a dirty pair of Wranglers, a red flannel shirt over long johns, and no coat. Because of his ruddy appearance and seeming indifference to the cold, Conner took him for a local.

"What gave me away?" Conner asked.

His new friend ordered a beer and pushed his cowboy hat back on his head. "You look like a city fella."

Shrewd dark eyes flicked over Conner's turtleneck sweater, his jeans, faded but clean, and his pristine leather hiking boots. "You come up to go skiing?"

"No." Conner considered telling him what he'd really come to Idaho to do, then decided against it. He hardly looked the type, and didn't want to get laughed out of town on his first night.

"Where ya from?"

"Napa Valley wine country."

"Where?"

For a moment, Conner had forgotten that he'd been relegated to the American equivalent of Siberia. "California," he said.

"That explains it."

"What?"

"You look like a Californian. Must be the tan."

Conner didn't have California to thank for the tan; he had his old UC Berkeley buddies, who'd just accompanied him to the Caribbean. But he wasn't *too* grateful, because he probably had his affiliation with those same people to thank for the lifestyle that had brought him to this point.

The cowboy downed half his beer, then wiped his foam mustache on his sleeve. "How long're you staying?"

"That depends on how long I last."

He chuckled. "Don't let the snow scare ya away."

Conner wasn't worried about the weather, miserable though it was. His family—his mother's *adopted* family—owned a three-million-dollar condo in Tahoe, so he'd been exposed to cold and snow, at least on occasion. It was the boredom he feared in Idaho, the lack of contact with the real world. From what he remembered, there weren't many people where he was going. In Dundee most folks were ranchers. They went to bed early, got up early, worked hard and rolled up the sidewalks on Sundays. How was he going to fit in there? How was he going to succeed?

His uncles, of course, were hoping, *betting,* he wouldn't.

"What do you do?" Conner asked to keep the conversation going.

The man told the bartender to bring him some chips and salsa. "I've done just about everything," he said. "Right now, I work for the county driving a plow."

Snow removal. That sounded exciting. Maybe he'd underestimated this place, Conner thought sarcastically.

"What about you?" his friend asked.

"I'm a dissolute heir to a great fortune," Conner told him, making himself into the joke he thought he was, even though he doubted he'd ever inherit a dime. His multimillionaire grandfather had no reason to give him anything— not when he had three sons and several *legitimate* grandchildren.

"A disso— what?" the man asked.

"A bum," Conner supplied.

The other man shrugged. "Least you're honest."

That was the one thing Conner had always been—painfully honest. But he didn't see it as a virtue. If only he could hide from the truth as well as his mother did, pretend the past had never occurred...

But he couldn't dwell on Vivian or Clive or anyone else. Idaho was a test to see if he really was the no-good, lazy individual his uncles claimed him to be. Could he beat his genetic legacy? Compete with the great Armstrongs? Only time would tell.

His cowboy friend started on the basket of chips, and Conner ordered another beer. He was almost finished with it and thinking about heading up to his room to see if hotels in Boise had Pay-Per-View, when the street door behind him opened again.

"Let's go somewhere else," a woman murmured. "There's hardly anyone here."

"It's getting late and it's storming. There's not going to be a big crowd anywhere," another female voice replied, this one more clearly. "Besides, hotel bars might not be the busiest in town, but you won't have to go anywhere to rent a room if you happen to get lucky."

Get lucky? Conner turned to see a tall redhead with a petite brunette. The redhead was saying something about the clientele of a hotel being transient and how perfect that was, but her words fell off the moment she noticed him.

"Omigod, there he is!" she cried.

Conner stiffened in surprise, wondering if the redhead thought she knew him from somewhere. Not very likely, he decided. He would have remembered her. This woman wasn't exactly the type to get lost in a crowd. Nearly six feet tall and bone-thin, she was dressed in a floor-length, fake leopard-skin coat, wore bright red lipstick, nail polish and high heels and had died her hair to match. She was mildly attractive despite all the fashion handicaps, but she certainly didn't look like anything he'd expected to find in Idaho.

She immediately started prying off the brunette's coat. Though the brunette obviously didn't want to relinquish it, she finally let go, probably hoping to save herself the humiliation of an all-out brawl.

At that point, Conner turned away. The redhead was sending him overtly interested looks, and he didn't want to be singled out by a woman who reminded him so much of Cruella De Vil. He had only one night in Boise, which made it pretty pointless to socialize. And he'd long since grown bored with easy women.

"I think someone's got her eye on you," his neighbor said with a chortle.

Conner shook his head and lifted his glass. "I'm not interested," he said, but then he caught a good look at the brunette in the mirror behind the bar and wasn't so sure. She had wide blue eyes, creamy white skin, a slightly upturned nose and a full bottom lip. Except for her eyes, which were striking because they were so light against the contrast of her dark hair, she wasn't stunningly attractive. But there was something about her that was wholesome, almost sweet, and it certainly had nothing to do with her dress.

Conner sucked air through his teeth in a silent whistle as he let his eyes wander lower. Dresses like that should be outlawed, he decided, noting that she'd already turned every male head in the place, including the cowboy's. Black, short and clingy, the skimpy number she had on left little to the imagination, and this woman definitely had the figure to pull it off. Conner couldn't help admiring her firm, trim shape and some of her softer curves—until he met her eyes in the mirror. Then she looked at him like a rabbit caught in his headlights, blushed and tried to reclaim her coat.

The redhead would have none of it. They moved across the room, where Conner could no longer hear what was being said, but some sort of argument ensued. The redhead rolled her eyes, and the way she kept glancing at him suggested he played some part in the conversation.

A prickling at the back of his neck told him it was time to go. He'd had his wild days. He'd put them behind him and was ready to find something more meaningful in life. But the distress on the brunette's face kept him in his seat. Most women who wore such revealing clothes *wanted* male attention. This one seemed completely out of her element.

Letting curiosity get the better of him, Conner decided to stick around for a few more minutes. He even ordered another beer. He could usually trust his instincts, and his instincts told him the excitement level in Idaho was about to spike.

DELANEY HAD NEVER BEEN more embarrassed. She wanted to cover the scandalous dress she'd borrowed from Rebecca's sister, drag Rebecca outside and head straight home, snowstorm or not. But now that they'd come this far, Rebecca wasn't about to let her off the hook.

"Why are we sitting way the hell over here?" she demanded when Delaney led them to a far corner table.

"Because I need a moment to collect myself."

"Collect yourself? Why? We just got here."

"I want to sit back and check out the scene, all right? Can I have some say over what happens tonight?"

"I guess." Rebecca conceded this small victory to Delaney by finally taking a seat, but that didn't stop her from looking over her shoulder every few seconds at the guy they'd spotted when they first came in.

"Would you quit being so obvious?" Delaney muttered. There were only twelve or fourteen other people in the whole place, mostly along the perimeter, but Delaney felt as if they were all staring at her. "You're drawing too much attention!"

"I'm not drawing attention. That dress is drawing attention. I'm just making sure our man doesn't go anywhere while you 'collect' yourself. He's *so* hot. He looks just like Hugh Jackman, don't you think? I love the way his hair curls above his collar."

The guy at the bar did look like Hugh Jackman. He had coffee-colored eyes and hair, with short sideburns. Plus high cheekbones, a narrow nose and square jaw. His body type seemed similar, too—all muscle and no fat. But that was half the problem. Why did Rebecca have to choose someone so intimidating?

"If you think he's so cute, you sleep with him," Delaney grumbled.

"I'm not the one who wants a baby," Rebecca reminded her. "At least, I'm not in any hurry."

Because Rebecca wasn't the one who'd been taken in but not legally adopted, who was going to be alone, who'd always been alone. "Well, I'm not ready for this," Delaney said. "We should've waited until tomorrow night or next week or—"

"Or never? You would've chickened out. I know you. You would've started thinking about how unfair it is not to be completely up front about your intentions and—"

"Because it *is* unfair."

"Except that it won't cost the guy you sleep with anything to make you the happiest woman on earth." Rebecca checked over her shoulder again. "Now, go talk to him."

Delaney's stomach plummeted to her knees. "Just like that?"

"Why not? What are you waiting for?"

A personality transplant. This just wasn't her. She'd never come on to a guy before. Which was probably why she'd die a virgin if she didn't make some changes soon, she told herself. Rebecca *had* managed to find a husband and *was* going to get married. Maybe she should take Rebecca's advice on this. But why did her friend have to choose a guy who looked like he could be Hugh Jackman's twin brother?

"He's at the bar," she told Rebecca. "A guy who sits at the bar is interested in serious drinking, not socializing. We'd better find someone else." But when Delaney surveyed the lounge, she realized how hopeless that would be.

Of the fourteen or so patrons, more than half were women. The men consisted of an elderly gentleman, a barrel-chested, bearded guy somewhere in his forties, two nerdy computer types who had their hair greased down and gave Delaney the creeps, and a redneck cowboy sitting next to the Hugh Jackman look-alike.

Rebecca cocked an eyebrow at her. ''If there's someone here you'd rather sleep with, go for it. But it looks to me like Hugh's our most eligible donor. He's only drinking a beer. That's hardly 'serious drinking.' And he seems friendly enough. He sort of smiled when we came in.''

''*Sort of* smiled? He ducked his head and turned away the second you zeroed in on him.''

''Well, he definitely smiled at us in the mirror afterward.''

Delaney didn't remember a smile. She remembered his eyes, though. They'd followed her, appraised her boldly.

''Go,'' Rebecca prodded. ''The worst that can happen is he tells you he's married. Then you politely excuse yourself and we try someone else.''

''I'm never going to get over this experience,'' Delaney moaned. ''I just know it.''

''Do you want a baby or not?''

She did. And she wanted to be pregnant before Rebecca left, so she'd have something positive to look forward to.

Taking a deep breath, she stood and forced herself to approach the bar. Better to get this over and done with, right?

She saw his gaze flick over her in the mirror, guessed he'd been expecting her—and felt like a complete fool. Especially since the guy sitting next to him was watching her far more eagerly, and she knew she wouldn't sleep with him if he was the last man on earth.

Relax. Pretend you're someone else, someone chic and bold and—she gulped—*easy.*

"Hi," she said, sliding onto the empty stool next to him. She'd been planning to order a drink to make her approach a little less obvious, but her timing wasn't good. The bartender had turned around and was busy fiddling with the television in the corner.

She glanced forlornly at his back, then braved a smile at the man she hoped would father her child.

He studied her for several seconds before responding. "Hi," he said, but he didn't return her smile or swivel toward her or do anything else to encourage her. It stung Delaney's pride enough to make her sit up and pretend confidence in what she was doing.

"You live around here?" she asked, keeping her focus strictly on him because the man in the red flannel shirt kept leaning forward to entice her with a battered grin. He might as well have been holding a sign that read "Take me," but Delaney simply wasn't interested. She'd do the artificial thing first.

"No, I'm just in town for the night," the younger man said. "What about you?"

Now that she was so close, she could tell his eyes weren't entirely brown. Gold flecks made them appear almost amber, and there was something inside them that seemed more worldly wise than Delaney would have expected for a man who seemed to be about her own age. After only a few seconds in his company, he reminded her much less of Hugh Jackman. He didn't possess the same relaxed smile or laid-back attitude. This man came across as intense, shrewd, even unforgiving, which added significantly to Delaney's anxiety.

I don't have to worry about his ability to forgive. I'm never going to see him again.

His eyes fell to the cleavage revealed by her dress, and she instinctively moved to cover herself. Rebecca had insisted she go without underwear—there wasn't any way to hide the lines and straps beneath the stretchy fabric—but the lack of her most basic apparel made her feel completely exposed. Leaning forward, she folded her arms on the bar and hid her chest behind them, just as Rebecca came to her rescue by engaging the leering cowboy and drawing him away to their table.

"I live a couple of hours from here," she responded automatically, then wanted to kick herself for being so truthful. The less he knew about her the better.

"Oh, really? Where?" Unless it was her imagination, his voice revealed a spark of interest.

"Jerome," she lied, picking a town on the opposite side of Boise.

"Oh."

The spark died, and an awkward silence followed, during which Delaney curled her fingers into her palms and thought of all the ways she planned to torture Rebecca for pushing her into this. She was going to tell Buddy that Rebecca had a snoring problem. She was going to hold Rebecca to her promise to quit smoking, starting immediately. She was going to unscrew the lid on their salt shaker and—and what? Delaney couldn't think of anything terrible enough, not while she was feeling like such a fool, but she knew Rebecca deserved whatever she came up with. If not for her, Delaney would be safe at home dreaming about a baby…and doing absolutely nothing to make it a reality.

That thought sobered her enough to keep her where she was. *One night, one man, remember? No big deal.*

"What can I get for you?" the bartender asked, finally making his way over.

Delaney ordered a club soda and opened her purse to get

her money, but the man surprised her by paying for it. "What are you and your friend doing in town?" he asked, once her drink had been delivered.

Delaney took a sip and focused on his hands, which circled his beer glass. They were big, strong hands. And he wasn't wearing a wedding ring. "Uh, it's a business trip," she said.

"And you're looking for something to relieve the boredom, is that it?"

Evidently he wasn't much for small talk. But Delaney didn't mind. Being direct could save a lot of time. Besides, if she had her guess, his type would be selfish and quick in the bedroom, which suited her just fine. She didn't want to enjoy the experience. That would make what she was doing seem even worse than it already was.

"I suppose so," she said, wishing her heart would quit jumping around in her chest. "You game?"

He took a drink of his beer. "What's your name?"

Delaney thought about using a false name, then decided against it. She didn't want the added worry of having to remember it, and as long as they remained on a first-name basis, she couldn't see any harm in telling him the truth. "Delaney."

"Delaney's some name. And that's some dress."

The way he said it, she couldn't be sure it was a compliment. He wasn't easy to read, but she was sort of grateful for that. His lackluster response made the initial contact difficult, but if she could just get him into a room, she wouldn't have a lot to worry about. He was too aloof to connect with her on a personal level. And he definitely seemed the type to take a brief encounter in stride. Rebecca might have been judging him on different criteria, but she was right—he was perfect for their purposes.

"And your name is…"

"Conner."

He didn't offer a last name, either, and Delaney took that as a sign that they were thinking along the same lines. "So, Conner," she said. "Do you want to…" She couldn't complete the question, but she figured he'd understand what she meant.

He raised his brows and looked over his shoulder. Rebecca was sitting with the cowboy, having a drink and talking while watching them surreptitiously. "Are you sure you *know* what you want?"

"What do you mean? Doesn't this dress say it all?"

"It says a lot," he admitted, "but the way your hands are shaking says even more."

"I've never done this before."

"Then, why are you starting now?"

Delaney hadn't expected such frank questions. All she'd hoped to do was catch a man's eye and dazzle him to the point that he'd give her what she wanted. Obviously Conner didn't dazzle easily.

"Why not?" she asked.

"Fair enough, but I've got to get up early. I think I'll pass," he said.

He stood, and she knew that in a moment, he'd leave and her best chance of making her plan work would disappear with him.

Swallowing hard, she caught his arm. "Okay, would *you* want to be a virgin at thirty?"

So THAT WAS DELANEY'S STORY. Conner had known something was up. All the warning bells in his head had been going off. But now that he understood her agenda, he could definitely see her point. He *wouldn't* want to be a virgin, not with one-third of his life already over.

Hesitating, Conner stared down at the hand that held him,

then at the honest appeal in the woman's face. He didn't want to be tempted, but he was. He'd been tempted since he'd seen her in the mirror, because of her eyes, not her dress. But he knew he was only setting himself up for more self-defeating behavior. One-night stands didn't do anything for him. He always woke in the morning feeling empty inside, as though he was missing something important. And yet here he was, hovering at the brink of taking the uninitiated Delaney to his room and giving her exactly what she was looking for, probably more than once.

"Don't you have a boyfriend?" he asked.

She gave him an "I'm not that low" look. "Do you think I'd approach a complete stranger if I did?"

Conner shrugged. "Some people get off on it."

"That's not my style."

Judging by the way she kept hiding behind her arms and chewing her lip, Conner believed her. She was far too nervous to be enjoying this. "You know it would be better to wait for someone who means something to you, don't you?"

"I'm thirty. I'm not sixteen," she said with just the right amount of pique to convince him he didn't need to coddle her.

"I realize that. I just don't want you to have any regrets later."

"Like I said, I'm thirty. I'm old enough to know what I want and to worry about my own regrets. I won't bother you with them."

"And if I still say no?"

"Then, I'll find someone else."

There he had it. She'd do it anyway. And hanging out at bars, shopping for a guy to relieve her of her virginity, was dangerous. If Delaney wasn't careful, she could wind up with someone who liked things rough. Or she could contract a communicable disease. At least Conner knew she'd be safe with him. He liked women, he treated them kindly and he was clean. He could do her this one favor, couldn't he?

He smiled at his thoughts, and she smiled shyly back. "What are we going to do with your friend?" he asked.

"Don't worry about Rebecca. She's engaged to be married. She'll just get a room by herself."

"You should know, I've never been with a virgin," he said, still half hoping to discourage her, "so if there are any special tricks for making it more comfortable the first time, I don't know them."

She couldn't quite meet his eyes. "I'm not asking for any special treatment. Whatever you normally do will be fine. I just want to, you know, get it over with."

Get it over with? No wonder Delaney was still a virgin. She was acting like she was about to go in for surgery, which, perversely enough, made Conner that much more eager to show her how good sex could be.

He glanced over to make sure the bartender was out of earshot. "Do you have protection?" he asked. Condoms weren't something he'd packed. Neither were they something he'd expected to need, at least not on his first night.

"You don't have to worry about that."

"You've already taken care of it?"

She nodded. "Unless I need to worry about protecting myself from—"

"You're not going to get anything from me."

Delaney seemed relieved. To her credit, his physical health had apparently been a big concern.

"That's great," she said. "So, are we good to go?"

She was back to the "get it over with" attitude, which

wasn't natural. She was too attractive to continue equating sex with having bamboo shoots shoved beneath her nails.

Maybe by morning, she'd have a different take on physical intimacy. Conner sure hoped so. "I'm in room 431," he said. "Tell your girlfriend goodbye and meet me there."

CHAPTER THREE

ROOM 431. For a minute, Delaney sat at the bar and stared at the doorway through which Conner had disappeared. She might have stayed there all night if not for Rebecca, who came up from behind to see what had happened.

"So?" she asked. "How'd it go?"

Delaney wasn't sure what to say. The cowboy Rebecca had drawn away was still at the table, but the bartender hovered close in case Rebecca intended to order a drink and Delaney didn't really want him or anyone else to know what she was about to do. She still couldn't believe it herself.

Taking Delaney by the elbow, Rebecca tried to steer her away from the bar, but Delaney wasn't ready to go anywhere yet. "Give me a shot of tequila," she told the bartender.

He seemed a little surprised that someone who'd just ordered soda water would suddenly go for the strong stuff, but he got her the drink, and she downed it in one gulp.

"I take it that's a yes," Rebecca said, pounding her on the back when she coughed and sputtered. "Or a very strong no."

"It's a yes," Delaney managed to say, when her eyes stopped watering. She hated tequila, but she needed something to calm her down so her legs would be capable of carrying her to room 431. "Give me one more," she told the bartender.

"Whoa, slow down, Laney. You don't want to pass out before you get there," Rebecca said, when Delaney swallowed the second shot as fast as the first.

"I'm done," Delaney croaked. Her eyes were watering all over again but the alcohol was doing a slow burn in her stomach, and she felt heartened already. Grabbing her purse, she slid off the stool. "What are you going to do while I'm...while I'm...busy?" she asked.

Rebecca frowned at the cowboy waiting for her at the table. "I'm going to lose Lover-boy there and get a room. I'll leave you a key with my room number at the front desk."

"Okay. I'll be in room 431. With Conner," Delaney added. Then she squared her shoulders and started for the door, her eyes on the elevators beyond, but Rebecca called her back.

"Will you be all right, Laney? You're whiter than a sheet."

"I'll be fine."

"The hard part's over, you know. You've just gotta—"

Delaney raised a hand. "I really don't want a pep talk at the moment. Not for this." She frowned. "I keep expecting to wake up and realize I've been dreaming."

"You'll thank me later."

"If it works."

"Just play your cards right, and it will."

Play her cards right? She was a virgin. She didn't know how to play this game at all. But she hadn't taken those assertiveness classes for nothing.

The lobby was empty except for a night clerk standing behind the check-in counter. He was clicking away on a computer and didn't look up as Delaney passed, despite the echo of her heels on the marble floor. She was glad; she didn't want to have to smile and nod and pretend she wasn't going to a stranger's room.

She kept her mind carefully blank as she rode the elevator and navigated the long narrow corridors of the fourth floor, but all her fears came flooding back when she finally stood in front of room 431.

This is it. Tomorrow I might be pregnant or I might be sorry.

With a deep breath to steady her nerves, she told herself to take a risk for once. This could bring her a baby. A baby! And Conner would never miss what he was giving her. He'd never even know.

On the other hand, there'd be no going back....

She was still hovering in indecision when a bellman came around the corner.

"You having trouble getting into your room, ma'am?"

"No, thanks. I'm fine."

"Okay. Have a good night." He passed, pulling an empty luggage cart, and turned toward the elevators, but Conner must have heard their exchange because he opened his door.

"I thought that might be you. I'm sorry," he said. "I didn't hear your knock."

Delaney didn't mention that she hadn't knocked, that she might never have knocked. She was too busy trying not to stare. Conner had taken a shower. He stood before her wearing nothing but a pair of faded blue jeans that had obviously been donned quickly—the top button was undone. His hair was combed but still wet, and she could tell he'd shaved, but it was his chest that made her mouth go dry. Broad and sculptured, with just a sprinkling of hair that narrowed into a thin line intersecting his navel, it looked like something she might've seen in a fitness magazine. Steam rolled out of the bathroom behind him, adding a bit of atmosphere, and Delaney could smell dampness and the scent of his shampoo.

"Smells good," she said before she could think.

He smiled, and this time it wasn't the social smile she'd seen fleetingly downstairs. It was sexy and sweet and nearly made her heart stop.

"I've been traveling all day, and I wanted to shave," he said.

That was nice of him. Nicer than she would've expected.

"Are you coming in?" he asked.

She glanced toward the elevator. A simple no could still end this. But Conner reached out to her, and she let him draw her inside.

The Bellemont was probably the nicest hotel in Boise. It was certainly more expensive than any Delaney had stayed in, but then she'd only stayed in one. When she was nine, Aunt Millie and some of the ladies from the Rotary Club had taken her to Disneyland. They'd rented a cheap motel because no one had much money, but there'd been a swimming pool and it had seemed like a castle to Delaney.

She circled the room, noting the striped wallpaper and crown molding, the king-size bed, the mahogany desk with rolling chair, the entertainment center that housed the television and snack bar, two nightstands with big brass lamps and an overstuffed chair next to a table on which lay a menu for room service. Picking up the menu, she leafed through it, as Conner folded his arms across his chest and leaned against the wall to watch her.

"You hungry?" he asked.

She looked up at him, then hurriedly away because he made such a spectacular sight with his powerful-looking shoulders and arms. "No. I've...I've never had room service before. I was just wondering what it's like."

"It's generally not the best food in the world, but it's

convenient," he said. His voice was amiable, kind, but there was curiosity in his eyes and he seemed to be taking in little things about her that she didn't even know she was giving away.

"Yeah, I'll bet." She gazed down the list of omelettes and pancakes, sandwiches and pasta entrées. "Looks like they have quite a selection. It's expensive, though, huh?"

"I take it you haven't traveled much."

"My mother moved around a lot, but we didn't stay in the kinds of places that have room service. Once we landed in Idaho, she was getting sick, so we stayed put. I've been to Disneyland, though." She smiled at the memory, which was one of the best of her life. "I've always wanted to go back," she admitted. Then, to counter the wistfulness of her words, she added, "I mean, when I have kids of my own."

She set the menu down. "Speaking of kids, do you want children someday?" She held her breath, thinking that his answer to this question would decide whether she stayed or quickly excused herself.

He shrugged, still leaning against the wall. "Maybe someday, but I'm certainly in no hurry. I have a lot to do before I'd be ready for something as monumental as that."

She nodded and some of the guilt twisting through her eased. See? He didn't want children right now. From the sound of it, he didn't want children for a long, long time. She wouldn't be denying him anything. And she had no guarantee that tonight would produce a baby, anyway. It would put an end to her virginity, however, and now that she was this close, that was reason enough to remain. Thirty years of celibacy was enough.

"Would you like a glass of wine?" he asked.

Delaney shook her head. She didn't dare drink more,

even though the tequila didn't seem to be having any effect. "No, thanks. I think we should, you know, get started."

He frowned. "Are you in some sort of hurry?"

She wanted to face the obstacle before her head-on, endure what was about to happen and put it behind her, but she couldn't say that, and she couldn't think of anything she could claim was pressing—not at midnight. "No, not really."

"Then, why don't you sit down and tell me a little about yourself first?"

"There's really nothing to tell," she said. The room suddenly seemed incredibly small, and she didn't know what else to do with herself so she perched on the edge of the bed.

"What happened to your mother? You said she was sick. I hope she got well." He casually shoved away from the wall and came to sit beside her, loosely folding his hands between his spread knees as they talked.

"No, she died when I was seven."

"I'm sorry."

Delaney followed his lead and clasped her hands in her lap, although the whiteness of her knuckles indicated that her grip was far tighter than his. The scent of soap on Conner's skin and of his aftershave was strangely provocative, and she could easily imagine how good it would feel if he took her in his arms—only she didn't *want* it to be that good. It had to be impersonal, unpleasurable, simply the means to an end. "It's okay. It happened a long time ago."

"What about the rest of your family? Do they live in Jerome, too?"

Delaney knew he was trying to put her at ease, and she appreciated the effort. Having this man so close and so nearly naked was certainly unsettling, but she didn't want to talk about her personal history. It wasn't a pleasant topic. She'd been foisted on the community at large, and the people of Dundee had been kind enough to look after her, to care about her. Which made her feel like she had to make it up to them somehow. She'd spent the whole of her adult life trying to repay a debt she could never completely discharge, and didn't want to be reminded of it now. Particularly since she felt she was betraying the same people she owed by doing something so far from what they'd expect of her, so far from what was right.

She opened her mouth to tell Conner she didn't want to talk about herself. But the tequila was finally siphoning off the tension in her body and making her a little dizzy at the same time, so she lay back on the bed and pretended she'd had the childhood she'd always wanted. What did it matter what kind of picture she painted for Conner? Their paths were never going to cross again.

She told him a fantastic tale about the wonderful father who'd raised her and six other siblings, the sisters who'd married and had children but were still close, the younger brothers who were going to high school. She told him she grew up on a farm with fresh fruit and vegetables and long days spent playing in the barn. She even told him she milked cows in the morning before school.

"I thought you said your mother moved around a lot."

"Oh, that was before," she said quickly, cursing the tequila for making her so fuzzy-headed. "After she passed away, I went to live with my father and his wife."

"I see. Sounds like, from that point on, you had the perfect childhood," he said. He was now lying on his side next to her, his head propped on one hand as he gazed down at her. They were close but not touching. He'd been listening—perhaps a little too carefully—and smiling and commenting, and surprisingly enough Delaney felt almost comfortable with him. She'd thought the tall tales she was spinning would push him away, keep him from glimpsing the real Delaney, but they'd done just the opposite because they'd revealed her most secret desires. She'd never revealed how badly she'd always wanted these things to Rebecca, nor certainly to anyone else. She occasionally dated in Dundee, but it was mostly group stuff—bowling league, softball league, weekends at the Honky Tonk. She generally preferred Billy Joe's company to that of most of her male friends. They always had a good time at the Honky Tonk, but he'd never made her stomach flutter, not like this.

"What about you?" she asked, trying to ignore the way Conner was looking at her, the fact that his gaze kept dropping to her lips as though he was waiting for the right moment to lean forward and kiss her. "What about your childhood?"

"Mine? Oh, it was perfect, too," he said. She thought she heard a trace of sarcasm in his voice, but her confusion was deepening because he'd started trailing one finger down the side of her face and over her lips, which she instinctively parted.

"Are you okay with this, Delaney?"

Was she okay? His touch made shivers shoot through her entire body. But wait—wasn't there some reason she shouldn't be doing this?

One night, one baby. The thought floated through her mind, but its meaning had changed completely. At this point, that one night hardly seemed like much of a sacrifice....

"I'm okay," she murmured.

"Good. Because I think this is going to be great. Better than I ever imagined," he said, and then he kissed her. It was a perfect kiss, a long, slow "I'm not going anywhere" kind of kiss, and it nearly melted Delaney's bones. Her eyelids drifted shut as his tongue met hers, and she flattened her hands against the hard muscles of his chest. He no longer reminded her of any movie star. But something warned her not to think of him as Conner, because women fell in love with men over less than he was doing to her now. She'd assumed that he'd be quick, abrupt and selfish, but he was just the opposite. He was taking his time, touching her, caressing her, kissing her.

By the time she felt his hand on her leg, moving slowly up her inner thigh, her head was spinning. Her body instinctively arched toward him, but he didn't hurry his pace. He seemed intent on going by degrees, almost painful degrees that nearly consumed her with need.

"Conner," she whispered, feeling as though she was hanging on to sanity by a very thin thread. She'd told herself not to use his name, to not even think it, but what could she do? It was printed across her closed eyelids like fireworks in the sky. She'd tried to distance herself by pretending he was Hugh Jackman, by telling herself that she was experiencing every woman's fantasy, nothing real, but it wasn't working. Even though she'd met him only an hour and a half earlier, Conner was Conner, and he was as real as a man could get.

"Let's do it now," she whispered, her voice throaty, almost hoarse.

He said something against her mouth about not fighting him, about letting it happen naturally, and started lifting her dress. She helped him by wriggling out of it, then tossed it onto the floor, focused on removing his clothes, as well. He stopped her long enough to let his gaze sweep over what he'd revealed, and his smile of satisfaction made heady pleasure course through Delaney, obliterating the shyness she'd expected. Conner made her feel so incredibly sexy, so desirable and yet safe, accepted. She wasn't supposed to be enjoying this but, heaven help her, she was. She'd never enjoyed anything more. She knew she'd pay in guilt come morning, but that didn't seem to matter, at least not now. Such realities hovered somewhere beyond her immediate thoughts, out on the fringes of her consciousness, and were completely forgotten when Conner finished taking off his pants and covered her with his naked body. Then, after a brief flash of pain, Delaney felt what she'd never experienced before—a man joined with her—and it was a reverent, powerful moment. The orphan was at last connected to another human being, physically and emotionally, and somehow she knew nothing would ever be the same again.

IT WAS CLOSE TO MORNING. Conner wasn't sure what had pulled him from sleep, but he certainly wasn't opposed to waking up, not with Delaney still in his bed and not when he felt so completely boneless, weightless and relaxed.

Delaney was lying on her side facing away from him, her breathing steady and even, and he was cradling her with his body, enjoying the feel of her backside pressed against him. He'd known when he invited her to his room that he wasn't doing it for the altruistic motives he'd kidded himself about in the bar, but he hadn't expected anything like the kind of emotionally charged hours they'd shared. Last night had not been a casual one-night stand. Conner wasn't sure if it was her innocence or her vulnerability or even something else, but Delaney had touched him deeply. She'd taken what they'd done far beyond the physical. And he had enough experience with women to know the difference.

Angling his head to see her face in the light that was just starting to creep through the crack in the draperies, Conner couldn't help smiling. He must have been blind not to think her absolutely stunning the moment she entered the bar last night. The more he stared at her, the more he liked what he saw. He loved the way her eyes closed and her lips parted when he caressed her, the dimple that flashed at him when she smiled, the swollen look of her mouth after he kissed her. And he liked a lot of other things—the sounds she made when he touched her, the tenderness she showed when they curled up together, the dreaminess in her voice when she talked about her family. Last night he'd been fully prepared to get up and head over to the Running Y Ranch and never see her again, but somewhere along the line, he'd changed his mind. Now he thought that letting her go too easily would be an unnecessary loss. Certainly he could find Jerome and take her out on occasion. Maybe she could even come up to Dundee once in a while. It would help pass the time until he returned to California.

He shifted to let the blood flow back into his arm, and Delaney started, then sat bolt upright, blinking and looking around. Reality seemed to descend on her when she caught sight of him. She grabbed the sheet and held it over her as though he'd just appeared and she hadn't made love with him all night.

"Morning," he said, reaching out to soothe her and gather her to him, but she dodged his hand and scooted to the far edge of the bed.

"Is something wrong?" he asked, raising himself into a sitting position.

She groaned and put a hand to her head. "I can't believe I did this," she said, but Conner could tell she wasn't talking to him. She eyed her dress lying on the floor, and then the sheet she was using to cover herself. Dropping the sheet, she streaked out of bed and scooped up her dress as she made a dash for the bathroom.

"Delaney?" he said, frowning in confusion. She'd been pretty jumpy when she first arrived last night, but she'd warmed up quickly enough, and the woman he'd made love to several times during the night hadn't been inhibited at all. Now she was blushing and covering herself as though he hadn't already seen her.

"I've got to leave," she muttered, as the sight of her delectable backside disappeared around the corner.

"Why? What's wrong?" he asked.

"This—everything!" she cried from inside the bathroom. She came out smoothing the skirt of her dress over her hips and dropped to the floor to find her shoes.

Conner felt a flicker of anger. Since she'd been a virgin, he could understand her having a certain amount of remorse, but he'd been careful to address that issue. And it wasn't as though he'd coerced her in any way. "I warned you about the regret," he said, wondering if he could have been clearer somehow.

"It's okay," she said. "It's not your fault."

"But I don't want you to be sorry about what happened," he told her. "It makes me feel as though I took advantage of you."

"Don't feel as though you— Don't feel anything. It doesn't matter. We're never going to see each other again, anyway."

That statement didn't make him any happier than her previous one. "Actually, I was going to talk to you about that," he said. "Will you slow down and give me a minute?"

She found one of her shoes and started forcing it onto her foot. "I can't. I have to go now."

"Where? I thought we'd order room service. Seemed like you were interested in that last night."

"I can't stay," she said, coming up with her other shoe. "But I owe you a big apology. For what it's worth, I'm sorry. Truly sorry."

"What are you sorry for?" he demanded. "I may be alone in this, but I enjoyed last night."

"I'm just sorry," she repeated. "And I'm going to kill Rebecca."

"Who's Rebecca? Your friend?"

"Never mind." She finally managed to get her other shoe on, grabbed her purse and started for the door but Conner jumped out of bed and intercepted her before she could leave.

"You're really going? Just like that?"

She wouldn't even look at him. She kept her eyes fastened on the door behind him. "I have to."

"At least give me your number," he said. "This is crazy."

"I can't."

"Why not? I won't be living far from here, and I'm willing to make the drive to Jerome. Come on, Delaney, I thought we had something here." He smiled, hoping she'd relent and stay a little longer—he had a couple of hours before the foreman from the ranch was due to pick him up—but she didn't. She remained stiff and unapproachable, and he knew she wouldn't let him hold her now for anything, even though he wanted to do exactly that.

She hid her eyes with one hand as though she was feeling trapped and couldn't decide what to do, but when she finally looked up at him, her expression softened. "All right. I'll leave my number on the desk."

He watched her cross to the pad and pen next to the room service menu, then searched for his jeans. He didn't understand her sudden modesty, but he was willing to respect it if that made her more comfortable. Maybe if he was dressed, she'd calm down.

"Here it is," she said. She ripped off the paper she'd

been writing on, folded it in half and stuck it in the pocket of the shirt he'd draped over the back of the chair.

He finished buttoning his jeans and followed her to the door. "I'll call you," he said, trying to give her the space she obviously needed.

"Good, okay. I'll talk to you later," she said, then slipped out without even a goodbye handshake.

Conner frowned as the door clicked shut behind her, then cursed. What had happened between her falling asleep and waking up? He'd never had a woman turn around so quickly. He'd had them become clingy and possessive or almost sickeningly sweet in their bid for more time, more things, more promises, but Delaney was the first to sleep with him, dress and run right out of his life.

At least he had her number. He'd wait a few days and then give her a call, he decided. But when he pulled the folded paper out of his shirt pocket and opened it he felt like she'd just kicked him in the stomach.

Delaney hadn't left her number. She'd written two small words: *Thank you.*

CHAPTER FOUR

DELANEY SHOVED THE DOOR out of Rebecca's grasp the moment she opened to her knock, and let it bang against the inside wall as she stormed through. "I can't believe I let you talk me into that!" she said. "What on earth was I thinking?"

"That a one-night stand is cheaper than artificial insemination?"

"Don't start with that stuff again," Delaney warned. "I was being an idiot."

"You were being assertive."

"I was being aggressive! I was lying and manipulating others to get what I want. That's not the same as being assertive, Beck."

Her friend looked a little sheepish. "Was it that bad?"

Delaney pivoted at the end of the bed and began to pace. "It was worse than bad. It was terrible."

"Terrible?" Rebecca echoed, tightening her bathrobe. "Don't tell me he was into whips and chains or something."

"No."

"Was he a selfish pig?" she said sympathetically.

Delaney shook her head. "He wasn't kinky or selfish. He was fabulous, a fantasy come to life. But that's the problem."

Rebecca's brows drew together in obvious confusion as she shoved her tangled hair out of her eyes. "Let me get this straight," she said. "He was good to you, and you think that's a problem?"

"It *is* a problem!" Delaney cried, rounding on her. "I feel like a horrible person, a lecher, a loser. He trusted me, and I betrayed him. I was lying to him the whole time."

Rebecca rubbed the sleep from her face and sank into the chair next to the round table that sported an *All About Boise* magazine and a giant bouquet of silk flowers. "It wasn't a *big* lie."

"I told him he didn't need to worry about birth control!"

"So it was sort of a big lie. But that was the whole point. If you'd told him the truth, he wouldn't have invited you up to his room."

"I wish he hadn't. I wish I'd never come here. I wish…" She stopped pacing and flopped onto the bed. "Oh God, what if I'm pregnant?"

Rebecca stood and leaned over her. "Wasn't that the point of this whole exercise?"

Delaney remembered Conner's surprise when she'd begun to leave his room, his earnest entreaty for her telephone number, and wished she could die. "No! If I'm pregnant, I'll never be able to forgive myself, never be able to forget what I've done. I'll have to stare into my child's eyes and know…" She was about to say *that deep down I'm no better than my mother,* but she stopped herself because she couldn't handle a philosophical discussion right now. She was too busy browbeating herself. "That I cheated his or her father."

"You're overreacting," Rebecca said. "You haven't hurt anyone. He had a good time, didn't he?"

"I'm not going to answer that question."

"I'm just saying, I'm sure he doesn't regret it."

"Whether he regrets it or not, he was a nice guy, Beck. I had no right to treat him the way I did."

Rebecca lit a cigarette. "How do you know he's such a nice guy? What do you really know about him, Laney? One night doesn't tell you anything."

Delaney thought her night had told her a few things about Conner. For one, he was generous. He'd been concerned about her enjoyment and what she might feel afterward. Two, he was loving and kind. He'd seemed as happy to hold her and keep her warm as he'd been to make love, which was a large part of what she'd liked about last night. Three, he was a good listener. He'd made her feel more important and understood than she ever had before.

And she'd taken advantage of him. "I have to go back there," she said. "I have to tell him what I've done." She climbed off the bed, but Rebecca blocked the door.

"You're crazy," she said. "He had a good time. Leave it alone. Do you think he wants you to drop a bomb like that? It's over, and he's gone on his merry way. Let him. I doubt that you're pregnant, anyway."

Delaney hesitated, trying to count how many times they'd made love. What were the chances that after five…no, six times, she'd be carrying his child?

Probably not very good, she decided. Besides, Conner didn't want children yet. He'd told her as much. Rebecca was right: Delaney would be doing him more of a favor at this point simply to let it go…and hope for the best.

So this was Dundee, where he'd been born and lived with his mother for the first six years of his life.

Conner frowned as Roy, the foreman of the Running Y, who'd picked him up just after breakfast in Boise, drove him through the center of town, where several buildings rose out of the surrounding mountains, leaning on each other like old men. Built of wood and painted red, brown or white, they ran along both sides of the street, fronted by a covered boardwalk that extended for several blocks like something out of an old western. Only the gas station down the street and the new A&W looked out of place or the least bit modern.

Modern? He thought of the spacious, Spanish-style villa he'd grown up in, with its expansive wings and gardens, inside swimming pool and tennis courts, and knew he'd been banished to hell.

Where he'd rot, if his uncles had their way.

Swallowing a bitter sigh, he glanced at his companion. Tall and lanky, Roy had red hair and a mustache that entirely covered his top lip. His freckled, sunburned complexion gave his face a leathery appearance and made him look older than the fifty-five or so he probably was. And he wore, like most other men within sight, a parka with a pair of Wranglers that were so tight his chewing tobacco stood out in marked relief.

Conner considered his own jeans, which were loose fitting by comparison, his Doc Martin loafers and Abercrombie sweatshirt, and knew he was going to blend in about as well as his clothes did.

"How much farther to the ranch?" he asked, breaking the silence that had fallen between them almost immediately after their brief greeting in Boise. He needed to dispel the lingering sense of loss and confusion he'd experienced since Delaney's sudden departure, and after a twenty-five year absence, he remembered the ranch and the cemetery where they'd buried his grandma, but not much about the town or surrounding area.

"'Nother ten miles or so round that mountain." He pointed to their right before slinging his arm casually over the steering wheel.

Conner gazed off in the distance. "Who lives there these days?"

"Only a handful of us. Ben, Grady, Isaiah and me live in the cabins behind the barn."

"No one stays at the main house?"

"Just Dottie. Least during the week. On weekends she stays with her son and his family in town."

"And just what does this Dottie do?"

"The cookin' and cleanin' and stuff. Takes care of the dogs and chickens, too."

"So there's just the five of you?"

Roy cast him a sideways glance. "Now there's you."

Conner was painfully aware of that fact. "I think I heard one of my uncles say that the Running Y is twenty thousand acres," he said. "Is that about right?"

Roy spat out the window as they rumbled to a stop at what appeared to be the town's biggest intersection. A brick municipal building with the date 1847 carved above its arched entry stood on one corner, across from two stately homes that looked as though they hailed from the same era and a redbrick building designated as the city library.

"Give or take a few," he said. "Not that twenty thousand acres is very big, far as ranches go. You want big, go to Texas."

"Where they raise Longhorns." Even Conner knew that. "What kind of cattle do we stock?" he asked. He'd been too angry at his grandfather and his uncles to reveal the slightest interest in returning to the Running Y by asking even the most basic questions.

The light turned green, but his companion squinted at him for a second or two before giving the pickup enough gas to roll through the intersection. "We've got about two thousand Bally-faced Herefords."

Bally-faced? Conner hadn't heard that term before, but he did, thankfully, recognize *Herefords.* Unless he was mistaken, they were the common reddish cattle seen in so many places. "Is the entire ranch fenced?" he asked, trying to imagine how one might manage such a large chunk of land.

Roy accelerated to their usual traveling speed of about forty-five miles per hour. Because of the load of hay Roy had picked up in Boise before appearing at Conner's hotel, Conner doubted the truck could go any faster.

"Parts are fenced," Roy said. "But some of the land is open range leased from the BLM, and I doubt they'd like us fencing it off."

"The BLM?"

Another squinty gaze. "The Bureau of Land Management. It operates state land. We hold the grazing rights for about ten thousand BLM acres down along the south pass."

"I see," Conner said, but he didn't see much. He'd thought owning a twenty-thousand-acre ranch meant owning twenty thousand acres of deeded property. Evidently that wasn't strictly the case.

What are the grazing rights worth? he wanted to ask. *How do we keep our cattle from straying if our property isn't completely fenced? How do we stop thieves and predators from stealing and slaughtering our Bally-faced Herefords? Did a few cowboys keep a constant vigil over them?*

There were hundreds of things he'd need to know. But he didn't ask anything more. His lack of knowledge wasn't exactly inspiring confidence in his foreman, and he was still too disgruntled about what had happened with Delaney this morning to handle the situation diplomatically.

There'd be plenty of time to learn how to run the ranch once he arrived, he supposed. At this point, he preferred his unhappy thoughts to Roy's resentment. But Roy wasn't ready to let the conversation lapse.

"Ever been out on a horse?" he asked as they rumbled along.

"On occasion," Conner told him.

"For work or for pleasure?"

It didn't take a crystal ball to see where Roy's questions were leading, and the implication of his words caused the irritation already rushing through Conner's blood to get the better of him. He'd gone against his saner judgment when he'd taken Delaney to his room last night, and she'd left him feeling jilted and used. He didn't need a crusty old cowboy to make him feel worthless, as well.

"What do you think?" he said.

"I don't think you look like much of a cowboy."

"Well, I guess I'll have to buy myself a belt buckle tomorrow."

Roy's furry eyebrows shot up, but he kept his eyes on the road as he shifted onto one hip to reach his chew. "It's gonna take a lot more than a belt buckle, son."

Conner recognized the challenge in the man's voice. Fixing him with a level gaze, he said, "I'll manage," even though, in all honesty, he couldn't blame Roy for resenting his lack of experience. The ranch was deeply in debt and would probably fail in far more capable hands. His grandfather had obviously sent the wrong man. Conner had known that from the beginning, and now he and Roy both knew it.

"You want to tell me a little about what's been going on, why we're so far from showing a profit?" Conner asked. As long as Roy had no illusions about his abilities, they might as well get down to the nitty-gritty.

The foreman took a pinch of tobacco, settled it between his cheek and gum and put his tin away before answering. "Price of beef's been falling. What with foreign competition and the price of feed after the drought last summer, we're not lookin' to have a good year."

"Is there any way to turn things around?" Conner asked

as they approached a black wrought-iron archway with the words "Running Y Ranch" inscribed on it.

Roy spat out the window as he slowed to make the turn. "That's what you're here for, ain't it?"

"YOU'LL HAVE TO MOVE BACK HERE with us. How else will you get by once Rebecca leaves?" Aunt Millie asked, watching Delaney closely.

Delaney paused in her dusting but kept her face purposefully averted from Aunt Millie, who sat propped up in bed, suffering from a touch of the flu or a cold or, more likely, simply the need for a little tender loving care.

"I'll get by," she said for probably the hundredth time and went back to dusting, hoping Aunt Millie would let the subject drop. But Delaney knew she wouldn't. Ever since Millie had heard about Rebecca's engagement, she'd been pressing Delaney to move home again. She'd never liked the fact that Delaney had moved out in the first place, especially to go and live with Rebecca. But Delaney wasn't about to return to the days of having Aunt Millie cluck over her constantly, monitoring her diet, her spending habits, her social success. Much as she loved Millie and Ralph, she liked her privacy and was determined to preserve it.

"But coming home for a few months would help you save a little money," Aunt Millie said. "What's wrong with saving money? You don't want to live all alone, do you?"

"I don't mind living alone. Can I get you anything else to eat?"

"No, I'm finished," Aunt Millie said, but she wasn't so easily distracted. The white-haired woman who'd raised Delaney was getting on in years. Her body was beginning to succumb to arthritis and advanced age, but nothing could diminish her iron will. "You could have your old room," she went on. "We haven't changed a thing in there, but we could, if you want. We could sew some new drapes, buy a new spread...."

The cornered feeling Delaney knew so well crept over her, along with a touch of resentment. If she'd wanted to move home, she would have done it by now. Why couldn't Millie understand that? Why did she have to keep pushing?

"The room's fine," she said.

"Think of the time we'd have. We never did finish putting that quilt together, you know."

Delaney imagined living under Aunt Millie's regime again, imagined Uncle Ralph sitting in front of the television most of the time, monopolizing the remote, while Millie insisted Delaney take her vitamins, eat her bran, get more sleep—and thought she might scream.

Then she felt guilty for wanting to scream because Aunt Millie and Uncle Ralph had been so good to her. They'd never formally adopted her; there'd been no one to contest their guardianship, so paying for the paperwork to be filed seemed unnecessary. But Millie and Ralph had given her their name and treated her as lovingly as a blood daughter.

God, she couldn't win.

"That house of yours is too drafty in the winter," Millie was saying. "I just freeze to death whenever I go there. You need to tell that landlord of yours that you're moving out because it's so cold. He should really do something about the insulation."

"I'll mention it," Delaney said, but she wasn't thinking about insulation. She'd role-played this exact situation online with her assertiveness training coach. She knew what she had to do. She had to tell Aunt Millie in a kind but firm manner that she wasn't moving home under any circumstances, and now was as good a time as any. But when she turned, she saw the hope on her adoptive mother's face and couldn't bring herself to say what she knew would hurt Millie, no matter how kindly she framed it.

"I'll think about it," she said instead, then mentally kicked herself. She was never going to overcome her passivity. She'd probably be the first person to fail a class that gave no grades.

"Ralph could borrow the neighbor's truck, so we wouldn't have any trouble moving your things," Millie said, struggling to lift the breakfast tray from across her lap.

Delaney put down her dusting cloth and went to help. "I'll get that," she said, setting it on the nightstand. "Are you sure you wouldn't like another cup of coffee?"

"No. Ralph says drinking so much coffee will kill me. But arthritis won't let me do much of anything else these days. I'm just sitting here getting fat."

Uncle Ralph was at the barbershop, probably drinking his own share of coffee while he complained about the rising price of gasoline to the same friends he'd met there every Sunday for the past thirty years. Dundee was nothing if not comfortable with routine.

"Uncle Ralph likes the way you look, and so do I," Delaney said, straightening the covers on Aunt Millie's bed.

Aunt Millie raised a gnarled hand to pat her arm. "You're a good girl, Laney. I've always been so proud of you. I knew the moment I saw you when you were just six years old that you were nothing like your mother. And you've never disappointed me."

Delaney felt the bonds of obligation grow a little tighter, tying her hands, trapping her in the mold Millie had created for her. And fear overwhelmed her as the memories she'd been trying so hard to suppress for the past twenty-four hours quickly surfaced—Conner standing at his hotel room door wearing only his jeans…Conner smiling above her…Conner's lips, his hands, his body…

She closed her eyes, feeling as though she might pass out. What if she was pregnant? What if she had to tell Aunt Millie and Uncle Ralph that their perfect little girl wasn't so perfect after all?

"It's getting kind of late," she said awkwardly, her face growing hot. "If I don't head home, there'll be people breaking down my door for pies. You think you'll be okay here until Uncle Ralph gets back?"

"Of course." Aunt Millie waved her away. "I've got my cross-stitch. And the books you brought me."

Delaney moved the stack of romances she'd checked out of the library closer to the bed so Aunt Millie could reach them, then did the same with the remote control to the television. "You want me to raise the blind a little higher?" she asked, hearing the reedy thinness of her voice and hoping Aunt Millie wouldn't notice it. "It's overcast right now, but the weather report said we're supposed to get some sun later this afternoon."

"That would be nice, dear."

Delaney raised the blind, put away the dust cloth, gathered the coupons Aunt Millie had clipped for the weekly grocery shopping—which Delaney did every Monday before work—and reclaimed the breakfast tray. "There's an apple pie in the fridge for your dessert," she said, dropping a quick kiss on Aunt Millie's lined cheek.

Then she ducked her head and hurried out of the room, eager to escape that loving smile and those adoring eyes, afraid that Aunt Millie would see what a fraud she really was. Afraid that if Aunt Millie looked too hard, she'd realize Delaney was her mother's daughter, after all.

CHAPTER FIVE

THE MEMORIES OF THOSE FEW YEARS when Conner had lived at the Running Y were far more vivid than he'd ever dreamed they would be. After all, he'd been only six when his grandmother died and the whole household had moved to California, and the twenty-five intervening years had changed him into another person entirely. The hopeful little boy who'd ridden behind his grandfather to rescue a stranded calf, whose job it was to feed the chickens and gather the eggs, was long gone. Yet something as simple as the crackling fire beneath the large stone mantel in the living room, the lingering scent of pine and smoke or a glimpse of the snow-covered mountains crouched protectively on either side of the house flooded him with images and snatches of conversation he thought he'd completely forgotten.

"Why do you get up so early, Grandpa?" he'd once asked, entering the very room in which he sat now, his grandfather's study, to find Clive hard at work, even though the sky beyond the windows was still black and dawn seemed hours away.

"Because I have a lot to do, son," his grandfather had replied, glancing up from the papers on the desk.

"No one else gets up so early."

"You do," he'd responded with a wink. "And that's why we Armstrongs are going to stay one step ahead of our competition. You're my future, Con."

You're my future. Such hope, such confidence. At the time, Conner had swelled with pride to think the same blood flowed through his veins. But that was before he'd found out he wasn't really an Armstrong at all, before his uncles had made it abundantly clear that he was nothing but a bastard, a ward, a *parasite*.

Other memories threatened, but Conner forced them from his mind and returned his attention to the ranch's account books, which lay open before him. As he'd feared, the financial picture wasn't good. His grandfather had bought the place over fifty years ago, when ranching was still profitable. It had given the old man his start, and he'd built an empire from there. But for the past five years, the cost of feed and hands had climbed steadily while the price of beef had fallen. Unless something significant happened, the ranch wasn't going to make it, and even a frat boy who'd spent most of his time at college trying *not* to learn could see that.

The end was coming, Conner thought. There wasn't a thing he could do to change the inevitable. Why was he even sitting here, going through the books, racking his brain for solutions?

Clive would tolerate the losses for only another year or so before he sold out. And Conner knew he was in much the same situation. Like the ranch, he'd started out full of promise but had eventually fallen into decline. He'd barely graduated from high school, had dropped out of college just as he was about to receive his diploma, and had spent more time traveling and playing than working. He'd drunk, gambled and squandered money. He'd spent his time driving fast cars and associating with even faster women. And his grandfather had finally drawn a line in the sand.

Tough love. What a concept. His grandfather loved the ranch more than he loved Conner.

Staring out the window, which looked over acres of pasture, Conner stopped fighting the past and let the memory of his last meeting with Clive play in his mind. His grandfather had summoned him to the office at the winery, where Conner's uncles already waited. Forty-three-year-old Dwight had offered him a seat, as though he were some sort of stranger. Thirty-eight-year-old Jonathan had smiled, obviously relishing a moment he'd anticipated. And the balding, thirty-five-year-old Stephen had come right out and told Conner that his wild days were over. If he didn't settle down and start contributing to the family, he'd be cut off from the Armstrongs forever.

Conner would have expected nothing less from his uncles. But his grandfather... What had happened in that meeting had twisted something inside him that Conner had thought long dead. Clive had sat behind his expansive desk, fingers steepled beneath his chin, watching and listening to everything that occurred. He'd nodded when Stephen announced that they were sending Conner to the Running Y, adding nothing until Conner stood to leave. Then he'd said only this—that he was sending Conner back to Dundee *where he belonged.*

Which was absolutely laughable because Conner didn't belong anywhere.

The telephone rang. Conner hesitated, expecting Dottie, the widow his grandfather paid to cook for the cowboys and manage the house to answer it, but she didn't seem to be available.

He picked up at the same time as the answering machine came on. "You've reached the Running Y. We're either out with the animals or running an errand in town—"

When Conner spoke, the machine automatically shut off. "Hello?"

"Conner? Is that you?"

His mother. She was as excited about his return to Dundee as her younger brothers were, but for entirely different reasons. An eternal optimist, she saw it as a great opportunity for him.

"Yeah, I made it," he said. "How are things at home?"

"The same. I'm more worried about things at the ranch. Is the situation as dire as we thought?"

"It's not good."

"When life hands you lemons, make lemonade."

Her cliché, as much as the unfailingly cheerful note in which it was spoken, confirmed what Conner had suspected for years—his mother was delusional. *Make lemonade?* "This was a setup," he said, feeling his irritation rise. "There's no way for me to win. You realize that, don't you?"

"I don't think Dad would set you up," she argued.

Of course he would. His grandfather was finally getting rid of him. Conner had known it would happen someday. But he wasn't going to argue with his mother, who was singularly devoted to the old guy. "Then he let Stephen, Jonathan and Dwight do it. Either way, the result is the same."

"The result is what you make it."

"Mom, you don't know anything about the beef market or ranching or—"

"I know your grandfather started with a lot less than what you have going for you now," she interrupted, and Conner dropped his head in his hands to massage his temple. Why had he answered the phone?

"I don't want to hear about the time Grandpa was too poor to buy a pair of shoes to wear to school, or the time he nearly froze his feet off trying to reach cattle that would've starved without the feed he carried," he said. "I've talked to Roy. He obviously knows how to manage a herd, so there's nothing I can improve on there. Rhonda, the accountant who works here three days a week, knows what she's doing, too. I've got the books in front of me now. Grandfather's money has been tracked to the penny, and receipts account for every expense. Coyotes are picking off a few steers, but our losses are in line with those suffered by other ranchers in the area. So I can't increase profits by improving the general running of the ranch.''

"Then, think of something else.''

"You want me to end the drought that's plagued the area for three years? Or why don't I figure out what to do about the competition from other countries that's driving down American beef prices?''

"I don't like the tone of your voice. You're being negative.''

"I'm being honest!''

"If you didn't think you had a real chance of succeeding, then why did you go?'' she asked impatiently.

It was a good question. Conner had asked himself the same thing a million times. He'd almost rebelled that day in the winery. Without the Armstrongs he'd simply be the son of a no-good auto mechanic who was spending his life in jail. He would have nothing to live up to, nothing to prove, nothing left to fear....

But there was his mother to consider. She'd given birth to Conner and kept him, despite the circumstances of his conception. And she'd loved him. That was the crux of the matter, wasn't it? He couldn't turn his back on her.

"I came to spite your brothers,'' he lied.

"Then, spite them,'' she said. "Make the ranch a miraculous success.''

Conner stifled a groan. Hadn't she heard what he'd just told her? There wasn't any way to save the ranch. "You're not listening,'' he said.

"I am listening. I've just heard enough. Quit looking for reasons to fail and decide to succeed."

She made it sound so easy....

"Dad wants to speak to you," she said. "Hang on."

"Wait," Conner said. "I have to go. Tell him I'll call him later." But she'd already set the phone down, presumably to get her father, and Conner forced himself to hold, even though he wasn't sure what he and his grandfather would say. They hadn't parted on the best of terms. They'd barely nodded at each other when Conner boarded the plane in San Francisco.

A voice came over the line, but it wasn't his grandfather's. It was his uncle Stephen. "Well, what do you know. My nomadic nephew's actually up on a Sunday and it's only, what, just past noon?"

Conner felt the muscles in his jaw tighten but fought the building tide of anger. When Conner was a child, Stephen and the others had constantly riled him until he used his fists or broke down in tears. As he grew older, he refused to give them the pleasure of knowing when anything they said or did bothered him.

"Did you need something specific, Stephen?" he asked, trying to sound as indifferent as possible.

"Dad was wondering if you got in okay. He was probably afraid you'd taken a detour to Vegas or something."

"No plans for Vegas yet."

"Give it a few days. I'm sure your stint in Dundee won't last long."

It had already lasted a day and a half longer than Conner wanted it to.

"So how are things there?" Stephen asked.

His uncle had phoned to hear that the situation was hopeless, of course, that Conner was defeated before he'd begun. And even though that was precisely the truth, as he'd just explained to his mother, Conner would be damned if he'd admit it now. "Great," he said. "Never better."

"If they were that good, the ranch would be turning a profit."

"It'll be turning a profit soon enough."

His uncle's surprised silence was well worth the lie.

"Yeah, well, we'll see," his uncle finally replied. "The last thirty years speak for them—"

"Did you have something important to say?" Conner said, cutting him off.

Stephen chuckled. "Not really. I'm just following directions. I know that's a novel concept for you, but the rest of us have always had to toe the line. Only little Con gets away with murder."

It was Conner's turn to laugh. "That's too juvenile, even for you, Stephen. When are you going to forget about me and live your own life?"

"I am living my own life. As far as I'm concerned, you don't even exist. At least, you won't in a few months, when you give up on the ranch and go on another party cruise or whatever."

"I guess I could spend more of my time brown-nosing, like you."

"Is that what you call doing my duty as my father's son?"

"You wouldn't know your duty if it bit you on the ass," Conner said. "You're too ready to line your own pockets, too eager to pick Grandfather's bones once he's gone. It's pathetic, really, that you're such a grasping bastard. No wonder I took myself out of the picture."

"You were never in the picture, Con, because *you're* the real bastard. My family's tolerated you all these years, for Vivian's sake, but do you think anyone's been happy about having a rape baby in the house? Everyone told her to put you up for adoption, and she should've listened.''

She *should* have listened. Conner had always believed that. Then he wouldn't have to face, daily, what had happened the night he was conceived, or know that he would never truly be part of the family in which he'd been raised.

Regardless, he was growing tired of his uncles' reminders. ''Feeling a little cocky now that I'm two states away, Stephen?''

''I've never been afraid of you,'' his uncle countered, but Conner knew his words weren't entirely true. Stephen and his brothers had plagued him his whole life with subtle barbs that kept Conner constantly aware of his status, but in recent years, they were generally careful not to go too far. At well over six feet, Conner had several inches on Stephen and Dwight, and almost half a foot on Jonathan, and though they all outweighed him—Jonathan by at least fifty pounds—they were soft.

''We'll have a talk about this again sometime when we're all together,'' Conner promised.

''I think we should do that.''

''I'm available any time you're ready, Uncle.''

Conner was expecting a sharp comeback, but the tone of Stephen's voice suddenly changed.

''Sure, I understand, Con,'' he said. ''I'm glad you're there safe and sound, and that you're willing to give the old ranch a try. You know how much it means to Dad.''

Confusion left Conner tongue-tied for a moment, but then he heard Clive's voice in the background and understood. His grandfather had entered the room, and Stephen had snapped into character, pretending to be the long-suffering, if not loving, uncle.

''You're such a greedy asshole,'' he said, sickened by the blatant playacting. God, this was what he'd rebelled against, wasn't it? This was why he'd forged his own path. Wild as his past had been, it had kept him, for the most part, far from the back-stabbing that went on among Clive's immediate family. His mother was still in the fray to protect his interests, she said, but Conner didn't care about his grandfather's money. The posturing and conniving of his uncles turned his stomach.

"I think just as much of you. You know that, Con," Stephen said, unmistakably smug at the double entendre. "And it's never going to change, is it? Now, here's Dad. He wants to talk to you."

Conner closed his eyes as he waited, bracing for what might come. He doubted his grandfather would say much. Clive had always been rather aloof and preoccupied, too busy to be bothered with family. But for some reason, maybe because Conner had worshipped him so much as a child, even the slightest criticism from him hurt far worse than anything Dwight or the others had to say.

"Con?"

Taking a deep breath, Conner flattened his hand and placed it on the desk in front of him. He stared at the ring his mother had given him just before he left. She'd said it was special to her, but she hadn't said why—only that she was giving it to him for luck, as a symbol of her love and support.

Some people were gluttons for punishment, weren't they?

"Con? You still there?" his grandfather demanded.

"Yeah, I'm here," Conner replied.

"How does the ranch look?"

"Good." For a moment, Conner was tempted to admit that in some ways it felt great to be back. There *was* something of home here, something he'd never identified with

California. But the days when they used to speak so freely to each other were history.

"What's Roy up to?" his grandfather asked.

"Taking care of business."

"He's a good cowboy. You can trust him."

"Yeah. I think he likes me," Conner said, taking care to keep his tongue-in-cheek tone apparent only to himself.

"An ounce of respect is worth a pound of love. You remember that, you'll do well."

"Right. Respect." After all, he'd done so much to command the respect of others.

"I meant what I said before you left here. You know that, don't you, Con?"

"About—"

"You get yourself together now and put your past behind you, you hear? It's time to grow up and be a man. I need you to save that ranch, Con. I don't want to lose it. It belongs in the family."

"You're coming through loud and clear," he said.

"Good. You see that it happens. Now, get back to work. I'll call you next week."

Conner hung up, then pressed his fingertips to his eyes. *If it belongs in the family, Clive, why the hell did you send me?*

CHAPTER SIX

DELANEY SIGHED IN EXHAUSTION as she slumped into the easy chair in her living room to sip a cup of hot cocoa. She'd made over twenty pies this week and had sold eighteen in less than five hours. Which meant she'd earned another $146 she could shove into her cookie jar against the time Rebecca left, when her expenses would nearly double. Though Dundee could pay her only so much to run the library, she made extra money selling her pies on the weekend. If she was careful, she should be able to get by. She certainly wasn't going to move back home.

The assertiveness evaluation she'd printed off the Internet earlier sat on the accent table next to her. After eyeing it over the rim of her cup, she finally set her hot cocoa aside and took up her pencil. She'd made progress in the assertiveness department, hadn't she? She might not have told Aunt Millie—yet—that she wasn't moving home, but going to Boise hadn't been a failure in *all* ways. As misguided as she'd been, she'd finally done something she wanted to do. And she'd lost her virginity. After thirty years, that had to be considered an accomplishment of sorts.

Smoothing a hand nervously over her stomach, she forced herself to stop thinking about Conner and the horrifying possibility of living with a daily reminder of that fateful night, and read the instructions on the questionnaire.

There are basically three modes of interpersonal behavior: passive, which is characterized by an overly nice or submissive quality; aggressive, which is often intimidating or manipulative; and assertive, which is bold, confident and fair behavior. To evaluate your natural tendencies, please answer the questions below according to how you would act in the situation given:

1. You are sharing an apartment with a friend. He or she borrows a garment of yours without asking and stains it. You find it wadded up on the floor of your closet. Would you—

   a. Accept the damage without comment because you really don't want an argument?

   b. Angrily destroy a garment belonging to your roommate in retaliation?

   c. Call your roommate and calmly explain that you have a problem with this type of behavior, that you work hard for your money and feel he/she should reimburse the cost of the garment and have the courtesy to ask before borrowing any clothes in the future?

What about extenuating circumstances? Delaney wondered. What if that friend was very generous with her possessions and not likely to mind having garments borrowed or even ruined? That would make *c* seem a little high-handed and condescending. Clothes were only clothes, and if that person was Rebecca, things would always even out in the end. But *b* was way off the scale of possible reactions, which left her with *a*. So she marked it and moved on.

2. You are waiting in line to go to a movie that has just debuted. It is getting rave reviews, and you have come early to get good seats. Two young teens cut in front of you in line, and then invite all their friends to join them. Do you—

    a. Allow them to cut in front of you because stopping them isn't worth making a scene.

    b. Shove them out of line.

    c. Kindly but firmly tell them that you purchased your tickets early and have been standing in line for some time, that they need to go to the back and take their turn, and that if necessary, you'll get the manager to enforce fairness.

Shove them out of line? Jeez, who made up these things? In any case, Rebecca typically went with her to the movies, which meant that if some teenagers crowded in front of them and really threatened their seating, Rebecca would tell them to haul their butts to the back of the line, and they'd do it. Delaney wouldn't have to say or do anything. But even if Rebecca wasn't around, Delaney couldn't see calling for a manager. Kids did that kind of thing all the time, and she couldn't imagine letting it upset her to the point of causing a problem. That'd be *a* again.

3. You are in the middle of watching your favorite television program. A good friend or significant other comes in and asks you to go with him or her to get the car washed. Would you—

    a. Turn off the television and go, knowing you'll miss the rest of your show?

    b. Criticize your friend for asking you during your favorite program and feel put out that he

or she couldn't intuit your desire to finish
the program?

c.   Tell him or her you'd love to go as soon as
your show is over.

Another tough one. Delaney chewed on the end of her
pencil and read through the options again. She'd care more
about being with a good friend or significant other than
watching any television show, but she was beginning to see
the pattern. If she put another *a*, she'd be categorized as
terribly passive, and passive was no longer a good word in
her vocabulary. So she finished the questionnaire with all
c answers and turned out amazingly assertive. The doorbell
saved her from going back to give honest responses.

"Good timing," she murmured, getting up. She set aside
the questionnaire, thinking it was stupid, anyway, then
opened the door to find Roy from the Running Y Ranch.

"Hi, Roy," she said. "I didn't think you were going to
make it today."

"I don't miss on the days you sell apple. You've got
one left, I hope."

"I do. I have a Dutch apple and a sour cream apple, but
that's about it."

"I'll take the Dutch."

"Come on in while I get it." She went to the freezer in
the small attached garage and brought back the pie he'd
requested. "Been busy?" she asked conversationally as she
wrote out his sales ticket.

He scowled. "You could say that. The owner's sent his
snot-nosed grandson out here for me to baby-sit."

"How old is he?"

"He's got to be thirty, but it's baby-sitting all the same."

"Why's that?"

"He's supposed to take over the ranch, but he don't know dollars from doughnuts."

Delaney handed him his pie. "He must not be a country boy."

"He's not. First day here, he asks me what kind of cattle we're runnin' and wants to know whether we've fenced the entire property."

She laughed. "Doesn't the BLM own part of it?"

"Yeah."

"Can he sit a horse?" she asked, accepting his eight dollars in exchange for the pie.

"From what I saw yesterday, he can, but only because he's as ornery as they are."

"Well, if he's that ornery, he might make a good cowboy, given time. How long is he planning to stay?"

"Hasn't said, but I give him three months. He's not used to gettin' his hands dirty, and there ain't no way a pretty boy like that's gonna last."

"Well, I hope you're rid of him soon."

"You and me both," he said, and with a tip of his hat, he stepped outside, where he nearly ran into Rebecca, who was coming up the walk.

"Hi, Roy," she said, grabbing his arm to steady herself so she didn't fall into the muddy flower bed. "I cut Dottie's hair today at the beauty parlor. Said you got company out at the ranch."

"We got trouble, you mean," he grumbled.

"Can't you use the help?"

"I need a cook for when Dottie's daughter has her baby and Dottie goes out of state to help her. I don't need someone who doesn't know a damn thing about cooking *or* ranching."

"Dottie didn't seem to think Clive's grandson is so bad," Rebecca said.

"That's 'cause she wants to set him up with her niece."

"So he's single?" Rebecca asked.

"Far as I know. But there's no need to break off with Buddy. This guy's a short-timer. He's just here to please Grandpa. Soon as his backside's sore enough from ridin', he'll head home to California. And the sooner the better, I say."

Delaney could understand Roy's frustration. These were hard times for ranchers, and he was a no-nonsense type who liked to get the job done. But his impatience with Dundee's newcomer made her feel a touch empathetic. She'd once been new. What would she have done if the town hadn't opened its arms to her?

"Wait a second, Roy," she said. "I have one pie left. Maybe I should send it with you for your guest. It might make him feel more welcome."

"I have bigger things to worry about than pampering the pampered," he retorted.

"It'll just take a minute."

"No, he's had everything he's ever wanted. And from what his uncles tell me, he hasn't been worth his keep since the day he was born."

"I said I want to send him a pie!"

Roy's eyes widened at her firm tone, and he looked questioningly at Rebecca.

Rebecca shrugged. "Assertiveness training," she said, squeezing around him to enter the house.

"Oh," he said. "Sure, send him a pie if it's that important to you."

Delaney nodded, feeling somewhat vindicated after that lousy questionnaire—and a little embarrassed about taking such a strong stand. "Beck, write him a quick welcome note for me," she said, and dashed off to the garage for the last pie.

CONNER WAS GETTING A HEADACHE. Breaking only for dinner, he'd spent hours in the study, researching the cattle industry on the Internet and looking for other avenues of income, like mining or farming. But nothing he'd found seemed plausible for the Running Y. There wasn't much silver or gold in the area. No molyndenum or industrial garnets or phosphate rock as there were in other parts of the state. And the rugged mountains made it too impractical to plant feed or other crops. Which meant Conner had to do something else. But what? He was running out of ideas.

Hoping for a revelation, he started visiting the Web sites of various cities in Idaho and bordering states, to gain familiarity with the area and make note of population, agriculture and industry. But after another hour of reading charts, graphs, maps and summaries, he sat back with a sigh and pressed his palms to his tired eyes.

You're crazy to be doing this, a voice in his head taunted, taking advantage of the quiet room and creeping discouragement. *If you think you'll finally prove yourself worthy of the Armstrong name, you're a fool. Nothing's going save this place. And if you own it, if you take it into your heart and soul, you'll walk away even emptier than when you came here.*

"Shut up," Conner said, teeth clenched.

But the voice merely laughed at him. *Don't risk it, man. Pack up and walk out. You know the routine. You've done it plenty of times before—*

There was a knock at the office door. "Conner? You in there?"

Roy. Just what he needed—more quality time with his foreman.

"Come in," he said, swiveling away from the computer.

The door opened and Roy strode in, boots thudding against the carpet. He carried a square white box, which he placed on the edge of Conner's desk. "Gal from town sent ya somethin'."

"What is it?" Conner asked.

"What's it look like?" he said, and left.

Conner stood, pulled the box closer and read the attached note.

Welcome to Dundee. I sell pies for $8 every Sunday, but this is a free sample. Number 8 Second Street. Delaney Lawson.

Delaney! Conner stiffened when he read the name. Surely this woman couldn't be the Delaney he'd met in Boise. That Delaney was from Jerome, which was nearly four hours away.

Crossing quickly to the door, Conner hollered down the hall and managed to catch Roy just before he headed outside, presumably to the small cabins beyond the barn.

"Who is this Delaney person?" he asked.

The two golden retrievers, Sundance and Champ, who belonged to the ranch, came charging down the hall, tails wagging.

"Just a gal in town," Roy said.

Dottie poked her head out of the kitchen, where she was still cleaning up the dinner dishes, judging by her wet hands. "Are you talking about Delaney Lawson?"

"She sent him a pie," Roy volunteered.

"Bless her heart." Dottie dried her hands on the towel slung over her shoulder. "That little Delaney's a dear thing. And she makes the best-tasting pie you'll ever want to eat. She used to win every baking ribbon at the fair and—"

"What does she look like?" Conner interrupted, too impatient to wait through what promised to be a litany of praise.

"She's pretty, but she's getting up in age and it doesn't look as though she's ever gonna marry. Spends all her time at the library or baking."

Delaney certainly wasn't "getting up in age" and didn't seem the type to closet herself away in a library. Besides, she'd said she was in Boise on business. He could be wrong, but he didn't think librarians traveled on business. At least, he wouldn't expect a librarian from a small town like Dundee to do so.

"Does she have any siblings?" he asked, racking his brain to remember the details he'd learned about his mystery woman's family.

"Not a one," Dottie answered. "Our little Laney was raised by Millie and Ralph Lawson. They're a gentle old couple who owned the drugstore for years and years. I remember stopping by there on my way home from school to buy candy when I was just a girl. They're retired now. Sold the store to the Livingstons, but Ralph and Millie still live in the same house they've always lived in, right off Front Street."

"They don't own a large farm?" Conner asked, finally giving in to the dogs' persistence and bending to give them each a pat. "They don't have any ties to Jerome?"

"Jerome?" Dottie echoed.

"They don't own a farm. They don't have any ties to Jerome," Roy insisted, still poised at the front door. "Laney's the town librarian, and she's the type that likes to look after people. She wanted to make you feel welcome, so she sent you a pie. That's it. Don't read anything more into this," he said, and the screen door slammed behind him.

"Roy's right," Dottie agreed. "I don't think Millie and Ralph have any kin in Jerome. And they've certainly never owned a farm."

"Of course." Conner straightened, feeling silly for pressing them so hard—and strangely disappointed at the same time. Dundee's Delaney probably wore thick glasses and thick-soled shoes. The townsfolk considered her too unappealing to find a husband. And now that he thought about it, the bold, loopy handwriting on the note that had arrived with the pie looked nothing like Delaney's neat "Thank you." Obviously, he had the wrong person.

"Is something wrong, Mr. Armstrong?" Dottie asked, and Conner realized he was still standing in the hall, staring off into space, picturing the Delaney he'd wanted it to be, the one with the smile he'd never forget.

"No, nothing," he said and forced a congenial nod before shooing Sundance and Champ away and turning back to his office. "Just thought I recognized the name."

"So? What does it say?" Rebecca demanded, and Delaney knew, from the sound of her voice that she was hovering just outside the bathroom door.

"Nothing yet. You're supposed to give it a few minutes," she said, gnawing anxiously on her bottom lip. She'd waited three weeks to take the in-home pregnancy test they'd driven nearly all the way to Boise to purchase. Now, at long last, the moment of truth had arrived. In less than two minutes, the little plastic indicator would turn pink—if Delaney was pregnant.

"I don't think you're pregnant. Your breasts haven't been sore, have they?" Rebecca said through the panel.

Delaney's breasts *had* seemed a little more sensitive than usual, but she couldn't exactly claim they'd been sore. Considering how badly she didn't want to be pregnant from that encounter at the Bellemont, it was entirely possible that her mind was playing tricks on her.

"I don't think so," she hedged. "But it's only been three

weeks. Is there supposed to be a difference in so short a time?''

''I don't know. But my sisters complained about being tired right from the start, and you've had your normal energy.''

''I guess,'' Delaney said. Actually, she'd been exhausted, but that was probably because she hadn't been sleeping well at night. She couldn't stop worrying about the possibility of a baby. She was going to feel terrible—even worse than she already did—about the way she'd deceived Conner if she found out she was indeed pregnant with his child. ''What other signs are there?''

''I don't know,'' Rebecca responded.

''I bet some people don't experience anything noticeable, not so soon,'' Delaney said. Now dressed, she braced herself emotionally and opened the door to let Rebecca in so their collective willpower might influence the results. ''Please don't turn pink. Please don't turn pink,'' she muttered as they both stood by the small vanity and stared hard at the plastic indicator.

''Pink means there's a baby?'' Rebecca asked.

''Pink means there's a baby,'' Delaney breathed.

''Isn't there a part of you that wants it to turn pink?''

''Not anymore. I just want to forget that I could ever—''

''It's turning pink,'' Rebecca interrupted.

Delaney gripped the sides of the sink. ''No, it's not,'' she said, ''because if it is, I'm going to go crazy with guilt. And if I go crazy, I'm going to come and live with you and Buddy and drive *you* crazy. And—''

Rebecca grabbed Delaney's arm so tightly it hurt. ''It's turning pink!'' she cried again. ''Look at it!''

Delaney leaned closer. What was at first barely a tinge became more obvious as she watched. ''Oh my gosh,'' she muttered and had to feel behind her for the toilet before her knees gave out. "I'm pregnant."

Rebecca stared at her. "Don't look so glum. This is—"

"If you say this is what I wanted, I'm going to kill you," Delaney interrupted.

"I thought it was what you wanted. You've been mooning over the idea of having a baby for the past few years and I…"

Her voice fell off, and Delaney suddenly realized, only because all her other thoughts were frozen with panic, that it had to be the first time she'd ever seen Rebecca at a loss for words.

"I'm going to have a baby," she said, the pronouncement ringing like a death knell in the small room.

Rebecca's smile looked forced. "That's not such a bad thing," she said. "I hated the idea of leaving you here alone. Now I can get married, knowing you'll be just as happy as I am."

"Happy?" Delaney echoed.

"Of course you'll be happy. You'll eventually forget about Conner and Boise and concentrate on the baby. And I'll be her godmother, which means I'll have to come back here for the birth and all the important occasions. It'll be perfect. What are you going to name her?"

Name her? Delaney hadn't thought past *Please, God, forgive me for my terrible mistake.* She couldn't even summon the energy to tell Rebecca how ludicrous her question was.

"Since Aunt Millie could never have kids, it might be nice to name the baby after her if it's a girl," Rebecca said cajolingly. "I mean, Millie's a bit dated and sounds almost as bad as Lula Jane or Myrtle, but—"

"Do you think you're helping?" Delaney asked.

Rebecca sat on the tile countertop and finally abandoned the pretense of "let's be happy about this." "Okay," she said. "So we have a problem. But if you really don't want the baby, you could always have an abortion."

Delaney shook her head. "Are you kidding? That's the last thing I'd ever do."

"Then, what do you suggest?"

"I need to find Conner. Tell him what I've done."

"How?"

"I don't know."

"Listen, Laney, it's too late for that. He's gone, and he's better off for it."

"How do we know he's better off?"

"He's living the life he wants to live without any interference from you, for one thing. And think about the baby. What if he sues you for custody someday? Would you be able to give up your child? Once he knows about the pregnancy, you won't be able to cut him out of your life, yet you have no way of knowing whether or not he'd be a good influence. Contacting him would only open a can of worms. What's done is done. You need to deal with it and move on."

Rebecca's words made sense. Conner wasn't ready for children. He'd told her that. He was simply a stranger who'd passed in and out of her life. She didn't know where he lived; she didn't know his last name. And he didn't know anything about her, either.

Getting hold of herself, she nodded. "Okay."

Rebecca squeezed her shoulder. "When do you think you'll let the secret out?"

"Not for a while," she said. "I have to come to terms with it myself first." She closed her eyes. "Aunt Millie and Uncle Ralph are going to die when they hear."

"What do you mean? They've been *begging* you for grandchildren."

"They mean the legitimate kind."

"I know, but they'll get used to this. Come on out of the bathroom. It's not the end of the world." Rebecca tugged on her hand until Delaney finally moved woodenly to the living room, where she sank, still numb and incredulous and sick inside, into her favorite easy chair, a castoff from Uncle Ralph when Aunt Millie bought him a new recliner for their fiftieth wedding anniversary.

"Maybe you should tell them right away and get it over with, so you don't have to dread it," Rebecca volunteered.

"Thanks for the suggestion, but I don't think so," Delaney replied. "I won't start to show for several months. No need to jump the gun and make a big announcement when something could still go wrong. A lot of women miscarry in their first trimester. Don't you think I should at least wait until I pass that milestone before opening myself up to the scorn of the whole town?"

"Makes sense," Rebecca admitted. "But if you wait too long, I'll be gone. I'm getting married in June, remember?"

Delaney folded her arms and leaned back, telling herself to take some deep, calming breaths. "How does your being gone affect when I should tell people about the baby?"

"If I'm here, they'll blame me and my influence, and you'll get off more easily. They'll say, 'Just look at Laney now, pregnant without a husband. We always knew what hangin' around that Sparks kid would do, but she wouldn't listen to us.'"

Delaney was too emotionally devastated to laugh at her friend's twangy imitation. And she sensed something serious, and very possibly painful, running beneath the words. Maybe being typecast a hellion in such a small town was as difficult as being typecast a Goody Two-shoes. No one gave Rebecca credit for her positive traits, and the townspeople, by refusing to adjust their image of her, didn't allow her room to grow and change. If Delaney and Rebecca took the poor kids from the trailer park to see a movie or picked up trash on the streets to help get ready for rodeo season, Delaney received the credit. If they were together and got pulled over for a traffic violation, no matter who was driving, it was Rebecca who took the blame. Life had been that way for so long, Delaney had grown accustomed to it. But something in Rebecca's voice made her consider the disparity now.

"Not everyone knows you as well as I do," she said softly, trying to set aside her own worries for a moment.

Rebecca shrugged. "Oh, yeah? Well, they've had more than thirty years to get to know me. Anyway, I don't care what they think." This time her words didn't ring entirely true. "I'm out of here in four months. But you have to stay behind, and I don't want them treating you like an outcast."

As they'd always treated Rebecca? Delaney hesitated, wondering how to soothe her friend's heartache, but knew there wasn't much she could say at this late date. The damage had already been done, bit by bit over the years. And Rebecca would never admit to being hurt in the first place, so they couldn't discuss it openly. All Delaney could do was reassure her that she wouldn't suffer the same fate— even though she had no guarantees and feared exactly that.

"If they do, it's okay," she lied. "You know why?"

Rebecca didn't answer, but her eyes betrayed her interest.

"Because this baby was my decision," she went on. "I let you push and prod, but deep down, I wanted to go to Conner's room or I wouldn't have done it. It's that simple. So, for better or worse, I have only myself to blame, and I'm willing to accept the responsibility."

As the worry in Rebecca's eyes began to clear, Delaney thought of the Assertiveness Evaluation she'd recently taken. Question: When you do something stupid, do you a) blame the person who talked you into it, b) smack the person who talked you into it, or c) take responsibility for your actions?

Delaney smiled. She'd just chosen *c*. Maybe she was becoming more assertive, after all.

CHAPTER SEVEN

"HOLD HIM DOWN, Dwight," Jonathan whispered, his mouth so close to Conner's ear that he could feel the air stir. "And cover his mouth or he'll start crying for his mama like the big baby he is."

Conner knew what was coming, but he wasn't even tempted to cry out. He knew that would only heighten his uncles' anger, make them more determined to get even with him later. He hadn't bothered to summon help in over two years, since he was seven. The fighting between him and his uncles upset his mother too much, made her cry, and his grandfather was never around long enough to do anything about it. But Jonathan and his brothers always said that bit about crying like a baby. And they said a lot of other things, too.

As Dwight pinned Conner's hands above his head on the floor of his bedroom, Conner heard Stephen laugh. "Come on, rape baby. You think you can get away? You think you can take the three of us?" he taunted. Only he didn't come *too* close. The last time he'd called Conner "rape baby," Conner had managed to squeeze out from under Dwight and bloody his nose, even though Stephen was four years older than he was.

But Dwight was prepared for him this time. And Jonathan was helping out, anchoring his feet. "Kick him, Steve," he told his younger brother. "Kick the stupid rape baby. He thinks he's got as much right to live here as we do.''

Conner winced at the explosion of pain in his ribs and began to fight in earnest. He knew the whole episode would end much more quickly if he remained inert and let his uncles have their fun, but he'd never been able to do that. The anger inside him was too great. Scorching hot, it seemed to erupt like a volcano. And then he was suddenly free of Dwight's and Jonathan's grips and swinging and swinging. But he couldn't hit anything....

Conner woke in a tangle of sheets, drenched in sweat and, at first, didn't know where he was. The Bahamas? Hawaii? Europe? He loved spending his uncles' inheritance, loved knowing how much it bothered them that he was out playing while they were back in Napa, working for their father and trying to make good. Maybe he *was* a rape baby. But because of that, his grandfather gave him certain latitude the others didn't get. And Conner was determined to ram it right down their throats.

He blinked at the ceiling, the modest furnishings in the room, the bronze sculpture of a horse and rider on the bureau, the dogs, who'd taken to sleeping in his room. He wasn't in the Bahamas. He wasn't even in California. He was in Nowhere, USA, where his past had finally caught up with him and the pain he'd felt in his dream was only the soreness of his muscles from having worked all day. Over the past few weeks, he'd tossed bale after bale of hay to hungry cattle. He'd sat a horse in the bitter dawn, hunched against a chill wind, and helped move the herd closer to the streams and creeks that weren't frozen over. He'd gone out searching for strays, the snow falling so thick he could hardly see Ray's horse in front of him. He'd even learned to shoe horses and run a small tractor. Then, after spending his daylight hours outside, he'd used the evenings to work on the computer or the telephone, looking for information that might lead to possible salvation for the ranch, a fourth-quarter, come-from-behind victory.

But he hadn't found anything very promising, and on quiet, lonely nights like this, the old nightmares mingled with memories and crowded in, as though they were conspiring to tell him that Dwight, Jonathan and Stephen would eventually win.

Slugging his pillow, Conner groaned and rolled over to face the window, listening to the wind and to the leafless trees outside clawing at the glass. He felt like he was one of those trees, as if Dwight, Jonathan and Stephen were tugging and pulling at him, trying to uproot him and blow him away....

Don't think about it, he told himself. *Give it a break.*

Closing his eyes, he forced all thought of the ranch, his grandfather, his mother, his uncles, his past—everything—from his mind and rejoiced in the only positive thing that had happened to him since he'd arrived in Idaho. Delaney. Now, *that* had been a night in a million. She might not have given him her number, but she'd left him plenty to remember her by, and thinking about her never failed to put a smile on his face.

But she wasn't the only woman in Idaho, right? Now that he'd spent some time learning his way around the ranch, he needed to get out and start meeting people. Surely Dundee had a singles scene that was at least mildly entertaining.

He finally drifted off to a more peaceful sleep, dreaming that Delaney was suddenly in his arms, once again a warm and willing partner. But when Conner opened his eyes in the morning, he realized dreaming wasn't enough. He didn't want another woman. He wanted Delaney. At least, he wanted the chance to get to know her, to be with her again. Which meant the only thing he could do was go to Jerome to find her.

THE NOTICE, *WHEN IT CAME,* looked innocent enough. It was just bad timing that Aunt Millie happened to call the moment Delaney slid the typewritten page out of its envelope.

"Oh, no!" she said as she read the two short paragraphs written on the city's embossed stationery. Her involuntary cry interrupted Aunt Millie, who was asking whether or not Delaney wanted to participate in her Bonco group this month.

"What it is, dear?"

"The city finally has the funds to remodel the library and expand the book collection," she said.

"That's good, isn't it? You've been wanting to expand the book collection for a long time."

"But they can't do it right now!"

"Why not?"

Delaney sank into a kitchen chair, feeling numb and even a little frightened. "Because on April fifteenth, they're closing it down for three whole months. And they're putting me on half pay." Half pay—when she needed to be saving as much money as she could for the baby...

"You can find something else to help you get by, can't you?" Aunt Millie responded. "You won't need much if you're living here."

Delaney caught the not-so-subtle hint, but didn't have the energy to comment on it or even worry about it. She had bigger things on her mind—like buying groceries and feeding her baby. "Dundee doesn't exactly have a booming economy."

"So, what will you do?" Aunt Millie asked, her voice starting to reflect Delaney's worry.

"I'll come up with something," Delaney said as calmly as possible. She couldn't deal with the prospect of Aunt Millie getting upset; she was too upset herself.

"I know you will. You're a mature, responsible person. Good things come to good people, Laney. I've always told you that."

Guilt assaulted Delaney, stabbing her right in the heart. She lied to Aunt Millie and Uncle Ralph every time she saw them by pretending nothing had changed. She'd never felt like such a fraud, and was finding it increasingly difficult to get through the day without blurting out her secret for everyone to hear—for better or worse. Especially when Aunt Millie started describing her as a saint.

"I'm too old to be living at home," she said suddenly.

"What, dear?"

"I said I'm too old to be living at home. I want to take care of myself. I'm *going* to take care of myself."

"I wasn't trying to steal your independence, Laney. I only thought—"

"I know what you thought. And it's sweet and wonderful and I appreciate it. But I just can't do it."

Silence.

Delaney closed her eyes, knowing this wasn't going well. But she was still reeling from the news about her job and didn't know how to improve her methods. Those stupid role-playing things never panned out the way she envisioned. She wasn't supposed to lose her job, for one thing.

"You and Uncle Ralph have a nice routine worked out and lots of peace and quiet, which you need at your age. I'm not going to disturb all that."

"You wouldn't disturb us, Laney. We *want* you here. Goodness knows how lonely it can get...."

Oh God, now the guilt. "Aunt Millie..."

The edge in her voice checked the flow of Millie's words. "What?"

Delaney sank into a kitchen chair, put her elbows on the table and dropped her head into her hands. "I'm sorry, but I'm not going to move back home. I like being on my own."

Another silence. Then Millie said, "But you need to be sensible, Laney. You've lost your job."

"Not exactly, and it's only for three months." She took a deep breath. "I'll figure it out. I'm thirty, Aunt Millie, not eighteen."

"You're sounding more and more like that friend of yours." Aunt Millie always referred to Rebecca as "that friend of yours."

"That friend of mine is getting married and moving out. There's no point in bringing her into this."

"I've never liked the fact that you two have been so close. She's not a good influence."

Delaney hated the split loyalty she felt whenever Aunt Millie spoke of Rebecca. She loved them both, but they didn't care for each other. "I don't want to talk about Rebecca."

"Anyone who dyes her hair that ungodly purplish color—"

"It's a dark shade of auburn," Delaney corrected.

"—is no kind of lady. I, for one, will be glad when she's gone."

Delaney felt exactly the opposite, but she didn't answer. She was too busy staring down at her notice from the city, wondering why they were talking about purple hair when she didn't know how she was going to buy diapers thirty-five weeks from now. She was barely making a living as it was. If she fell behind while she was pregnant...

"Poor Mayor Sparks has sure had his hands full with her," Aunt Millie was saying.

"What's she ever done to you?" Delaney finally blurted, her irritation getting the best of her.

"Nothing."

"Then, what do you have against her?"

"You mean besides the time she ran away with that biker? She stayed in his room at the hotel for *three* nights before they left. And they weren't even engaged."

Delaney squeezed her eyes shut, trying not to think about Millie's reaction once she learned the truth: *I don't know why I ever took her in. I should've known, what with her mother and all….*

"People make mistakes, Aunt Millie. I don't think they set out to make bad choices, it's just—" she hesitated "—it's just that they're…trying to fill the holes inside them. You know?"

"What are you talking about—holes? You're not yourself. What's wrong with you?"

Delaney shoved a hand through her hair and let her breath seep out in a long sigh. "I have something I need to tell you," she said. "But I need to do it in person."

THE TICKING OF THE CLOCK sounded abnormally loud as Delaney sat in Aunt Millie and Uncle Ralph's kitchen, waiting for Ralph to return from the hardware store. He'd been gone when she arrived. Aunt Millie was there, though. She sat across from her, drinking tea; Delaney's own cup stood untouched on the table at her elbow.

"Are you sick?" Aunt Millie asked, breaking the uncomfortable silence.

"No." Delaney glanced down at the dark tea in her cup, then out the front window at the gently falling snow. She felt her stomach tense when she saw Ralph's big Cadillac turn the corner and make its way up the slippery street.

"There he is," Aunt Millie said.

"Yeah." That single word was all Delaney could muster. She was wondering how to tell the people who'd raised her, good churchgoing, law-abiding folk, that she was having a child out of wedlock, knowing it would humiliate and embarrass them in front of all their friends. *Delaney would never run off like that flighty Rebecca,* they'd always brag. *Delaney's such a good girl.... How Delaney could've had a mother like that, I'll never know....*

Delaney swallowed a sigh. Breaking the news was just the beginning. She'd also have to explain how it had happened. Aunt Millie and Uncle Ralph knew she hadn't been dating anyone—at least, not steadily—which certainly wouldn't reflect well on her when she announced that she was having a baby.

Delaney toyed with the sugar while she waited for Ralph to park the car and come in, letting the spoon clink against the sides of the old-fashioned porcelain bowl.

"Stop that. It's making me nervous," Aunt Millie said, and Delaney put the spoon down.

Outside, Delaney could hear Uncle Ralph stamping the snow off his boots. The door opened and closed, the floor creaked, then he appeared in the kitchen.

"Well, if it isn't our little Laney. How are you, girl?" he said, his face creasing into a ready smile the moment he saw her. "Millie didn't tell me you were coming for dinner."

"I'm not here for dinner," she said, standing to give him the hug he expected.

"You're not? Just came by to see the old folks, huh?"

Delaney perched on the edge of her chair as Uncle Ralph

glanced at Aunt Millie and finally seemed to grasp that this wasn't a social visit. "What is it?" he asked his wife.

Aunt Millie shrugged. "Ask Laney."

Short and wiry and nearly seventy-five, Uncle Ralph rubbed the bald dome of his head and turned his soft brown eyes to Delaney. "Is something wrong?"

She was tempted to tell him about the library closing and try to distract him with that bit of bad news. But Delaney refused to be such a coward. She needed to take responsibility for her actions, get it over with.

"I'm going to have a baby," she said, as loudly and clearly as she could.

Aunt Millie spilled her tea, and Uncle Ralph rushed to help mop up the hot liquid before it could burn her.

"Come again?" he said, when the immediate crisis was over.

Delaney curled her nails into her palms. "I'm pregnant."

Both jaws sagged wide open and two sets of dentures nearly tumbled out onto the floor.

Aunt Millie seemed to recover first. "Did you say what I think you said, Laney?" she asked, her voice sounding oddly strangled.

Delaney nodded. "I'm sorry."

Uncle Ralph finally closed his mouth. "Does this mean you're getting married?" he asked tentatively.

Delaney sat up straighter and shook her head. "I'm afraid not."

"But how could that be?" Aunt Millie asked. "Who…I mean how…I mean you—"

"Out of *wedlock?*" Uncle Ralph cut in.

"It…it was just a one-night thing, a mistake," Delaney said.

"Damn right it was a mistake," he nearly shouted. "Who did this to you?"

"A man I met in Boise."

"Then, we'll find him, make him own up to—"

Delaney stood. "No. What happened was my fault. I take full responsibility."

Uncle Ralph didn't seem to know what to say. He turned to Aunt Millie. "How could this have happened?"

"I don't know," Aunt Millie said. "She's always been so good."

"I'm still the same person," Delaney said.

"You're not the same person," Aunt Millie replied. "I don't know what's gotten into you, but you're not the same person at all!"

The high pitch of her voice indicated impending tears. Delaney winced as Uncle Ralph put a protective arm around his wife. "How could you do this?" he asked. "Didn't we teach you better? Hasn't Millie been a good mother to you?"

"You've both been good to me," Delaney said. "And I'm grateful."

"Well, this is a heck of a way to show it," he said.

Then Millie started to cry in earnest, and he took her in his arms and tried to comfort her, and Delaney didn't know what else to do except leave.

EVIDENTLY DELANEY'S NAME was as unusual as Conner had thought. No one he'd met in Jerome had heard of a Delaney. But it was a much bigger town than he'd expected from her description. He couldn't ask all 18,000 residents. And she might live in an outlying area. Or it was possible that her family wasn't as well-known as she'd made it sound. He couldn't be sure. He only knew that it was late, and he was tired and angry with himself for wasting so much time trying to find a woman who obviously didn't want to be found. If she'd been interested in seeing him again, she would've left her phone number. He should just forget her and keep his mind on what he was doing.

The warmth of the heater threatened to put him to sleep. Rolling down the window of the ranch's old pickup, he let the cold night air revive him, and fiddled with the radio, looking for a station that didn't play country music. But before he could settle on anything, the voice in the back of his mind started in on him again.

It's Friday night, man, and look at you. You're driving a beat-up truck down a long stretch of road, heading back to an empty house. It's pathetic what the old man's reduced you to. Haven't you steeped yourself in isolation, sweat and hard work long enough? Isn't it time for a little fun?

A little fun? Conner eyed the Honky Tonk as he drove into town, heard the music spilling out its doors. A drink would reward him for all his hard work—and anesthetize him against the hopelessness that edged closer every day.

Why not, Con? Just one drink.

He turned into the gravel drive and parked alongside a row of pickup trucks that looked as dented and work-worn as his. He knew from the condition they were in that the trucks had been used to carry hay and fencing, tools and tack. The men who drove them, the men inside the bar, would resemble him, too, now that he was wearing cowboy boots and a pair of snug-fitting jeans. He hadn't taken to chewing tobacco, knew he never would, but after the sunburns he'd suffered on his face and neck, he was already on the hunt for a good hat.

Maybe the town was rubbing off on him more than he thought. Maybe he *was* turning into a real cowboy. There were times when it seemed he was slowly becoming part of the ranch, or the ranch was slowly becoming part of him, but he was fighting the transformation almost as much as he wanted to embrace it. Belonging would only make matters worse.

A drunken cowboy came stumbling out of the bar. Staring at the street, he swayed unsteadily on his feet, as though he was about to stumble off the curb.

Someone in a passing Cadillac honked; startled, the man stepped back and crumpled to his knees.

Conner shook his head, his desire to numb his senses with alcohol suddenly waning.

Come on, the voice in his head complained. *You said one drink. One drink isn't going to hurt anything.*

But he knew he'd never stop at one drink. He'd spent enough hours in clubs and bars to know that. Besides, there weren't any answers in places like this. If there were, he'd have found them by now. He needed to go home and get a good night's rest so he'd be worth something in the morning. They had cattle to move again, and with the way the temperature was dropping, they'd probably have to fill the water troughs, as well.

Getting out of his truck, Conner strode over to the inert cowboy and hauled him to his feet so he wouldn't pass out and freeze to death on the sidewalk. "Come on, buddy," he said. "If you can tell me where you live, I'll drive you home."

The man mumbled something about a trailer behind the single-screen movie theater a few blocks away, so Conner started guiding him toward the truck. But as soon as their boots began to crunch on gravel, the cowboy jerked out of his grasp.

"Where we going?" he asked, his tone belligerent, his words so slurred Conner could barely understand him.

"Home," Conner said, calmly propelling him forward.

"What for?" the guy demanded.

When they reached the truck, Conner opened the passenger door. "Because it's time for bed. Five-thirty in the morning comes pretty early when you've got to be at work," he said, then grimaced at his own words. What the hell was the matter with him? He was sounding like his grandfather. Worse, he'd let a woman from a one-night stand send him on a wild-goose chase. He was giving up drinking, dammit, *by choice*. And he was going home to bed, alone, at barely ten o'clock.

Evidently more than his style of clothing had changed. But he noticed, for once, that the voice in his head had nothing to say.

CHAPTER EIGHT

"WHERE CAN I GET a good haircut?" Conner asked Roy, who was riding shotgun in the pickup as they made their way into town after work the next day.

"There's the beauty shop. And then there's the barbershop," he said.

"Where do you go?"

"The barbershop."

Conner sent him a meaningful glance. "In that case, I'm going to the beauty shop."

Roy's mouth twitched as though he was tempted to smile, but he didn't. After six weeks of working together, Roy seemed to be softening toward him, although why Conner cared so much about the opinion of a crusty old cowboy, he couldn't say.

"You want a city-boy haircut to go with that city-boy face?" Roy asked, curling up the brim of his hat on both sides.

"You think I'd prefer the butch you've got?" Conner said.

This time Roy did laugh. "Don't blame me if you come out looking like Goldilocks."

"I'll take my chances."

They rode another few blocks before Roy pointed to a glass-fronted building with pink awnings. "That's the place you want—Hair and Now. They'll fix you up with ribbons and bows."

"What'll you do while I'm in there?"

"I sure as hell ain't gonna wait for you, not with all those ladies jawin' about neighborhood gossip. Just take me to the hardware store. I gotta get some stuff to repair the barn door. It's about to come off its hinges. Then I'll swing by the café and grab a burger. We'll have missed dinner by the time we get home, so you might want to join me there later."

"Sounds good," Conner said, and drove him to Ellerson's Hardware before doubling back to Hair and Now, where he parked on the street and sauntered inside to find a handful of women. One was doing an older lady's nails in the corner, the noxious chemicals strong enough to burn his nostrils and sting his eyes. Another, a blonde, was trimming a young girl's bangs, laughing and talking as though the pungent odor didn't affect her. And a third, wearing the customary pink smock of a hairdresser, was sitting under an old-fashioned dryer with a section of her hair up in rollers, reading a magazine. She was the only one who didn't look up when the bell jingled over the door.

"I think I should get this kind of dress," she said. "It isn't white, but then, white's so boring, you know? Who says a wedding dress has to be white?" She flipped her magazine around to show everyone, but they were all staring at Conner. And then she saw him, too, and leapt out of her chair, dropping the magazine in the process.

"What are *you* doing here?" she cried.

Conner's brows shot up in surprise. It was the woman who'd walked into the Bellemont with Delaney. What was her name? Raylynn or Rhonda or—something with an *R*. He'd have recognized her anywhere. Not many women were so tall, for one thing. And not many colored their hair such a distinctive shade of…whatever it was.

"Hey, can you tell me how to reach Delaney?" he asked, delighted that he'd happened to run into her again.

"Laney's the town librarian," the blonde volunteered. "Just go down the street another block and—"

"Katie, I'll handle this," Rebecca interrupted, and unless Conner was mistaken, he detected an edge of panic in her voice.

"Wait a second," he said, taking in the stricken look on her face, Katie's words and his lack of success in Jermome. "What's—" And then, before he could even finish his sentence, the truth hit him with startling clarity: There *weren't* two Delaneys! The Delaney who'd sent him the pie was the one he'd taken to bed at the Bellemont.

CONNER WAS FURIOUS. Evidently Delaney wasn't what she'd appeared to be. She wasn't the daughter of a prominent farmer, as she'd claimed. She had no brothers or sisters, going to high school or otherwise. She didn't live in Jerome; she lived right here in Dundee. Yet she'd seemed so sincere. He'd believed everything she told him, but now all he knew for sure was that she'd wanted to have sex with him, and he'd stupidly obliged.

What a fool! Stephen had probably hired her to intercept him at the hotel and lead him astray, hoping he'd never show up at the ranch. But either his uncle hadn't coached her well or he hadn't paid her enough, because, instead of tightening the noose, she'd abandoned the project before it could interfere with his arrival in Dundee.

"I want to talk to her," he said. "Is she at the library right now?"

Rebecca sent what looked like a silencing glare to the others, the blonde in particular, then hurried toward him and tried to drag him outside.

"Let's go somewhere we can talk privately."

Conner's first impulse was to resist, simply for the sake of resisting. But he was at least halfway convinced that Rebecca could resolve a lot of his confusion. And the women in the shop were staring at them both, looking more than eager to hear the whole story. He didn't see any need to broadcast the fact that he'd been so easily conned.

He allowed her to guide him out and around the building, toward an old Firebird. He waited while she unlocked the doors. Then she slipped behind the wheel, and he took the passenger seat, assuming they'd talk in the lot. But as soon as he'd closed his door, she started the engine and began to back out of the parking space.

"Where are we going?" he asked.

"For a drive."

"You have curlers in your hair."

"Who cares?" she said scornfully. "This town has seen me looking worse."

Somehow, Conner didn't doubt it.

They drove for several minutes, heading out toward the open road, an old disco tape playing in the equally dated tape deck, while the defroster worked overtime to clear the ice from the edges of the windshield.

"So?" he said when they'd driven several miles, too impatient to wait any longer. He'd taken Delaney at her word, had remembered her fondly, *frequently*—even gone searching for her in Jerome. And here she was, living in Dundee, only ten miles or so from the ranch. He still couldn't believe it and hated what it might mean.

"So, what?" she said.

"You want to tell me what's going on?"

Rebecca didn't answer right away, but her expression was grim, which wasn't a pretty sight on a woman with rollers on top of her head and loose sections of purplish hair hanging limp at the sides.

"I'm thinking," she finally said.

"What's to think about?" he asked as the town behind them began to recede in his mirror. "Just tell me why Delaney lied to me. Does it have anything to do with my uncles?"

"Your uncles?"

"Stephen, Dwight, Jonathan. Those names ring a bell?"

Rebecca shook her head, a vague expression on her face, then turned onto an icy dirt road that bisected a large, snow-blanketed piece of farmland.

"Did they?" he persisted, as she pulled to a stop.

She cut the engine. "I don't know who you're talking about."

"So what's all this about? Why were you and Delaney in Boise that night if you live way the hell out here? Why did Delaney want to be with me instead of hooking up with someone a little closer to home? And why was she in such a hurry to get away when it was all over?"

He wasn't sure what he expected to come out of her mouth—some kind of weak excuse, probably—but what she said surprised him.

"Well, Delaney doesn't want this to get out. This is a small town, and she doesn't want everyone feeling sorry for her, whispering, 'Poor Delaney' all the time. But if you can keep a secret..."

"I can keep a secret," he assured her.

"Laney has a terminal illness."

"What?" he croaked.

"She has cancer."

That took him aback, quickly deflating his anger and making him feel terrible, until he remembered that Delaney and Rebecca didn't possess a great deal of credibility. After everything that had happened, he wasn't willing to trust either woman much farther than he could throw her, but Rebecca's statement *could* be true.

"What kind?" he asked skeptically.

"It's…um…" Her gaze lowered to the pack of cigarettes on her console. "In her lungs."

He crossed his arms and shifted to lean against the door so he could scrutinize her more closely. "She doesn't smoke."

"She used to."

Delaney didn't *seem* like a smoker. But on the off chance that Rebecca was telling the truth, Conner thought it better to play along. "How does the future look for her?" he asked.

Rebecca knotted her hands and stared down at them, as though she found the subject almost too painful to talk about. "Not good. She has less than a year."

"So why would a dying woman drive two hours to get herself laid?"

"She wanted a last hurrah."

"That couldn't have happened closer to home?"

"She knows everyone around here."

"Doesn't someone who's facing cancer have more important things on her mind than seducing a stranger?"

She unknotted her hands to rub her arms against the cold. She hadn't bothered to grab any kind of jacket when they'd fled the salon, but damned if Conner was going to offer her his. He still wasn't sure he liked this woman.

"She wanted to try it once, to see what it was like. You might have guessed she isn't exactly an old pro in the bedroom."

"I had some inkling," he said.

"Well, we were just trying to have a little fun before the…you know, the end." Her voice dipped reverently on that last word, which hit Conner hard enough to put a lump in his throat even though he was almost certain he didn't believe her.

"How terrible," he said, still watching her closely. "I'm sorry."

Rebecca nodded and blinked rapidly, as if she were about to cry.

Conner reached out to take her hand, knowing he'd feel like a complete jerk later if he found out she'd been telling the truth and he hadn't done what he could to comfort her.

"It is terrible," she said, managing a few very real tears, which served to confuse Conner even more.

"I'm not sure what to think," he admitted. "I knew she was a virgin, of course, but she didn't say anything about the rest of it."

"She was a virgin?" Rebecca said, her voice suddenly strident.

"You didn't know?"

She pulled away to wipe her eyes. "No. But it figures, don't you think? She didn't want to take her virginity to the grave."

"But she seemed in perfect health. Isn't chemotherapy and radiation hard on a body?"

Rebecca squinted into the distance. "Yeah, well, she's a naturalist. She doesn't believe in ruining her quality of life, and the cancer's not to the point that it's painful, you know?"

The tears had been pretty convincing, but…something still didn't seem right.

"Have you ever met Stephen Armstrong?" he asked.

"Who?"

"My uncle."

"I told you I don't know anything about your uncles.

Where would I meet this Stephen? And what does he have to do with anything?''

"That's what I want to know. And I'm wondering why Delaney didn't tell me about the cancer." He remembered her saying *"Would you want to be a virgin at thirty?"* That was the line that had finally hooked him. But she could've said *"I have only a year to live"* just as easily.

"Telling someone you're dying is hardly an aphrodisiac," Rebecca pointed out. "Besides, she didn't want you to do it out of *pity.*"

She seemed to have an answer for everything. "So you're not making this up," he said.

"Why would I do that?"

Conner couldn't imagine. He thought again of his uncles, but either he'd underestimated Rebecca's lying ability or she really didn't know them.

They sat in silence for a few minutes, Conner torn between sadness and raging doubt. Then Rebecca started the car.

"Well, I have to get back or my hair's gonna be fried."

"That doesn't make you sound as though you're very worried about your friend," he said.

"I've had longer to adjust."

"I'm going to the library. I want to see her."

She shook her head adamantly. "No, the doctors wouldn't like that. Any kind of upset could take years off her life."

"I thought she only had a year."

"I mean months. It could take *months* off her life."

"But I wouldn't upset her."

"There's no reason to risk it," she said. "What do you want with her, anyway?"

"Maybe I want a second date. Maybe I'm not a love-'em-and-leave-'em kind of guy."

She rolled her eyes. "You are *totally* a love-'em-and-leave-'em kind of guy."

Was it that obvious? "Okay, maybe I haven't been Mr. Commitment in the past. But I'd really like to get to know Delaney. She was…different."

"Why would you want to get to know someone who's dying in a few months? What's the point?"

Conner arched a brow at her. "What's the *point?* How unfeeling is that?"

"It's practical," she said. "Practical is my nature."

"And it's my nature to support my friends through crises such as cancer."

"Right." She sounded even less persuaded by his excuses than he was by hers. "Well, Laney's got lots of friends." She turned onto the highway. "Don't get me wrong. I'm sorry you probably had to drive quite a distance to find her. And I can't believe she gave away enough details that you *could* find her," she added under her breath. "But Boise wasn't supposed to be a forever kind of thing, you know?"

"It's not like I signed a no-contact clause," he muttered.

"Stalking is sort of an unstated taboo."

"I'm not stalking her!"

"Then, go back to wherever you live and leave her alone. She wants to spend her last days with the people she already loves, and you need to respect that."

With an exaggerated sigh, Conner turned up his palms in surrender. "Okay, I'll keep my distance," he said. "I'm no stalker. But in a town this size, we're bound to run into each other eventually."

She lowered the volume on the tape deck. "Why?"

"Because I live here now."

"Oh God," she said, and Conner had to grab the wheel before she ran them off the road.

"WHY DO YOU keep staring at me?" Delaney asked, looking up from the pregnancy book she was reading in her recliner.

Rebecca returned her attention to the television program she'd been watching from the couch. "I'm not staring at you."

Delaney went back to reading, but soon felt her friend's gaze on her again. "What is it?" she asked impatiently.

"Nothing," Rebecca said. "I was just wondering when you were going for your first doctor's appointment."

"Not for another ten days or so."

"Oh. Right." She nodded, then asked, "How have you been feeling?"

"Good." Physically, anyway. "Why?"

Rebecca grimaced. "No reason. Just checking."

Prickles swept up Delaney's spine. Rebecca wasn't acting like herself. "What's wrong?" she asked. "Something happen at work today?"

"What makes you think something happened at work? Did one of the other stylists call? Katie or someone?"

"I haven't heard from anyone. You just seem…I don't know…edgy."

"If I'm edgy it's only because I haven't had a cigarette since I got home." Rebecca flipped off the television, scooped her pack of Camels and her lighter off the coffee table and headed for the back porch, where she always did her smoking in deference to Delaney and the owner of the house, who'd asked her not to smoke inside. Now that Delaney was pregnant, she was doubly cautious about not smoking in her presence.

But Delaney doubted that one trip outside with Rebecca would hurt the baby. She grabbed their parkas from the pegs that lined the small, old-fashioned mudroom and followed her onto the porch. "Did you and Buddy have a fight?" she pressed.

"No." Rebecca slipped into the coat Delaney handed her and shook a cigarette out of her pack.

"So what's wrong?"

Her lighter momentarily illuminated her face, which bore a rather pensive expression. "What do you know about Clive Armstrong's grandson?" she asked, sitting on the top step of the porch and holding her cigarette away from Delaney.

"Nothing, really. Have you met him?" Delaney donned her coat, then stared out over the leafless trees, buried stumps and snow-covered fence the moonlight revealed in their small backyard. Spring was going to be late this year. The weather was still snowy and cold, although it was nearing the end of March.

Rebecca paused. "No," she said at last.

Delaney shoved her hands in her pockets for warmth. "Then, why did you bring him up?"

Rebecca's cigarette glowed eerily in the darkness. "You sent him that pie. I was just wondering if he ever responded."

"No."

"Good." Rebecca turned her head and blew out a stream of smoke. "No one knows about the baby, right?"

"Just Aunt Millie and Uncle Ralph. I told them last week."

Rebecca looked stricken. "You did?"

Delaney nodded.

"Why didn't you mention it?"

"I don't know. I guess I didn't want to relive the experience." She'd simply pushed that painful confrontation to the back of her mind and tried to concentrate on the more immediate problem of a job.

"So how'd it go?" Rebecca asked.

Delaney shrugged. "Pretty much as I'd expected."

"That bad, huh?"

"They're still not talking to me. Millie called once, but only to tell me not to let word of the baby get out. She's afraid the city will fire me instead of putting me on half pay, and I won't be able to find another job."

"This is the twenty-first century, for crying out loud," Rebecca said. "The city isn't going to fire you. Having an illegitimate baby has nothing to do with how well you perform your job."

"We live in a small town," Delaney reminded her. "Getting fired over something like this is a very real possibility."

"But you were a virgin, for Pete's sake! They can't fry you for making one mistake."

Delaney felt she could certainly argue that point, but a tug of apprehension led her thoughts in a different direction. "How did you know?" she asked.

Rebecca scowled at her. "How'd I know what?"

"That I was a virgin."

Her friend gazed off into space, her strange reaction, as much as the way she'd been behaving all night, telling Delaney that something significant was wrong. "What's going on with you?" she demanded. "How'd you know I was a virgin?"

More silence.

The telephone rang, and Rebecca got to her feet and tossed her cigarette onto the cement steps, then ground it out. "There's Buddy," she said. "Thank God."

But Delaney grabbed her by the arm before she could disappear into the house. "Call him back," she said. "Something's going on, and I want to know what it is."

Rebecca surprised Delaney by not arguing. "I have bad news," she said simply, turning to face her.

"I'm getting used to bad news."

"I mean, this is *really* bad news."

How could anything be worse than what had happened already? "What is it?" Delaney asked.

"Remember Conner?"

Delaney gave her a "get real" look. "Of course I remember Conner. He's only the father of my baby."

"Well…"

An expression crossed Rebecca's face that said this was definitely going to hurt, and Delaney sucked in a breath to brace herself.

"He's here," she said.

"He's where?"

"In Dundee, at the Running Y Ranch."

Delaney grabbed the railing to steady herself. "He's *what?*"

"You heard me."

"What's he doing there?"

"He's Clive Armstrong's grandson."

The blood rushed to Delaney's head, and she bent over to combat the sudden dizziness so she wouldn't pass out. "Conner's the snot-nosed brat Roy mentioned?"

"One and the same."

Closing her eyes, Delaney shook her head, trying to make some sense of the cataclysmic events of the past six weeks. One mistake and the rest of her life was falling down like dominoes…. "And you weren't going to let me know?" she said.

"I didn't want you running over there to tell him about the baby. You heard what Roy said that day he came for the pie. He said Conner won't last. That he's no good. He'll probably head back to California before you even start to show." She squeezed Delaney's hand. "I think you should keep your mouth shut and just let him go."

Delaney didn't know what to think. She felt as though

she'd just been leveled by a two-by-four. "Where did you see him?"

"At the beauty shop."

"Did he see you?"

Rebecca raised her eyebrows. "He recognized me right away. But don't worry. I don't think he'll bother you."

"Why not?"

"I told him you need your privacy because you're dying of cancer."

"You *what?*"

"I needed to come up with something," she said, a defensive note creeping into her voice. "He was angry about all the lies you already told him and was going straight to the library to confront you."

"So you told him I've got *cancer?*"

"Yeah."

"How long did you give me to live?"

"A year."

"Great," Delaney said. "Now the whole town can start planning my funeral. That should solve everything."

CHAPTER NINE

WHAT IF DELANEY did have cancer? Conner wondered, scanning both sides of the road as he rumbled into town in the old pickup he drove everywhere. Then he'd feel terrible—worse than terrible—for not treating the situation with the proper gravity. But no matter how hard he tried to believe Rebecca, he just couldn't convince himself that the woman he'd held in his arms was only months away from the end of her life. Delaney had seemed nervous, yes, but she'd also seemed healthy, passionate and unencumbered by anything so emotionally devastating.

Still, what better explanation did he have for all the lies? When he'd spoken to Stephen last night and mentioned meeting Delaney Lawson, the name hadn't evoked any response. He'd even called Dwight and Jonathan and received similar reactions from both of them. He highly doubted the three Super Egos would miss the chance to taunt him about falling so neatly into their trap, even if it hadn't achieved the results they were hoping for. Which led him to believe that his uncles weren't involved. But if *they* weren't involved, something else had to account for Delaney's and Rebecca's strange behavior. And the thought of what that "something else" might be made him uneasy.

She could've been doing exactly what she'd said—dispensing with her virginity. Or she could've heard from someone at the ranch that he was coming to town, that Roy was picking him up at the Bellemont, and purposely intercepted him. Since Delaney lived in Dundee, she knew his grandfather had money, and would probably assume he did, too.

He frowned, remembering their conversation in the bar, when he'd mentioned birth control. "You don't have to worry about that," she'd said. And they hadn't. But what if...

That was crazy, he decided, slinging an arm over the steering wheel as he drove. If she'd purposely gotten herself pregnant in hopes of coming after him for money, why hadn't she contacted him by now?

He let his breath go in a long sigh. Maybe he didn't want to know what Delaney Lawson was all about. Maybe he'd be better off heading back to the ranch and minding his own business.

But he didn't turn around. The library was on his right, and an old Volvo still sat in the lot.

He pulled into the alley that ran along the back of the building and parked where he could watch the front door. Then he cranked the heater and folded his arms to wait. If she didn't come out in the next ten minutes, he'd go home and let the future take care of itself. But one minute ticked on to the next, and he was still there after half an hour.

Did he want to go in? Would he be sorry if he did?

Sitting in the cold certainly wasn't doing him any good.

He got out and slammed the truck door, then walked through the patchy snow to the entrance. A placard in the window said the library closed at eight on Wednesdays, which was nearly two hours ago. But when he tried the door, he found it unlocked.

THE LIBRARY HAD ALWAYS BEEN Delaney's safe haven, even when she was a child, and it still was. Between Aunt Millie muttering *"What's this world coming to?"* and

"Just when you thought you knew someone," and Uncle Ralph closing himself in his bedroom until she left, she couldn't visit her childhood home. With Rebecca insisting she shouldn't tell Conner about the baby, that he'd probably leave town, anyway—haranguing her on the subject—she didn't feel like going back to her own house, either. And then there was her fear of running into him before she could decide *what* to do. With all of that, she'd rather just stay at work. She wanted to hide out in the peace and quiet of the library for the rest of her pregnancy. Especially now that Mrs. Minike, her most devoted volunteer, had gone home.

Stretching out on the floor in one of the wider aisles, she turned to the books she'd piled next to her, hoping to distract herself from her worries, if for only a few minutes. She'd been so overwhelmed by the negative consequences of what she'd done, she'd scarcely had time to consider the positive—the fact that she was actually going to have a baby.

She gazed down at the cover of *Your Pregnancy Week by Week,* entranced by the photograph of a fetus in its mother's womb. *What a miracle!* She traced the baby's tiny fingers and toes, marveling at the absolute perfection.

Page One started from the beginning and showed a picture of a sperm penetrating an egg.

One Month: What's happening
This week—or sometime soon—the momentous meeting takes place: the sperm breaks through the egg and fertilization occurs. A baby is in the making!

That had already happened to her. She thumbed ahead to see what was coming next and couldn't help smiling at the words and illustrations. The fetus grew fingernails during week eleven, kicked for the first time in week nineteen and could laugh at three months—

"Hello? Anyone here? Delaney?"

Quickly shoving her books beneath a nearby cart, Delaney sprang to her feet, her heart beating wildly. She knew that voice. It had been over six weeks since she'd heard Conner speak, but she would've recognized his baritone anywhere.

"The library closed at eight," she called, to buy herself a few precious seconds. What was she going to do? What was she going to say? She double-checked to make sure the books she'd been reading were well out of sight, then hovered there in indecision.

"Delaney? Can I talk to you? It's Conner Armstrong."

Biting her lip, she forced herself to start toward the front desk. She had no choice. She had to deal with this situation, and she had to do it now.

When she emerged from the stacks and saw him standing there, wearing a heavy coat, jeans and boots, she felt apprehension—and a sudden, undeniable excitement. That excitement seemed to bubble up from the part of her that didn't know this sudden appearance was a catastrophe, the part of her that clung to the memories of their time together and knew it had been special.

He looked good. Better than ever. Somehow, just seeing him evoked every wicked sensation she'd experienced at his hands. But he wasn't smiling. Suspicion marked his features, making him seem more like the Conner she'd spoken to at the bar than the one she'd known in his room.

"Rebecca told me you were in town," she said.

"I thought she might, although I'm sure that came as no surprise to you."

"I'm sorry?"

"The fact that I'm here in Dundee, that I live at the

ranch. That couldn't have been a surprise. You knew I was
Clive Armstrong's grandson, right? That's why you intercepted me in Boise, why you never asked anything about
me.''

She'd picked him up because, in that setting, he was the
obvious choice, and she hadn't asked anything about him
because she hadn't *wanted* to know. She'd been afraid that
knowing him would make him too hard to forget, and she
was right. She might not have heard his hopes and dreams,
where he came from or where he was going. But she'd
learned other details that were just as significant—how he
liked to be touched; the tenderness and caring he hid behind
a façade of indifference, the security he offered when he
wrapped his arms around her and pulled her close while he
slept.

''I had no idea who you were when we met in that bar,''
she said. ''I intercepted you because…because you seemed
the type who might—''

''Be an easy mark?''

Delaney winced at the accusation in his tone. ''I wanted
a one-night stand and you were there.''

''If it was that simple, why all the lies?''

Feeling her neck and cheeks warm with embarrassment
as she recalled the make-believe childhood she'd created
for his benefit, Delaney managed a brittle smile. Inside all
those lies she'd actually revealed her heart, the real Delaney. But he wouldn't realize that. She didn't want him to.
She showed others the Delaney they wanted to see, the one
she knew they'd accept.

''I'm sorry about that. Really I am.''

His brows lifted. ''That's it? That's all you've got to say?
I'm *sorry?*''

She had to tell him. She couldn't stand here and lie to
him again, couldn't pass him on the streets as she grew

bigger and bigger with his child. It was difficult enough living with what she'd done when she'd expected never to see him again.

"I—I wasn't looking for an ongoing relationship," she explained. "I told you those lies because I didn't want you to be able to find me. I wanted to walk away and never look back—"

"You're not going to tell me you have cancer, are you? Because I'm getting a real bad feeling about this."

"No, I don't have cancer. Rebecca just…well, she came up with that one on her own."

He hesitated, his amber eyes searching her face. "So you're healthy. There's nothing wrong with you?"

She nodded.

"You just wanted to lose your virginity in Boise and went to greater lengths than most to make sure I wouldn't stalk you later or something, right?"

Somehow Delaney sensed that he'd already guessed the truth. She could tell. He didn't want to face the obvious, was trying to talk himself out of it, hoping she'd help him even if it meant more lies. But the stark reality of the situation stood between them.

When she didn't answer, he thrust a hand through his hair. "You were trying to get pregnant, weren't you?" he asked.

"Yes."

He briefly closed his eyes. "And did it work?"

Everything Rebecca had told her over the past few days about the perils of Conner's learning about the baby—the possible custody battles, the difficulty of sharing a child, the fear that he might not be the best influence, even the negative comments Roy had made about him—seemed to float to the forefront of Delaney's mind. She didn't want to do anything that would risk the security of her baby's future. But the truth was the truth. She couldn't get around it anymore. She'd cheated him, and her sense of justice demanded she admit it.

"Yes," she said.

He gulped air into his lungs as though she'd slugged him, then jammed his hands in his pockets and whirled toward the door. Delaney thought he was going to walk out on her without another word, but after only two steps he turned back. "I can't believe you did this," he said. "I can't believe any woman would do this."

The loathing in his voice hurt even more than Delaney had imagined it would. "I'm sorry."

"And what the hell do you hope to gain from it?"

"Nothing," she said. "I just want the baby. That's all. That's all I've ever wanted."

"Yeah, right," he said, and strode out. Then silence fell again. But the peace was gone.

REBECCA WAS ON THE TELEPHONE—with Buddy, no doubt—when Delaney slipped through the door, deposited her purse and coat on the bench that was the only piece of furniture in their small entryway, and tried to slip through the living room to her bedroom. She didn't feel like talking, but Rebecca glanced up when she entered, took one look at her, and told Buddy she had to go.

"Go ahead and talk to Buddy. I'm okay," Delaney lied, but Rebecca hung up anyway.

"What happened?" she asked, turning down the volume of a Sara McLachlan CD playing in the background.

"Nothing," Delaney said.

Rebecca shook her head. "I'm not buying that, Laney. You look as white as a ghost. And the library closed hours ago. Where've you been?"

"At the library," she said. "Conner came by."

"Oh, Laney, you didn't tell him, did you?" Rebecca wailed.

"I had to. How can I keep his baby a secret from him?"

Rebecca smacked her forehead with her open palm and fell back on the couch. "I knew it. You thought I was crazy to come up with the cancer thing, but—"

"You *were* crazy to come up with the cancer thing," Delaney argued. "If word of that got around, it could break Aunt Millie's heart."

"But it was working. It kept Conner Armstrong away from you."

"For a whole week? Big deal."

Rebecca rubbed her hands on her jeans. "I can't believe it. This is exactly what I was afraid of. Now you're going to tell me he was mad as hell. And of course he was. Who wouldn't be? But it didn't *have* to be this way. He didn't have to find out!"

Delaney threw up her hands. "We don't know that he's going back to California, Beck. What if he sticks around? Then he would've found out eventually. Don't you think he would've wondered when he saw me carrying a baby around?"

Rebecca groaned and covered her eyes, but didn't answer, and Delaney started to pace the area rug that covered the scarred hardwood floor. What was she going to do now? She had no idea how Conner was likely to respond, Aunt Millie and Uncle Ralph weren't speaking to her, and she had no job.

Rebecca was the first to break the silence. "Have you ever thought of leaving Dundee?" she asked. "You could move to a big city, start over, escape Conner and Aunt Millie and all the judgmental bull you're going to go through living in such a small town once everyone learns about the baby." She leaned over to reach the stereo and turned off Sara McLachlan, but Delaney caught her hopeful glance. "You could even move to Nebraska with me."

Delaney sat in her easy chair and crossed her legs, willing the tension to ebb from her tired muscles. For days she'd walked around feeling as though one more setback might make her unravel completely. "You know I'd like to come to Nebraska," she said. "But I can't leave here. Aunt Millie might be angry with me right now, but she and Uncle Ralph need someone to take care of them. And so do their friends."

"Their *friends?*"

"Mrs. Shipley's kids went away to college and never came back. Who's going to look after her?"

"That's up to her family."

"She didn't say that about me when my mother died. Nor did she say it throughout all the years she took me under her wing at the library."

"You were six when your mother died, and you were always a great help to her in the library!"

"I needed someone, and she was there. Now she needs me."

"So you're telling me that even if Aunt Millie and her self-righteous friends put you down, find fault and judge you, you're going to stay put and take care of them."

"They're not all self-righteous. Mrs. Shipley will probably just assume that Conner's no good. And the others, well, it's just what they've been taught. I'm going to help them out regardless."

"That's nuts." Rebecca shook her head. "Especially now that Conner lives here."

"Maybe, but I can't leave. Besides, I do like my job— if I can just get through the remodelling. Where else can I work noon to eight Monday to Friday, have weekends to myself and be my own boss?"

"You're not really your own boss. You're afraid you're going to be fired."

"In practice, I have a lot of autonomy," Delaney said.

Rebecca twirled her hair around and around her fingers, something she did when she wanted a cigarette but couldn't or wouldn't let herself smoke. "So who knows about the baby?" she asked.

"You, me, Conner, Aunt Millie and Uncle Ralph."

"And who knows that Conner's the father?"

"Just you, me and Conner. And I want to leave it that way, okay?"

Rebecca's lips turned down. "You're the one telling everyone."

"Well, you're the one who works at a beauty salon and does more gossiping than hair care. And I don't want Aunt Millie and Uncle Ralph to find out—certainly not until they get used to the idea of me having a baby on my own. If I told them now, Aunt Millie would probably make Uncle Ralph march over to the Running Y and demand that Conner marry me." She noticed Rebecca's agitated hair-twirling again and said, "Why don't you go have a cigarette?"

Rebecca didn't budge. "I can't."

"Why not?"

She shrugged impatiently. "I quit."

Delaney let her head fall back on the chair. "Oh Lord, not now." Rebecca had tried to quit several times before. She always lasted a few weeks, then caved in, and those weeks were hell for both of them. She'd eat like a horse, litter the house with empty ice cream containers and cookie and candy bar wrappers and complain about the smallest things, slowly driving Delaney crazy.

"That's some support, Laney," Rebecca said in a sarcastic voice.

"You know I want you to quit. I've been after you to give up smoking for years. But right now, I can't deal with you constantly chewing your nails and twisting your hair and bouncing your knee. Can't we get through this Conner mess first? One nervous wreck at a time is enough in this house, and I got there before you."

"I won't be difficult," Rebecca insisted. "I have more resolve. I can do it."

Delaney was afraid for her friend's health. And she didn't particularly relish the smell of smoke that trailed into the house on Rebecca's hair and clothes. But Rebecca had been smoking since she was sixteen. It wasn't an easy habit to break. They already knew that from past failures.

"Why now?" Delaney asked.

Rebecca picked up the remote and turned on the television.

"Why now, Beck?" Delaney pressed. "Is it because I'm pregnant?"

"That's part of it." Rebecca blew her short bangs off her forehead. "And I saw Josh today. At the drugstore."

Josh. Rebecca hadn't talked about him for a couple of months, but that didn't necessarily mean anything. He and Rebecca went way back, to their childhoods. And somehow, whenever he became involved in anything that included Rebecca, the world tilted a little off its axis.

"Did you speak to him?" she asked, wondering why a recent sighting of Josh would be a factor in giving up cigarettes.

She nodded. "He stopped to congratulate me on my upcoming marriage."

"That was nice of him," Delaney murmured, but Rebecca offered nothing more, and what she'd said so far didn't explain why this chance meeting was significant. "Is he still with Mary Thornton?" she asked, probing for the connection.

"Yeah. She was with him." Rebecca made a face. "All that perkiness makes me want to slap her, you know? Doesn't she get on your nerves?"

Delaney had never been fond of Mary, either, but she was a little surprised that Rebecca seemed to feel so strongly about her all of a sudden. "So how does this connect with your new resolve to quit smoking?"

"I think Mary whispered something to Josh about me always smelling like smoke."

So *that* was the story. What Mary said had gotten to Rebecca. But why? Rebecca didn't care what other people thought. Especially Josh. Delaney had grown up with the two of them, had witnessed how they competed and goaded and snubbed each other. Although, there was that one night when Rebecca and Josh had danced at the Honky Tonk, and finally left together. But ever since Buddy came on the scene, Delaney had figured that was all in the past.

"I'm guessing they'll be getting married soon," Rebecca said.

"Probably," Delaney agreed. "I'm surprised Josh has waited as long as he has to find a wife."

"He's been too involved in building his business. He's driven, doesn't do anything halfway."

Was that admiration Delaney detected? She shook her head in confusion. One minute, Rebecca's tone was disparaging, the next it was almost...wistful. "Does this have something to do with that night the two of you left the Honky Tonk and went to his place?" she asked.

Rebecca's hair-twirling suddenly sped up. "It didn't mean anything to me. You know that."

Uneasiness crept up Delaney's spine, and it had nothing

to do with the blatant worry she felt about her own situation. Was Rebecca rushing toward certain marital disaster?

Delaney hesitated, but what needed to be said needed to be said. Better now than after the wedding. "Beck, if you have any kind of feelings for Josh—"

"Stop it!" Rebecca said. "I don't feel anything for him. I've never even *liked* him."

"It wouldn't be fair to Buddy if—"

"I *said* I don't feel anything for him. He belongs with Mary Thornton or someone just like her. She fits into the Dundee mold. She'd never do anything that would so much as raise his eyebrows. I'm not like that, and we both know it."

"But do you love Buddy?" Delaney asked.

"Of course I do." Then she stood and headed to her room, leaving a *Seinfeld* rerun on the TV. "I'm going to bed."

Delaney didn't respond. She'd always taken Rebecca at her word when it came to Josh Hill. But she was beginning to wonder: Was Rebecca telling the truth when she said she felt nothing for him? Or did she like him just a little too much?

CHAPTER TEN

"YOU OUT OF SORTS?" Roy asked, lingering after supper instead of going directly to his house in back as he usually did.

"Why do you ask?" Conner replied, slouching lower on the brown leather sofa in the ranch's main living room and taking a long swallow of his beer.

Roy stepped over the two dogs lounging at Conner's feet and carried his beer to the chair closest to the fire that raged, hot and crackling, in the huge stone fireplace. "Been brooding most of the day."

He had good reason to brood, but he'd be damned if he was going to tell anybody about it. His family had sent him to save the ranch, and he'd knocked up the town librarian instead. The second they found out he was involved in yet another scandal, his grandfather would probably follow through with his promise to cut him off.

"Maybe I'm beginning to take after you."

"Somehow, I doubt that."

Conner prodded Sundance to move over and stretched his legs, hoping the fire's heat would ease the stiffness in his muscles and help his anger to dissipate. He hadn't slept a wink last night, and he and Roy had hauled water and feed to cattle all day. He was exhausted. But not exhausted enough to forget what Delaney had said to him last night, what she'd done to him.

"So?" Roy said, interrupting the incessant question—

what the hell am I going to do now?—that had been consuming Conner's thoughts for nearly twenty-four hours.

"So, what?" he replied, taking another sip of his beer.

"You gonna tell me what's the matter?"

He swallowed and drank some more. Maybe he'd get drunk and forget the whole thing. Maybe he'd call up a few old friends and run off for Europe, let his grandfather and uncles have the damn ranch and everything else.

That's it. Give it up before everyone finds out it was starting to mean something to you, the voice in his head quickly agreed.

"It doesn't mean anything to me. None of it means anything to me."

"Pardon?" Roy said.

Conner grimaced. "Nothing."

Roy snorted and tilted his bottle, but made no move to stand or go. Conner stared into the flames, seeing Delaney's face and hating himself for falling into her carefully laid trap. That skimpy black dress…

"Maybe we could raise horses," Roy said, out of the blue.

Conner shifted his gaze to the older man's weathered face. "What?"

"You asked if there was any way to turn this place around."

Two months ago! Conner arched his brows. "I thought I was in this on my own."

"Well, maybe I like your new haircut. Or maybe I'm starting to enjoy your cheerful personality."

Conner didn't answer. He'd gone to the barbershop instead of the salon to avoid seeing Rebecca again, and hated his new haircut. But a bad haircut was the least of his troubles. His uncles were going to have a heyday when they heard about the baby.

"I've been thinking that the Hill brothers seem to be doing mighty well for themselves," Roy went on. "They raise horses, you know. Thoroughbreds."

Did Conner care about this anymore? No. He didn't want to hear it. Roy's suggestion had come too late to make any difference.

Roy shifted forward in his seat and leaned his elbows on his knees, as though he believed that might help him gain Conner's attention. "You remember, you met Josh at the feed store when we were there last."

Conner did remember a man a couple of inches taller, wearing a demin shirt and a tan cowboy hat, but he could barely manage a grunt.

"They own almost a hundred brood mares and a million-dollar racehorse," Roy said with a whistle that made the dogs' ears perk up. "You should see the stud fees they're charging."

"I'll have to look into it," he said, so that Roy would shut up and go away. Conner had already thought of raising horses, but they didn't have the capital it would take to get started, and Josh and Mike Hill had a pretty firm hold on that sector of the market, anyway. Why did Roy have to open up to him tonight of all nights?

"There's one other thing that might help some," Roy volunteered.

Conner didn't answer. He was too busy going over the conversation between him and Delaney in Boise. *"Do you have protection?"*…*"You don't have to worry about that."*

Why the hell hadn't he insisted they buy some condoms?

Because she'd told him she was a virgin and that she'd taken care of birth control.

She *had been* a virgin. She hadn't lied about that.

"Conner? Are you listening?"

He wondered how long it would be before she hit him up for money. "Hmm?" he said.

"I was saying that a lot of people come to hunt and fish once summer gets here. They camp along the creek below the south pass. We've never charged anyone to use our land—people have helped themselves for years—but they gather our wood for fires and often leave their garbage behind. We could establish some campsites and charge sixteen, eighteen dollars a night."

"We'd have to police it, collect payment and run off anyone who won't pony up," Conner said automatically, not particularly excited by the idea. Finding a solution for the ranch didn't matter anymore, unless he could do it overnight.

"True, but we could make two, three hundred bucks a night," Roy said.

Conner glanced at him. "How? The Bureau of Land Management controls a chunk of the south pass, and the government doesn't charge for camping, does it?"

Roy fingered his mustache, then smiled. "Learned something since you've been here, have ya?"

"It doesn't take a rocket scientist to know we're not going to make any money selling something people can get for free."

"I would've thought so, too, until water started going for two and three dollars a gallon."

"That doesn't happen around here."

"We still trust our water. That's why people want to come here. But if we start charging campers, maybe the BLM will follow suit. Even if they don't, it'd be worth it— if only to get visitors to stick with the free BLM sites so we won't have to clean up after them."

Conner nodded, marginally interested because the idea seemed to have some merit, but in the end, his dark mood won out, and they sat in silence until Roy finished his beer. Setting his bottle down, the foreman finally stood to go, but Conner stopped him with a question.

"How well do you know Delaney Lawson?"

"She grew up here, for the most part," Roy said. "She's a real nice girl, has a drink at the Honky Tonk now and then, bakes a great pie. She's single, if that's what you're after. You interested?"

In making her pay for what she'd done to him, maybe. Conner didn't answer. "What about Rebecca?"

"Hang out at the Honky Tonk or the barbershop or even the convenience store long enough and you'll learn all you want to know about Rebecca Woods," Roy said. "Her daddy's the mayor."

"So she's locally famous?"

"I'd say it's more like she's—" his lips twisted into a wry grin as he shoved his hands in his pockets and jingled his change "—notorious."

"How's that?"

"When she was, oh, 'bout seventeen, she ran away with a biker, but she was too hard to handle, even for him. He sent her packing right away." Chuckling, he scratched his head where his hat had left what looked like a permanent imprint. "She's getting married soon, though. And believe me, you don't want to hook up with her, anyway. Just ask Josh Hill. They've had a feud going for as long as I can remember. The whole town stays out of their way."

"What's wrong with Rebecca? Besides her hair?"

He shrugged. "She's wild. She set the high school on fire trying to burn the mascot symbol into the football field, and dyed Mrs. Reese's hair blue the night before she was supposed to chair a meeting for the Daughters of the American Revolution, and—"

"The hair thing wasn't an accident?" Conner asked.

Roy shook his head. "Mrs. Reese's son was dating Rebecca, and Mrs. Reese stepped in to make sure it didn't come to anything. The blue hair was Rebecca's way of saying thank you."

Then, maybe Rebecca could identify with his desire for revenge, Conner thought.

Roy stretched his hands toward the fire, mistaking Conner's smile for interest in his story. "It all turned out for the best, though. I can't see Byron Reese with Rebecca. He works at the bank with his father, but he's too much of a mama's boy."

"Rebecca lives with Delaney, doesn't she?"

"Yeah, they've been friends for years."

"And they're completely loyal to each other."

"You got that right. Gilbert Tripp once backed his truck into Delaney's car at the Quick Mart, then tried to drive away before Rebecca and Delaney could get out of the store. Rebecca got behind the wheel and chased him down. He gave her some excuse about how Delaney had parked wrong and the accident was really her fault. Rebecca pulled him out of the truck by the shirtfront and gave him a black eye."

Conner considered this tidbit of information as he finished his beer and started on the bottle he had waiting in reserve. "No kidding?"

"That's our Rebecca."

"Who'd want to marry a woman like that?" Conner asked.

"A man who doesn't know any better. A man from out of state. She's moving to Nebraska after the wedding."

"When's that?"

"In June, I think. Dottie would know," he said, as Dottie came in from the kitchen carrying a bowl of ice cream for each of them.

"What would I know?" she asked as Sundance stood and started wagging his tail. Champ stayed where he was but thumped his tail against the floor.

"The date of Rebecca's wedding," Roy said.

"June twenty-sixth. Then she's off to Nebraska."

Conner declined the ice cream in favor of continuing to nurse his beer, but Roy accepted a bowl.

"I don't know what I'm going to do once she's gone," Dottie said, propping one fist on her hip. "No one can get my hair to hold a perm the way she can. Poor Delaney will miss her, too. They've been like Siamese twins ever since they started grade school."

Conner didn't say it, but he thought Dottie's hair would do well to lose the perm. And he wasn't too sad for Delaney, either.

"Bring your bowl to the sink when you're done," Dottie told Roy, and turned back to the kitchen. She paused at the door. "You two make any progress on finding someone to take over for me while I'm gone? Lydia could have that baby anytime, you know."

Conner scowled. He didn't have the patience to deal with domestic matters at the moment.

Fortunately, Roy answered for him. "We've been pretty busy, but we'll start looking right away."

"Unless you want to go hungry, you'd better. How's your grandfather, Conner?" Dottie asked.

Roy cocked an eyebrow at Conner, as if to say that was one question he couldn't answer for him, and Conner sighed. "Fine."

"I thought we'd see more of him now that you're here, but the ornery old coot hasn't been out once."

Conner didn't want to talk about Clive. It reminded him too much of all the effort he'd put into the place these past two months, effort that was now a waste. The Delaney situation would make him look as though he hadn't shaped up at all.

"You got a headache?" Dottie asked, when Conner pressed his fingertips to his temples. "You want me to get you a couple Tylenol?"

"No, thanks." Suddenly he stood, because he couldn't sit still another minute. "I'm going out," he said. "See you both in the morning."

"MR. ARMSTRONG?" The high-pitched voice came through the phone a little too loudly, as though the caller had a hearing problem, and Conner yanked the handset back a few inches to stop the sound from grating through his hangover like a buzz saw.

Wincing, he tried to clear the cotton out of his mouth so he could speak. "Yes?" he said, wondering what time it was. Roy had come to collect him at the Honky Tonk at closing, just as if Conner had asked him to be there. But Conner hadn't asked him to do anything and still didn't understand how Roy knew exactly where to find him.

In a town this size, it probably wasn't very difficult to locate someone, he decided. However, he was a little mystified as to *why* Roy had come. What did it matter to him if Conner made it home or not?

He blinked and trained bleary eyes on his alarm clock. Seven o'clock. Why would someone bother him so early on a Sunday?

"This is Millie Lawson," the voice was saying. "You probably don't know me, but I'm a friend of your grandfather's. He used to come into my store all the time."

"Who?" he said, pulling the blankets higher to cut the chill.

"Millie Lawson."

He groped through his mind, trying to place the name but couldn't. "What can I do for you, Mrs. Lawson?"

"Actually, I'm not calling for me. I'm calling for my daughter, Delaney."

Delaney's name caused Conner's sleepiness to fall away almost instantly. He shoved himself into a sitting position, which he regretted when the pounding in his head threatened to level him again.

Here it comes, he thought, lying back to ease the pain. Delaney's first appeal for money.

"Let me guess," he said. "She needs a few thousand dollars to tide her over."

"What?"

"This is about money, isn't it?"

"I guess," she said. "If you're talking about Dottie's job. From what I understand that pays a pretty good salary."

Her words took a moment to sink in. "Dottie's what?" he asked.

"Her job. I heard Dottie Richens tell Elzina Brown and Sheila Smith at Bridge Club the other night that you're looking for someone to take over for her while she attends the birth of her new grandbaby," she explained. "I was hoping you'd consider my daughter for that position."

"Delaney, er, your daughter doesn't have a job?"

"She's the town librarian, but the library's closing down for remodeling in another week."

"Which means she'll be out of work."

"Exactly."

"And you want her to work here."

"She's attractive, bright and well-read. And she can cook. Not many young women can cook these days," she added proudly.

Delaney was also a few other things he wasn't going to mention. "Why doesn't she call me herself?"

"Well, I haven't told her about this yet. I was hoping you'd be willing to come to Easter dinner next Sunday afternoon at my place so you can meet her."

Conner shoved a hand through his hair, wondering what was going on here. Were the two of them setting him up? Delaney had said she wanted nothing from him. He knew better than that, but this kind of approach seemed a little odd. It was uncomfortable being suspicious of a seventy-something-year-old woman who sounded sweeter than sugar.

"I'm a little confused," he admitted.

"I'm sorry, dear. It's just that I wanted to talk to you before I brought Delaney into it because there's something you should know."

"What's that?"

"Well, I hesitate to say anything because this information shouldn't reach certain ears, but…"

"But what?"

She cleared her throat. "Delaney has a few…physical limitations."

"What kind of physical limitations?"

"Well, Dottie mentioned that she sprays for bugs, even on the outside of the house. But I don't think Delaney should do that. Or clean the oven, either. And she certainly shouldn't carry anything too heavy."

Conner pinched the bridge of his nose. This Millie person wasn't making sense. Maybe she was senile. "Why don't you want her to spray for bugs?" he said.

"Because it could harm her unborn child. Delaney's expecting a baby—out of wedlock," she added, as though she was terribly embarrassed but felt it necessary to clarify the exact nature of Delaney's "physical limitations."

Conner hesitated. How was he supposed to respond to *this?*

"I'd appreciate it if you could keep that to yourself."

"Uh…sure. No problem."

"And if you could find it in your heart to overlook her situation," Millie went on, "I'd be most grateful. I'm really quite worried about her. My Laney's not the kind of girl this would make her seem, mind you. But she's gotten herself into a bit of a…mess."

She wasn't the only one she'd gotten into a mess. "I'd be happy to consider her for the position."

"That's wonderful. And you'll come to dinner on Easter?"

"Sure," he said. "What time?"

CHAPTER ELEVEN

DELANEY SIGHED as she pulled into Aunt Millie's driveway. Millie had insisted she come for dinner today, but Delaney wasn't in the mood to endure any more silent disapproval. She'd made extra pies because it was Easter, expecting a boon in business that hadn't materialized. Every inquiry she'd made into finding a new job had resulted in another dead end. And morning sickness was beginning to plague her—all day.

Opening the glove compartment, she withdrew the films of the ultrasound she'd had done in Boise a few days earlier, and let the sight of them buoy her spirits. Mostly black, they revealed little to the untrained eye. But Delaney had insisted on keeping them as a memento of seeing her baby's heartbeat for the first time.

Closing her eyes, she pictured the fluttering white flashes she'd seen on the screen and felt the same emotions she'd experienced in the doctor's office. Soon she'd have a baby of her own. There was something wonderful about that, even though—ever since she'd talked to Conner at the library—she felt as though she was holding her breath, waiting for the sky to fall. He hardly seemed the type to let what she'd done to him go easily. But the longer she went without hearing from him, the more hopeful she became.

Shoving the ultrasound films back into her glove compartment, she gathered the berry pies she'd brought, and got out. Judging by the cars in the drive, the whole gang was here. Lula and Vern Peterson's blue sedan sat parked a few feet from her bumper, along with Ruby McCarrel's old Cadillac and an unfamiliar, nondescript white pickup.

Movement in the front window told Delaney she'd been seen, so she started up the drive. She'd grown up with Aunt Millie's friends and loved them all. The stooped and withered Vern, who wore his polyester slacks pulled almost to his chest, had helped Uncle Ralph teach her how to drive. When she was twelve, the small, spry Ruby had shown her how to shave her legs—since Millie hadn't kept up with the practice. And Lula, silver-blue hair always shining and perfectly coiffed, had bought her the most expensive pair of shoes she'd ever owned, for the Homecoming Dance during her sophomore year. They'd all gone with her on the trip to Disneyland, too, even chipped in for souvenirs. But, of course, they'd moved a little faster in those days. Vern had stood taller, his bones less noticeable through his thin skin; Lula had still been wearing high heels everywhere, forever careful to match them with her handbags; and Ruby...well, Ruby hadn't changed much. She still dyed her hair a harsh black, painted on her eyebrows and wore bright red lipstick.

They'd all been good to her, but because of the coming baby and her job situation and her strained relationship with Aunt Millie and Uncle Ralph, Delaney had too much on her mind to tolerate their slow pace today. She'd meet the newest addition to their group, whoever was driving the white pickup, eat and help clean up, then grab a newspaper and head home, she decided. She needed to keep looking for a way to make some additional income during the next few months. Certainly there had to be *something* she could do while the library was closed.

"There you are," Uncle Ralph said as soon as she set foot on the doorstep. He'd spoken very little to her since she'd told them about the baby, but he seemed congenial enough today. Delaney wondered what had happened to soften him, then saw Vern hovering behind him at the door.

"We were just coming to fetch you," he added.

"Am I late?" she asked.

"Not yet," Vern said.

"Then, what's the hurry?"

"There's someone here we want you to meet." Uncle Ralph took one of her pies and held the door.

Delaney hesitated on the stoop, surprised by their apparent eagerness. "Who is it?"

"This is the fella who—" Ralph started, but Aunt Millie's voice rang out from the living room, interrupting him.

"Laney? Come in, dear. Hurry. We've been waiting for you."

Were Aunt Millie and her friends up to their old matchmaking tricks? Surely not while Delaney was pregnant! Aunt Millie had once mentioned wanting to introduce her to Preston Willigut, her piano tuner. Maybe they'd invited him to come for dinner. But the only pair of young eyes that looked up when she entered the room didn't belong to Preston. Golden-brown and framed with thick lashes, they belonged to Conner Armstrong.

Oh, no. Delaney stopped abruptly.

"We have a special guest today," Millie announced, her round face positively beaming. "And he's going to help us out with your...little problem."

"My little problem?" Delaney repeated, hearing the words echo in her head.

"You know, with the library closing? You don't have to worry about that anymore. Conner says you can come out and work for him at the ranch while Dottie goes to Utah to be with her daughter. Isn't that nice of him?"

Delaney's knees buckled, and she put a hand on the piano so she wouldn't sink to the ground like a deflated balloon. "I don't need his help," she said.

"Is that any way to respond to such a kindness?" Millie said disapprovingly.

"He's Clive Armstrong's grandson," Lula supplied, as though that might make a difference. "And don't worry, he isn't going to tell anyone about the baby."

Lula knew about the baby? Had Aunt Millie told *everyone?* What happened to keeping the baby a secret?

"Nope. I won't tell anyone," Conner confirmed, his voice calm and low.

Even in her panic, Delaney could see he liked having her at a disadvantage. He smiled, but there wasn't a hint of warmth in his eyes, and for the first time she felt worse than guilty about what she'd done. She felt uneasy. What was he up to?

Standing, he extended his hand. "Conner Armstrong. It's a pleasure to meet you."

She accepted the handshake but avoided his steely gaze, going along with the pretense that they'd never met; she was reeling too badly to do otherwise. Aunt Millie had obviously taken her entire circle of friends into her confidence about the baby and Delaney's job situation, and now they were determined to solve her problems, whether Delaney wanted their help or not.

"Your secret's safe with us, too," Ruby put in, but if Aunt Millie couldn't keep news of the baby to herself even when she thought it could cost Delaney her job, Delaney had no faith in the rest of them. By this time tomorrow, all of Dundee would be talking about her.

"I thought you didn't want me to tell anyone about the baby," Delaney said.

"That was before," Aunt Millie answered. "Now it

doesn't matter because Conner here is very understanding. Aren't you, dear?''

"Very," he said.

Delaney barely suppressed a groan. "So, everyone ready to eat?" she asked, breaking eye contact with Conner. Fortunately, almost everyone present, except Delaney and Conner, read the newspaper with the aid of a large magnifying glass. So if there was anything in her expression or manner to betray the fact that she already knew Conner—intimately— no one seemed to notice. The last thing she needed was to have that secret revealed now, in front of the entire geriatric society of Dundee. As far as she was concerned, there was no need for *anyone* to know those details. The two of them had to get together and talk, decide whether or not Conner wanted to pursue his rights as a father.

"Don't you want to talk about the job?" Ruby asked.

"I don't need a job," Delaney said, a little too quickly.

Aunt Millie peered at her in surprise. "You've found something?"

"No, but I will."

"Why keep looking? This is perfect," she argued. "Dottie'll be gone for at least four weeks. And Conner says you can stay on even after she returns, till Thanksgiving, if the city won't take you back. You won't get a more generous offer than that."

Thanksgiving was nearly eight months away. The significance of that particular number terrified Delaney. In other words, he'd let her stay until after the baby was born—*his* baby. What was he trying to do?

"We can talk about the job over dinner," Aunt Millie finally conceded. "Ruby made a turkey, and we don't want to let it sit for too long. It's going to be dry enough as it is."

"My turkey's never dry," Ruby said.

"It's always dry," Aunt Millie insisted. "That's why I

asked you to bring a meat loaf. But you couldn't do that. Oh, no. You had to bring your dry old turkey.''

Ruby drew herself up to her full five feet two inches. ''I make the best turkey in the world. And you'd know it too, Millie Lawson, except you can't cook your way out of a paper bag, which is why you always ask me to bring the meat in the first place.''

Delaney almost intervened to keep the peace—it was her usual role—but today she was actually grateful for the distraction. Conner was staring at her, his dislike thinly veiled, and she didn't want to think about what might be going through his mind.

''Millie's a wonderful cook,'' Uncle Ralph said. ''And I love your dry turkey, Ruby. Let's not argue in front of company.''

''It's not dry,'' Ruby said.

''Ralph's right about the arguing,'' Lula chipped in. ''Those of you who can't hold a civil tongue in your heads won't get one of my homemade rolls.''

Everyone quieted down then, because they knew Lula's rolls were easily the best part of the whole meal, and Aunt Millie seemed to remember her reason for having this dinner.

''Delaney could have cooked this entire meal and done an excellent job of it,'' she told Conner, ''but Sunday's her day to sell pies.'' She guided him to a seat at the table opposite Delaney. He sat down, and Millie took the chair beside him, no doubt so she could continue to bend his ear with Delaney's many attributes. ''And she can clean, too.''

''Being able to cook and clean is definitely a plus,'' he said. ''But domestic abilities fall far behind honesty, in my book. I don't think I can work with anyone I can't trust.''

Delaney let her gaze dart to his face, but he didn't add anything and pretended to settle for Lula's response, which was a supremely confident "Oh, you can trust our Laney. There isn't a dishonest bone in her body. To tell you the truth, we don't know how she even got herself in this... predicament. She's never been one of those—" her voice fell to a whisper "—loose women."

"So she's pregnant," Ruby said, waving her hand as though they were making a big deal out of nothing. "At least she's not doing drugs."

A muscle had jumped in Conner's cheek at the word *pregnant.* "I'm sure I can trust her," he said smoothly, but the undercurrent in his voice made Delaney squirm.

The conversation turned to the fact that Delaney could ride a horse and had experience with animals, since she'd been in 4-H and had done some barrel-racing as a teenager. But Delaney kept her eyes on her plate, purposely ignoring the funny anecdotes and comments Conner chose to share as other topics arose. He pretended to be enjoying himself as much as Aunt Millie and everyone else, but Delaney knew better. She could see that he was making a concerted effort to win everyone over, which he did with ease. Why he'd bother, she couldn't say.

"What's wrong?" Uncle Ralph asked, looking concerned as she helped him carry the dishes into the kitchen.

"Nothing," she muttered, pushing through the swinging door.

"You hardly touched your food." He put his load of dishes in the sink. "And you've been quiet as a mouse. Why are you letting those old ladies out there do all the talking?"

"Conner's been doing his share," Delaney grumbled, resenting Conner's easy charm and quick wit because she knew he was using them as some kind of weapon.

"Don't you like him?" Uncle Ralph asked.

"He's okay, I guess," she said, but at the moment, she

didn't like him at all. Obviously she'd made a mistake in telling him about the baby. She should've listened to Rebecca and forgotten her scruples about having forgotten her scruples.

"Nice of him to let you take over Dottie's position. He hasn't even started interviewing yet."

"I'm not sure we should count on his help," Delaney said.

"Why not?"

"Because he probably won't last long around here. Roy, out at the ranch, says he's going back to California soon."

Uncle Ralph raised his eyebrows. "That's odd. He's not talking like he's going back anytime soon."

Delaney had noted the same thing, and it worried her more than anything else. She didn't want to live with his hostility for years to come. "I can find another job," she told him, infusing her voice with false confidence as she rinsed the plates and loaded them in the dishwasher. "I don't want to bank on something that's still so tentative."

"All we have to do is ask him. A woman in your situation can't be too choosy."

Aunt Millie yelled for the pie server, and Uncle Ralph immediately grabbed it and left the kitchen.

Delaney took as long as she possibly could with the dishes, but the time still came when she had to return to the dining room.

"Conner said you can start Monday," Ruby told her the moment she appeared, passing her a piece of pie.

"I can't start on Monday," Delaney said. "I'm working at the library for another two weeks."

"Then, start when you can. I'm not in a big hurry," Conner said.

Delaney gritted her teeth at the self-satisfied smile that curled his lips and shoved a bite of pie into her mouth, stalling until she could think of a refusal Aunt Millie and Uncle Ralph might accept. Now that they felt they'd found the perfect solution, they weren't going to give up. And Conner was taking full advantage.

"I'd be better off looking for something closer," she said. "The ranch is several miles out of town, and the roads will be icy that early in the morning. My tires aren't great," she added, hoping for a little support from Uncle Ralph, who was always worried about the tread on people's tires.

"It's nearly spring," Ralph said instead. "You don't have to worry about the roads."

"And you could do what Dottie does—spend the week at the ranch and go home only on weekends," Conner suggested.

"We were just saying that having you stay would probably be the best solution," Aunt Millie chimed in. "You know, to cut down on the driving."

Delaney folded her napkin, unable to take another bite. "Actually, I still have my pie business. I'd need to come home at night to bake—"

"It would be smarter to bake at the ranch," Conner said, sounding downright solicitous. "You'll have a big kitchen and lots of time."

"See? It's ideal!" Ruby said. "And he's promised to match the salary you've been making at the library. With what you'll be getting from the city besides, you won't have to sell pies if you don't want to and you'll still be able to save for the baby."

Delaney managed a weak smile, but the thanks that sprang to her lips was too sarcastic to utter. "That's very generous, but—"

Conner looked up at her, hitting her with the full force of his amber eyes and the dark emotion that lurked behind them. "Is there a problem?"

Aunt Millie rushed to reassure him. "Of course there's no problem," she said. "She'll start week after next, as soon as the library closes."

"What a nice young man you've turned out to be," Vern told Conner.

Yeah, what a guy, Delaney thought. Conner believed he had her cornered, and he wasn't about to let her escape. But she'd show him. She'd show them all with a quick and absolute refusal.

Except, she couldn't think of a single objection they couldn't easily override. Conner was being too reasonable. And she was afraid that if she pushed him, he'd end up telling the room at large that he was the father of her baby. Worse, he might explain exactly *how* he had come to be the father of her baby and destroy everyone's good opinion of her in one fell swoop.

All over one mistake...

"Why not come out to the ranch tomorrow so we can show you around?" he asked, his manner deceptively casual.

"Will Dottie be there?" Delaney asked.

"For another few weeks." His grin made her feel unsettled. "After that, we'll be on our own."

Delaney nodded weakly. "Great."

"No problem," he said. "Happy Easter."

HER HEAD WAS GOING TO EXPLODE if the ringing didn't stop. Shooting out an arm from beneath the comforter Rebecca must've thrown over her sometime during the night, Delaney almost fell off the couch as she fumbled around on the coffee table, searching for the telephone. She sighed in blessed relief when she succeeded in disconnecting it from its base and restoring silence.

A few seconds later she remembered that the ringing of

a telephone generally meant someone was on the other end of the line.

"'Lo?" she mumbled, barely managing to bring the receiver to her ear without knocking herself on the head with it.

"Rebecca?"

Aunt Millie's hearing was getting worse all the time. Delaney squinted at the clock above the television, surprised to find it after ten, then promptly squeezed her eyes shut in an effort to stop the room from spinning. *Morning sickness on top of a bad night. Wonderful.*

"Hi, Aunt Millie," she said. "It's me, Delaney."

"You sound funny. Did I wake you?"

From the dead. "No, I mean, yes, but I have to get up, anyway. I need to do some housework before I go to the library."

"I was just wondering what time you were going out to the Armstrong ranch."

The ranch. Conner. God, it hadn't been a dream. "I'm not sure. I'll have to give him a call."

"Want me to arrange it for you?"

"No!" Delaney shoved her tangled hair out of her face and struggled to a sitting position. "You've done enough, thanks. I'll handle it from here."

There was a long silence, during which Delaney realized, rather belatedly, that Aunt Millie was treating her in an almost normal manner. Yesterday, she'd even given her a hug goodbye. "I know you're trying to help," she added. "And I appreciate it."

"Well, I love you, you know that."

"I do."

"I still don't agree with what you've done, though."

"Of course not." Even Delaney didn't agree with what she'd done. But she was left with the consequences of it, and those consequences just seemed to keep coming and coming and coming.

"You'll probably lose your job over this."

"Maybe."

Another pause. "So that's not good. But I think I'll enjoy having a grandbaby. I'm not getting any younger. Sooner's probably better than later, huh?"

Delaney smiled in spite of the ball of nerves that had lodged in the pit of her stomach at the mention of Conner. "I needed to hear that," she said. "Tell Uncle Ralph I wouldn't mind if he were to forgive me, too."

"Ralph thinks you're about the best thing since sliced bread. He'll come around."

Delaney felt her throat tighten at this matter-of-fact pronouncement. They still loved her, bless their wonderful old hearts. "You two have always been there for me."

"And we're not going anywhere, least not till we don't have any choice in the matter." She chuckled. "Call Conner Armstrong and make sure you get that job. It's exactly what you need, especially since you're having a baby."

His baby. Conner's job was the last thing she wanted, but Delaney wasn't going to argue now that Aunt Millie had decided to let bygones be bygones. She promised to call back once she'd talked to him, then hung up and sat staring at the phone while the ball of nerves in her stomach turned to acid.

Hi, Conner. We don't know each other. We have nothing in common. So maybe you'd be willing to go about your business and just forget about me and our baby....

Hi, Conner. Just calling to say there's no need for you to get involved in my life. I can take care of this baby just fine on my own.

Yeah, right. Like he was going to buy that. He knew she didn't even have a reliable job.

Taking a deep breath for courage, she picked up the receiver, hoping something brilliant would occur to her—or that Conner would already be gone for the day. But Dottie answered on the first ring and assured her that he was just out in the barn.

"I'll get him," she said. "He's been expecting your call."

Don't throw up...don't throw up, Delaney encouraged herself while she waited, but as soon as she heard Conner's voice, she had to dash for the bathroom.

Unfortunately, he was still there when she returned.

"Where'd you go?" he asked.

She tried to catch her breath and ignore the nausea so she could think straight. "I'm not feeling very well."

"I hear pregnancy will do that to a woman."

"So I'm learning."

"Sorry if I'm having a difficult time dredging up much sympathy. When are you coming out here?"

Delaney grimaced as the unrest in her stomach increased. Not again..."I'm not coming out," she said. "I think we should talk."

"Isn't it a little late for that? Talking's not going to solve anything at this point."

"Any chance you'd believe this baby isn't yours, after all?"

"No."

"I didn't think so. What about the possibility that you might forget about us and go on your way?"

"Next to nil."

Delaney released her breath. "That's what I thought."

"At least we understand each other."

"In what way?"

"In the only way that matters. We've played the game by your rules up till now, but that's about to change."

He sounded like a stranger to her—an angry, unfathomable stranger. And he very nearly was one. "Listen," she said. "I'm *really* sorry. I didn't mean to hurt anyone."

"Right. Well, you might be *really, really* sorry, but sorry's not going to cover something like this."

"You have every right to be upset, but please know that I wasn't trying to trap you into marriage, if that's what you think. And I wasn't planning to go after you for money—"

"Oh, no? Were you planning to go straight to my grandfather, instead?"

"I don't know what you're talking about," Delaney said. "I'm not out to cause any trouble."

"You're definitely correct there, Miss Delaney from Jerome with the big family living on the farm with the fresh milk and all that other bullshit," he said. "Because I plan to make sure of it. How much did Stephen pay you, anyway?"

"I don't know any Stephen."

"Of course not. It doesn't matter, anyway. You're going to stay out here at the ranch until you have that baby, then you're going to turn it over to me and walk away. You got that? We'll deal with this little problem my way."

Terror shot through Delaney's veins. Regardless of what she'd done in Boise, she should've realized the risks she was taking when she told Conner about the baby. "I won't *ever* walk away from my baby," she said. "That's something you need to understand."

"Well, we'll see about that," he said. "For now, just pack your bags as soon as the library closes for remodeling, and come on out."

"I'm not going to stay with you out there in the middle of nowhere."

"In case you haven't noticed, you're already in the middle of nowhere. Or is that what you liked about me—did you think I'd be your ticket out?"

"I don't want a ticket out! I'm staying right here."

"Not there, exactly. You're going to move to the ranch with me, or you won't be able to live in this town for the scandal I'll cause. Poor Aunt Millie and Uncle Ralph and your dear old friends won't be able to hold up their heads in public when I'm finished with you."

Delaney imagined the embarrassment Conner could heap on Aunt Millie's already stooped shoulders because of *her*, and hesitated. Conner was angry—or maybe *livid* was a better word—but he'd calm down, and then he'd have to listen to her. She'd *make* him listen, convince him that she'd had no intention of involving him or his grandfather in her baby's future. Convince him she wasn't interested in his family's money.

"Fine." She relented. "I'll fill in for Dottie until she gets back, but that's all I can promise."

"See you in two weeks, *sweetheart*," he said, then the phone clicked in her ear.

She was still holding the receiver when Rebecca appeared at the end of the hallway, wearing a pair of boxers and a T-shirt.

"I thought that might be Buddy," she said, her hair sticking out on all sides.

"No." Delaney hung up and covered her face with her hands. What was she going to do?

"So who was it?" Rebecca asked.

"Conner."

Delaney peeked through her fingers long enough to see Rebecca's surprised expression. "What did he want?"

"He said I'd better move out to the ranch as soon as the library closes or all hell will break loose."

Rebecca shook her head. "I told you that you should've stuck with the cancer story," she grumbled, and shuffled back to bed.

Then Delaney called Aunt Millie to tell her the good news.

CHAPTER TWELVE

TWO WEEKS LATER, Delaney was on her way to the ranch. Encompassing most of two mountains and a good portion of the valley between, it looked beautiful with the green of spring. Yellow wildflowers waved on the hillsides and the trees were just regaining their leaves. But she hadn't come to enjoy the scenery.

Slowing at the gate that led to the house, she wiped away the moisture on her lip, wondering how she could be sweating in forty-degree weather. She tossed a nervous glance at the suitcases she'd piled in the back seat. She had enough clothes in those bags to spend all of spring away from home, and probably summer, too, but she didn't intend to stay with Conner any longer than it took to gain his confidence and cooperation. It was just that packing had been therapeutic—all those neat folds and familiar steps to and from her closet—so she'd gotten carried away.

As she turned into the rutted drive, she recognized the white pickup that had been parked in front of Aunt Millie's house when she'd come to dinner on Easter Sunday, and wished she had the nerve to ram it. She'd always weighed her actions carefully, stifled the dramatic, avoided anything that would make her look bad, anything that would make others look bad, anything that would be hurtful or foolish or require an apology. Anything, in short, with even the slightest negative consequences. But she was tired of all that. For some reason, she wanted to throw the biggest tan-

trum anyone had ever seen. All she'd ever wanted was a
baby of her own. She'd lived a good life, followed the
Golden Rule, gone to church, sacrificed for the good of the
community. Was one baby too much to ask?

Evidently it was. Since that night in Boise, everything
had started rolling downhill and was only gathering speed.
Now she was a hostage to her baby's father. Judging by
the cryptic message he'd left on her answering machine last
night, saying she'd better report for work by eight o'clock
sharp, Conner planned to make the most of whatever power
he imagined he possessed.

If he thought he'd take her baby, however, he had another think coming! She put a hand to her belly. No one,
no one, was going to stand between her and this child.

Delaney parked to the side so the other vehicles in the
drive—an old Chevy Suburban and a brown pickup truck
with the tailgate down—could still get past her. Shoving
the gearshift into park, she got out and collected her luggage. She dragged all three pieces to the front step, then
punched the doorbell about ten times without pause, feeling
vaguely satisfied when Conner answered, looking harried
and still in the process of buttoning his flannel shirt.

"Give me a damn minute, will you?" he snapped, scowl-
ing at her.

"Eight o'clock sharp," she said with a smile. Then she
pushed one piece of luggage closer to the entrance. "What
do you want me to do with this stuff?"

Without answering or bothering to finish buttoning his
shirt, he reached out and grabbed the suitcases. Carrying
them as easily as if they were empty, shirttails flapping as
he walked, he led her down a long hall and into a medium-
size bedroom.

Delaney forced herself to keep up with his quick strides
and then stood at the door while he deposited her things

on a double bed. Beneath the thick white molding that circled the room, flowered wallpaper—giant yellow and white
gardenias from the looks of them—covered the walls.
Green curtains, faded along the hem, framed the room's
one window; a small television sat on a highboy Duncan
Phyfe dresser opposite the bed; and various knickknacks
cluttered the mirrored dresser to the right of the entrance.
A quick peek told Delaney that the door beyond the mirrored dresser opened into a walk-in closet, but from what
she could see, there was no adjoining bath. All in all, the
room looked clean, even if it had been furnished twenty
years earlier and never updated.

"This is your new home for the next seven or eight
months," Conner said. "Unpack, then meet me in the
kitchen."

Delaney didn't want to unpack. She wanted to sit down
with him and have a heart-to-heart talk about those seven
or eight months he'd mentioned—and the baby who'd ar-
rive when that time was up. But Conner seemed to be in
some sort of hurry, and she knew better than to waylay him
just yet. Maybe his preoccupation had something to do with
the terrible stench she'd noticed coming from the kitchen.

"Is Dottie here?" she asked as he passed her.

"No. Her daughter went into labor early. She flew to
Salt Lake Saturday night." He headed out of the room, and
Delaney followed as far as the hall.

"So who's cooking?" she called after him.

"I am."

"Now I know why you wanted me here on time."

He didn't answer, so she went back into her room and
sat disconsolately on the chenille bedspread, where she remained for several minutes, staring at her bags. She could
unpack, as he'd suggested, but somehow unpacking did not
strike her as therapeutic. Unpacking meant she'd be doing

exactly what she'd been told. So she folded her arms in defiance, then realized Conner probably didn't care whether she unpacked or not as long as she stayed at the ranch. And, unfortunately, for her reputation's sake and for Aunt Millie and Uncle Ralph, she did have to stay there. At least for now.

Standing, she wandered around the room, examining framed prints by a man named W.H. Bartlett, scenes that looked like pencil sketches of London a century or more ago. Then she checked the bedding beneath the chenille spread to find three handmade quilts, tested the television and finally searched for a bathroom, which she found at the end of the hall. After about twenty minutes, she knew she should probably make her way to the kitchen, but the same stubborn streak that had stopped her from unpacking sent her back to her room. If Conner wanted to see her, he could damn well come and fetch her.

Footsteps in the hall sent a prickle down Delaney's spine. She turned, expecting Conner to appear and growl at her the way he had when she'd rung the bell earlier. But it was Roy who stuck his head through the doorway. "Conner's burned just about everything he's laid his hands on in there," he said, nodding toward the kitchen. "Would you see what you can salvage of our breakfast? At this rate, the cattle will starve by the time we get out there."

Frustrated that Conner had sidestepped her small rebellion so easily, she considered her options. She could refuse and have it out with him here and now, while Roy—and whoever else was here—listened in. Or she could comply and bide her time until a better opportunity presented itself.

She thought of Uncle Ralph, who, before leaving for the barbershop yesterday, had congratulated her on the new job, as though she was almost completely back in his good graces. She thought of her original plan to win Conner over and realized that plan hadn't included a knock-down drag-out fight. Then she thought of her dwindling savings and the possibility of earning some money while she was here, and nodded. She had almost seven months before the baby came—plenty of time to gain control of the situation.

"I'm coming," she said. "What's that terrible smell?"

"You'll see."

BURNT OATMEAL. Delaney swallowed hard and tried not to look at the hot cereal that had boiled over onto the stove. She wanted to show these cowboys that she could cook, that as low as Conner thought she was, she still had some redeeming qualities. But she wouldn't be able to do that if every time she smelled food her morning sickness reasserted itself. Putting one hand on the counter to steady herself, she smiled weakly at the four men who lounged around the table drinking coffee, hoping she didn't look as green as she felt and wondering what, if anything, Conner had told them about her.

"Hi." She recognized a stocky, dark-haired man balancing on two legs of his chair, and the man to his right, who was taller and had a slighter build, from the Honky Tonk, but she'd never actually met them before. Roy introduced the stocky man as Grady, the other as Ben, then motioned to the slender blond cowboy closest to her and said, "This here's Isaiah."

She mumbled that it was good to meet them, while searching her mind for a meal she could cook that would be fast and easy, and would smell nothing like oatmeal. "Anybody interested in an omelette?"

"I'll eat anything before I'll eat that," Isaiah responded, punching a finger toward Conner's breakfast.

Conner ignored him. Turning the page of a magazine on

the table next to him, he took another bite of his oatmeal as though it tasted just fine, and kept reading.

"Omelettes it is, then," she said, infusing her voice with as mu, n cheer as she could manage under the circumstances.

Roy helped her find a frying pan, eggs, butter, cheese, onions, bacon and a spatula. By the time Conner had finished his oatmeal and set his bowl in the sink, she was half done with the first omelette.

"Would you like one?" she asked him.

The look he gave her said he didn't want anything from her. "Meet you boys out back," he told the others, and left.

Delaney watched him go, wondering if seven months was going to be long enough to get through to him. He had every right to be angry, but if he'd just listen to her, *believe* her…

How could she expect him to believe her when she'd done nothing except lie to him from the moment they met? She *had* tricked him, even if it wasn't for money, as he thought.

"Don't worry about him. He's still learning his way around," Roy told her with a wink. "He'll settle down."

Delaney forced a smile. She *couldn't* worry about Conner—at least, not too much. Not now. It was all she could do to finish cooking their breakfast before running for the bathroom.

THE BARN SMELLED of manure and animals. The first time Conner had stood inside it, he'd immediately compared the smell to the scent of moist, rich earth so prevalent in Napa—and thought the place stunk to high heaven. He'd wondered how anyone tolerated it. But somehow, the smell of the barn didn't bother him anymore. Ironically enough, he sort of *liked* it. There was comfort to be found here, something that spoke of sweat and hard work, of the land, of his heritage.

Breathing deeply, Conner tried to forget about his nasty-tasting breakfast, and Delaney and her much more tempting omelettes, and even Roy's silent disapproval of his surliness toward their new cook.

He hefted his saddle from the rack, preparing to ride. Roy and the others didn't understand what was going on. They didn't know how Delaney had used him. And they had no idea what sort of bind he was in now. If he was going to save the ranch, he had to do it fast, before the secret of Delaney's pregnancy got out, or he wouldn't have the chance. What she'd done had effectively cut the fuse his grandfather had given him to a fraction of its original length.

Trigger, his horse, nickered as Conner settled the saddle on his back. He patted the gelding's neck and started cinching the girth strap, eager now that he was away from the house to get out on the open range. There, nothing except the rugged beauty of the mountains, his breath misting in the cold and the solid feel of his horse moving beneath him seemed of any consequence—but the telephone interrupted him before he could get away.

Taking a moment to finish with the saddle, he glanced over his shoulder at the wall, where the flashing light and constant ringing told him someone—Roy?—was patching a call through to him from the house. There were several more short bursts before he reached the phone, but when he finally brought the receiver to his ear, he wished he hadn't bothered. It was Stephen, his uncle.

"What's up?" Conner asked. "Is my mom okay?" His uncles contacted him once a week or so to check on his progress, but they typically called at night.

"She's fine, if you can call someone who lives like a hermit fine. She really should find something to do with her life. Devoting herself to Grandfather and you is noble, but he isn't going to be around forever, and we both know how much joy *you've* brought her."

Conner felt a muscle in his cheek begin to twitch. "And you'd make any mother proud, is that it, Stephen?"

"Just stating the facts."

"I'm aware of the facts. Why'd you call?"

"To tell you that we've made a few decisions on our end regarding the ranch."

Conner felt a tremor of foreboding. "What kind of decisions?"

"Grandfather met with a Realtor yesterday, who—"

"He what?" Conner broke in.

"He met with a Realtor who specializes in large spreads, and—"

"Why?"

Stephen chuckled. "Surely even you aren't that obtuse, Con."

"Grandfather gave me a year. It's only been a couple of months. What the hell is he doing meeting with a Realtor so early? Is he thinking of selling out?"

"I set up the meeting." Stephen sounded smug. "With as long as it's taking this type of investment property to sell, we need to put the ranch on the market right away. Unless we get lucky, it'll take a year to liquidate it as it is."

"Grandfather doesn't want to sell."

"Well, he's a little sentimental about it, I admit. But he's a businessman. He knows we'll have to sell eventually. Why prolong the inevitable?"

"Are you putting on the pressure because you're afraid the ranch is whittling away your inheritance, Stephen?"

Conner asked, watching but barely seeing Champ chase a chicken out of the barn. "Or are you afraid I might actually be able to do something out here if I'm given a real chance?"

"As if you, of all people, *could* do anything, Con."

"Then, what's your hurry?"

"It's all dollars and cents. Nothing personal, of course."

Like hell it was nothing personal. It had always been personal with his uncles. Stephen was getting nervous because Conner had actually stayed and was trying to make a success of the ranch. "When does it go on the market?" he asked.

"We're supposed to sign the listing agreement next week."

"How much are you asking?"

"We haven't decided yet. The Realtor is still gathering some comparables. But if I have my say, we'll price it to move fast."

Conner stared around him at the animals and the tack and the hay, breathed in the smell he'd once found so unpleasant, and felt sick inside. His grandfather had no confidence in him, after all. He'd known that in the beginning, but somehow he'd started to believe... It didn't matter what he believed. Clive was going to sell out. He was staring at the truth now, and when word of Delaney's pregnancy spread, his uncles would have even more fuel to use against him.

He'd known better than to try. He'd known Stephen and his other uncles would band together and win in the end. How could he ever compensate for their vast resources and unity? Remembering all the beatings they'd given him growing up, the fighting he'd done just to establish some kind of equilibrium and the futility of his resistance, he wondered why he'd ever tried to change. They'd boxed him out from the beginning. They would always box him out.

FROM HER BEDROOM, Delaney heard the men come in, noted Conner's voice among the others, and felt the tension in her body increase. She'd spent all day figuring out the kitchen and the house, had made a big meal of mashed potatoes and gravy, pot roast, candied carrots, spinach soufflé and Lula's homemade rolls, had visited the barn, fed the dogs, gathered the eggs from the chicken coop and taken an inventory of the cellar. She'd even baked a couple of pies. Overall, it had been a good day. She'd managed to get a lot done despite her morning sickness, and didn't mind the work. The ranch had a pleasant, homey atmosphere that felt as inviting as a toasty log cabin. But she hated feeling so unsettled about her future. She needed to talk to Conner, and she couldn't let him put her off much longer. After dinner...

Pulling on a clean sweater, she visited the mirror in the bathroom to run a comb through her hair, then hurried down the hall toward the kitchen. She needed to get these cowboys fed so they'd disperse. Then she and Conner would be alone.

Roy raised his head the moment she came in and whistled. "You look pretty as a picture, Laney. And the food smells great."

Out of the corner of her eye, Delaney saw Conner scowl, but she refused to give him a second thought. She was too busy taking the pot roast and vegetables out of the oven and transferring the food from pans into bowls. Shoving a serving spoon into each bowl, she placed everything on the long wooden table that ran the length of the room and motioned for Roy, Grady and the others to take a seat.

The young Isaiah, who'd been watching her since she

came in, smiled shyly at her. "Is there anything I can help you with, Ms. Delaney?"

Conner's scowl darkened, but Delaney's smile brightened in direct proportion. "A simple first name is fine with me. No need to be formal. I think everything's ready. Just take a seat and enjoy."

"Aren't you going to eat with us?" he asked.

"No, not tonight." Delaney was too nervous to eat and didn't want to risk having the food make her sick. She wanted to feel her best when she faced Conner tonight.

Isaiah caught her eye again. "Well, this looks mighty fancy, Delaney. I appreciate the effort that went into cooking up something so fine."

"Thanks," she said.

"Sure hope you plan on sticking around. I mean, it isn't every day a cowboy can find such a pretty lady to do his cookin'—"

"Oh, for God's sake, would you sit down and eat?" Conner snapped.

Surprised by the sudden outburst, everyone paused to look at him, but he ignored the attention, grabbed the closest bowl and began ladling carrots onto his plate as though he hadn't said a word.

Delaney quickly slipped out. She didn't want to antagonize Conner before she had a chance to talk to him. She wanted him to be fair and amenable—as far as he was capable. But when she sat down in the living room to wait until she could go back to the kitchen and clean up, she soon realized that she could hear almost everything they said.

"What's gotten into you?" Roy asked.

Delaney didn't have to be in the same room to know he was talking to Conner.

"Nothing," Conner mumbled.

"I was just paying the lady a compliment," Isaiah said. "Somethin' the matter with that?"

"You're too young for her," Conner said. "Stay away."

From the sudden silence, Delaney guessed the others had stopped eating and were staring at Conner. Her jaw had certainly dropped.

"What difference does it make to you?" Isaiah asked. "Having a beautiful woman in the house might turn *you* into a bear, but it doesn't affect me the same way. I wouldn't mind getting to know her a little better."

"You're only twenty-two!"

"So? Maybe I like older women."

"I said to stay away from her."

Delaney wondered if Isaiah would argue, but he immediately backed down. "Whatever," he said, a shrug in his voice.

The conversation lapsed. Forks clinked against plates, spoons scraped bowls and chairs occasionally squeaked, but no one spoke again until Roy and the others began to file out.

"Thanks for dinner, Laney... Dinner was mighty tasty... See you bright and early tomorrow morning...." they murmured as they passed her.

Delaney gave them each a polite goodbye, then ducked into the kitchen to find Conner still at the table, staring off into space. Finally, *finally,* they were alone.

"Can we talk now?" she asked.

He didn't answer.

"Did you hear me? We're going to have to talk sometime."

"I don't have anything to say to you."

"Then, maybe you can listen."

"I think I've heard about all I want to hear. Or is this when you tell me where to send my monthly check?"

"I don't want your money," she said. "If money's all you're worried about, then relax, because as far as I'm concerned you're released from all liability, all obligation, everything. I'll even put it in writing. I want this baby all to myself."

He stood and slid the chair under the table. "Then, that's the last thing you're going to get," he said softly and left.

DELANEY TOSSED AND TURNED for two hours before giving up on sleep. After her conversation with Conner this evening, she'd been tempted to toss her belongings in her car and head home. He'd thrown down the gauntlet, and fear that he meant exactly what he said made Delaney want to fight him.

But common sense told her she'd be better off biding her time. Conner had a lot more resources than she did—she didn't even have a job at the moment, other than the one he was providing—which meant he had a good chance of winning any custody suit. And some part deep inside her still clung to the memory of him as a man who could be as gentle as he was now being harsh. She remembered how he'd put her at ease in Boise by drawing her out and talking to her before making any kind of physical move, how he'd gone to great pains to make sure she enjoyed their lovemaking, how he'd seemed so disappointed when she wouldn't stay for breakfast…. Surely, he'd get over his initial anger, and they'd be able to work something out.

Kicking off the covers, Delaney got out of bed, pulled on her robe and headed down the hall to the kitchen. Maybe if she had a cup of tea she'd be able to relax. But her morning sickness wouldn't allow her to drink more than a few sips, and she ended up sitting in the living room in the dark, staring at the dying embers of the evening fire.

To avoid the steady ticking of the clock, reminding her

that she'd pay for her lack of sleep in the morning, she called Rebecca, thinking she'd hang up if Rebecca didn't answer by the third ring. But Rebecca picked up right away, and the alert sound of her voice and the music playing in the background told Delaney she hadn't been sleeping.

"What are you doing up so late?" Delaney asked.

"I just got off the phone with Buddy."

"How is he?"

"Good. Said to tell you hello. We're talking about moving up the date of our wedding."

"Why?" Lying down, Delaney pulled the lap blanket that was normally folded over the back of the couch around her shoulders, feeling strangely bereft at the prospect of Rebecca marrying and moving away, leaving her here with the disaster she'd created.

"Now that you're going to be gone most of the time, there really doesn't seem to be any point in waiting. It's boring here without you. And I'm eager to start my new life."

Delaney heard a familiar pause and knew Rebecca was smoking. "I thought you gave up cigarettes," she said.

"That was last week."

"What about smoking in the house?"

"Just one won't hurt anything. What's happening with our sperm donor?"

"Nothing. He hates me."

"And that's a surprise?"

"Not really."

"Are you going to stay there?"

Delaney snuggled deeper beneath the blanket, finally feeling a little sleepy. "I'm not sure. The ranch is nice, but—" she yawned "—Conner is not."

CHAPTER THIRTEEN

FOR THE FIRST TIME since he'd moved to the ranch, Conner thought he'd rather stay out in the freezing cold than return to the house. Delaney had been there for three days already, but he wasn't any more comfortable having her around now than when she'd first crossed the threshold. What man could be happy living with a woman who'd used him so calculatedly? Every time he saw her, a sense of betrayal settled so deep in his bones it kept his anger in a constant simmer. The fact that he couldn't simply tell her to stay the hell out of his life made matters even worse. In less than seven months, there'd be a child to consider—*his* child.

And he wasn't father material. He didn't even know if he'd have a job this summer. Stephen had called again last night to say they'd signed the listing papers. Once the ranch sold, Conner didn't know what he'd do. He wasn't going back to Napa, though. He was finished visiting the same old haunts, finished with the shallow people he'd partied with, finished with his uncles, the family fights, the jealousy and the greed. If living out in the middle of nowhere had taught him anything, it had taught him that he liked wide open spaces.

But having a kid would change things considerably. Kids needed money, care, supervision, a sense of belonging—

"What's that look for?" Roy asked, pulling his horse alongside Conner's.

Conner wondered how Roy could even see his face. It was after five and getting dark, and he had his cowboy hat pulled low against the wind, the collar of his sheepskin coat turned up. "What look?"

"The one that says the chip on your shoulder is growing bigger by the minute."

Conner considered the older man, then squinted at the others riding ahead of them. "Stephen called last night."

Roy spat at the ground. "He did? You tell him we're designating some campsites and charging to use them?"

Conner shook his head. "It wouldn't have done any good. They're planning to sell out," he said.

"They're *what?*"

"They're listing the ranch for sale."

Roy's mouth flattened into a short, straight line. "And you're gonna let 'em?"

"It's not my decision."

Roy rode for several minutes without speaking. "So basically you're giving up?" he finally said.

The accusation in his voice irritated Conner. He clenched his jaw, knowing it didn't take much to get a rise out of him lately. "What else can I do? It's not my ranch."

"Have you ever thought about making it your ranch?"

Conner scowled at him. "You know I don't have that kind of money."

"Since when has something like money ever stopped an Armstrong?"

Conner halted Trigger. Roy slowed and turned toward him. The wind whipped at their horses' manes, their clothes, their cold, raw faces, but Conner didn't feel a thing. "I'm not an Armstrong," he said, wondering what the hell Roy was getting at. Anyone who'd been around as long as Roy had heard about his father, knew where he'd come from. They knew his mother was adopted, too.

When Conner was angry, most people slunk away rather than taking him on in a direct confrontation. Evidently that didn't hold true for Roy. He looked Conner in the eye and even brought his horse a little closer.

"Maybe you're not an Armstrong," he said. "But you remind me a lot of your grandfather all the same. And the Running Y is a mighty fine place to raise a child." Saluting him with a hand to his hat, he started to wheel his horse around, but Conner stopped him with a question.

"Who told you about the baby?"

Roy grinned. "You're not in California anymore," he said. Then he kicked his horse into a gallop and rode on ahead to join the others.

IT WAS UNBELIEVABLE, really, everything that had happened since he'd arrived in Dundee, Conner thought. He'd stopped drinking. He'd stopped sleeping in late. He'd stopped wasting inordinate amounts of time and money. He'd given up fast cars and fast women. Yet it was *now* that he faced having an illegitimate child? Now that he faced his life's greatest dilemma? How ironic was that?

He probably shouldn't be so surprised, he told himself, putting down his pencil and closing the account books he'd been double-checking for the past hour. Sure, he'd taken his share of risks, but he'd never had a woman like Delaney working against him. He kept thinking he should've seen disaster coming, but how? He'd been in a bar, new in town, minding his own business, even doing a little soul-searching when—*wham!*—she struck out of nowhere, wearing that little black number.

If she'd been a more experienced woman, he might have suspected something. But a virgin? That part of the puzzle didn't quite fit. Conner wanted to paint her as cold and calculating because it was easier that way—easier to maintain a firm defense, easier to plan what he was going to do about the baby without taking her into consideration. But the memory of that night hardly supported a cold and calculating Delaney, and the longer she worked for him, the harder that image was to maintain.

Stacking the invoices that had yet to be paid on the side of his blotter, he rocked back in his chair and closed his eyes. Any sympathy he felt was because she was always sick, he decided. Any man would feel sorry for a woman who was constantly ill. Delaney spent more time in the bathroom than she did in the kitchen, and she was losing weight. Dark smudges underscored her eyes, she acted as though she could scarcely smell food without retching and she wasn't sleeping well. He often heard her rambling about the house at night, noticed the fatigue in her face come morning. Yeah, it was only natural he'd feel a little sympathetic....

But she'd brought this on herself, dammit!

"Roy said your grandfather's putting the ranch up for sale."

Conner's eyes flew open to see the object of his thoughts standing in the doorway of his office, wearing a gray sweatsuit that covered her completely yet managed to make her body appear soft and inviting. It was nearly midnight. He hadn't expected to be interrupted by anyone, least of all Delaney, whom he avoided as much as possible. Why hadn't he heard her approach?

A quick glance at her feet told him she was barefoot, and he felt the impulse to tell her to put on some slippers so she wouldn't catch pneumonia and make matters worse. But he knew he had no right to say anything.

"Is it true?" she asked when he didn't answer.

"Is what true?" He'd forgotten her question. She'd moved and the gentle sway of her breasts indicated she wasn't wearing a bra. For a moment the mental image of her naked flashed into his brain and robbed him of coherent thought.

"That you and your family are selling the ranch?"

He cleared his throat and opened the account books again, to distract himself from the fact that, despite everything, he still found her appealing. It was easier to keep his distance when he wasn't remembering the more intimate details of their past.

"Yes, we are. We've already listed it."

Having satisfied her curiosity, he thought she'd leave so he could go back to convincing himself that she was cold and calculating. But she didn't move and her gaze never faltered from his face.

"How long do you think it'll take to sell?"

"No telling. It could take a month. It could take a year."

"And then what's going to happen?"

He shrugged as if the ranch didn't mean anything to him. What good did it do to care? It was out of his hands, not his decision to make…. *So you're giving up?*

"Someone else takes over," he said, loudly enough to drown out the echo of Roy's words in his head.

"And you'll go back to California?"

Dropping the pretense that he didn't have time for the interruption, he linked his hands behind his head and crossed his legs in front of him. "That remains to be seen. Did you think you'd get rid of me that easily?"

"Stop it," she said. "I didn't have to tell you."

"About the baby?"

"Yeah."

"You did if you want any kind of financial help."

"You know I don't."

"Well, I would've found out about the baby eventually," he said.

"Maybe. Maybe not."

He considered her freshly scrubbed look, remembered the body those baggy sweats concealed and realized that suddenly he was having difficulty remaining angry.

"So why'd you do it?" he asked. "Why'd you tell me?"

"Because I feel bad about what I did. I wanted a baby and I got tired of waiting around for it, so I decided to make it happen on my own. I was wrong. But you should understand something else."

"What's that?" he asked.

"I won't let anything come between me and this child," she said.

Turning, she walked out of his office, and Conner stared after her, amazed at the jumble of emotions she left in her wake. When he thought about what Delaney had done, he still felt betrayed. When he thought about the time they'd spent together, he seemed almost willing to forgive her. When he thought about the ranch and the baby and the future...

He rubbed his temples. Who would've believed he could care so much?

THE NEXT MORNING, Conner wasn't particularly pleased to find Rebecca instead of Delaney in the kitchen, preparing eggs, bacon and toast.

"Where's Delaney?" he asked, pouring himself a cup of coffee.

Rebecca considered him, then went back to turning the bacon that was sizzling and popping in the frying pan on the front burner.

"Where's Delaney?" he asked again, and she finally deigned to answer.

"She had a doctor's appointment."

He almost said *"Good,"* but caught himself just in time.

He'd been worried about the weight loss and wondering why her doctor wasn't doing something to help with the nausea.

He took his usual place at the table with Roy, Grady, Ben and Isaiah, who were each cradling a cup of coffee while waiting for breakfast. "You didn't have to fill in for her. She could've told me she needed the morning off."

Rebecca widened her eyes. "Maybe she didn't want to ask you for anything."

"I can think of a few things she should've asked me two and a half months ago," he grumbled under his breath.

But Rebecca heard him. Spatula in hand, she leaned against the counter and addressed his comment, even though it wasn't specifically directed at her. "What happened two and a half months ago was more my fault than hers."

Conner glanced at the others. "Let's not talk about it right now."

"Why not?" she countered. "It's not like I'd be telling them anything new. It's all over town."

His co-workers stared into their cups as though coffee had suddenly become very fascinating. All except Roy, who seemed to have difficulty biting back a smile.

Conner shot him a dark look to see if that might help him regain his composure. "I don't care what's going around town. It's my business."

"Fine. I'm just trying to tell you that I put her up to it."

"Great. So I have you to blame?"

She shrugged. "You can blame me if you want. Just quit feeling so sorry for yourself. I mean, you enjoyed what happened as much as she did."

This time Conner was sure he heard a chuckle from Roy, and though he couldn't quite see their faces, he had no doubt the others were smiling behind their mugs.

Standing, he strode across the room, wrested the spatula out of Rebecca's hand and made a great point of giving it to Roy. "Watch the food," he said, then dragged her into the hall.

"Whether or not I enjoyed myself in Boise is beside the point," he whispered harshly, once they were alone. "I thought Delaney and I had an understanding about what was going on in that room."

"You did. And she's mostly lived by that understanding. You're the one who showed up and then proceeded to throw a wrench into everything."

"I didn't put a wrench into anything. She changed my life forever—I had no choice in the matter."

"You took a risk, okay? You trusted a complete stranger. But whether or not it changes your life is up to you."

Conner pulled her a little farther down the hall, afraid the others could still hear. "What the hell is that supposed to mean?"

"All Delaney wants is the baby. That's all she ever wanted. It was between you and artificial insemination, okay? And let's be honest, your services were a lot cheaper."

Incredulous, Conner shook his head. "I knew she was using me, but this is ridiculous."

"Oh, come on. You were using each other, and you both knew that from the start."

"Mutual pleasure is one thing. A baby is another," he replied.

"Only because you found out about it. You were supposed to live happily ever after in ignorant bliss. But then Delaney's conscience kicked in and...and you know the rest. So you see? This is all a big misunderstanding. If you ask me, you should forget any of this ever happened."

"I'm going to have a baby in less than seven months, and you think I should forget about it?"

"Why not? You're obviously unhappy about the situation. So walk away. Nothing's stopping you. Certainly not Delaney."

Conner frowned. "You have a strange way of looking at things, Rebecca. But somehow, that doesn't surprise me."

"Just walk away and Delaney will never contact you again, okay?"

"That's what she wants?"

"That's what she wants."

What Rebecca said should've made him feel better, but it made him feel worse. It stung that he could be so insignificant now, especially when Delaney had made him feel anything but insignificant the night they'd created the baby. But he couldn't have it both ways. This was what he really wanted—wasn't it?

What if he took the escape Rebecca was offering him, walked away and forgot about Delaney and the baby? Everything that weighed so heavily on his mind—his doubts about being a good father, his fear of the repercussions within his family, his uncertainty over the future, or at least some of it—could simply fade away. And turning his back on this situation was nothing more than most people would expect of him.

But somehow he couldn't do it. He couldn't walk away. Not from his child.

"Sorry," he said. "She took a risk, too. And no child of mine is going to grow up without its father."

"I THINK YOU MIGHT BE in trouble," Rebecca said as soon as Delaney returned from her doctor's appointment.

"What trouble?" Delaney asked, depositing a bag of groceries on the kitchen table.

"Not so loud," Rebecca warned. "Conner didn't go out with the others after breakfast. He's just down the hall."

"What's he doing?"

"I don't know."

"So why am I in trouble?"

Rebecca gave her arm a sympathetic squeeze. "He's not willing to back off and leave you alone, Laney."

"What's he going to do?"

"I don't know, but he told me this baby isn't going to grow up without its father."

"That could be a good thing," Delaney said, trying to be hopeful.

"If that's what you want to believe," Rebecca replied. "You know what I think? I think you were crazy to give him the power to hurt you. I tried to—"

Delaney cut Rebecca off with a warning look. "Don't say it. Don't say *I told you so*. I'm not in the mood."

Rebecca grabbed her jacket from one of the hooks along the far wall. "Okay, I won't. I know how it feels to hear it. People have been shaking their heads at me for years." She grinned. "But I told you so."

Delaney propped a hand on her hip. "You're also the one who said 'What are the odds of running into Joe Schmoe Donor from Boise way out here in Dundee?'"

A guilty expression washed over Rebecca's face, and she quickly changed the subject. "How are your assertiveness training lessons going?"

"I dropped out."

"Why?"

"Because life is teaching me everything I need to know."

Rebecca chuckled. "We make quite a pair, don't we? I'm too bold and you're not bold enough."

"If Conner tries to take this baby away from me, he'll find out just how bold I can be," Delaney vowed, but she'd scarcely gotten the words out of her mouth when the louvered door swung open and Conner came in from the hall.

Delaney gave Rebecca an apprehensive look, wondering how much he'd overheard, but if he'd caught any of their conversation, he gave no indication.

"What did the doctor say?" he asked.

Surprised by the question, Delaney exchanged another glance with Rebecca. "Nothing, really. He gave me a prescription for some prenatal vitamins. That's about it."

He hooked his thumbs in his pockets and leaned one shoulder against the wall near the entrance. "Did he say anything about the weight you've lost?"

Conner had noticed? "He's hoping the morning sickness will ease. It usually does."

"Who's your doctor?"

"His name's Wiseman. He's in Boise."

"Isn't there a closer obstetrician?"

"There's a general practitioner who delivers babies," Delaney said. "But I don't want to go to him. The whole town will know my situation in a matter of hours if I do. And I'm not in any hurry to spread the word. Why rush to be snubbed?"

"I think it's a little late to keep this under your hat," Conner said.

Delaney felt a jolt of anxiety. "Why?"

"Someone's talking. Roy mentioned the baby to me just the other day."

"He knows I'm pregnant?"

"He knows more than that. He knows I'm the father."

"But how—" Delaney started, then stopped. Rebecca

had been awfully quiet during this conversation. Surely she hadn't mentioned anything to anyone at the salon.... "Rebecca?"

Ducking her head, Rebecca grabbed her purse. "Wow, is it that late already? Gotta go. I've got appointments lined up all day."

"How could you, Beck?" Delaney asked. "I *told* you not to tell anyone."

Rebecca jerked her head at Conner. "Well, he already knew, so the danger was over. And everyone was guessing that it was Billy Joe or Bobby, because we've been seen with them so often. No one would believe me when I said they had it all wrong." She shrugged. "So I gave them a few details."

"Like..."

"The father of your baby's new in town, someone they'd never suspect, stuff like that."

"In other words, you led them straight to Conner."

"Would you rather have them think it was Billy Joe or Bobby?" Rebecca asked.

"No," Conner said. Then he shoved away from the wall and left the room.

"No?" Rebecca repeated, her eyes round. "What are we supposed to make of that?"

Delaney shook her head. "I really don't know."

CHAPTER FOURTEEN

WITH DELANEY and everyone else gone, the night was far too quiet as Conner sat in his study, halfheartedly flipping through the latest issue of *Idaho Cattlemen.* Since coming to Dundee, he'd pored through every ranching magazine he could lay hands on, trying to learn the business, trying to gain some bit of information that might help him put the Running Y in the black. But now that his grandfather had listed the ranch for sale, he no longer saw any reason to bang his head against that wall. Roy might think he was giving up too easily, but he knew his uncles. They wouldn't be happy until they had the money from the ranch to invest in another hotel or office building or winery in California. They didn't care that the Running Y hailed back to Clive's roots, that it stood for something beyond profit. To them, it was all about dollars and cents. Nothing else mattered.

So why was the idea of letting go bothering him so much? With the ranch on the market, he no longer had to worry about failing. The big question—whether or not he could follow in his grandfather's footsteps—would never be answered, and he could simply tread water until the ranch and all its problems disappeared. For whatever reason, his uncles had given him a graceful out. But somehow, taking that out made Conner feel more like a failure than if he'd kept fighting.

He tossed the magazine aside and considered calling his mother. He wanted someone to tell him there wasn't anything more he could do, that the fate of the Running Y was out of his hands. Then maybe he could really let himself off the hook. But he knew she'd probably agree with Roy about giving up too soon, so he frowned and shoved the phone away. He couldn't beat Stephen, Jonathan and Dwight. Not when they stood together. They'd always had too big an advantage.

"You gonna sit there all night, staring into space?" Roy said, poking his head through the doorway. He smelled as if he'd doused himself with an entire bottle of Brut cologne.

Conner blinked and focused on his foreman. "I thought you went into town with the others."

"No, Isaiah has a date, and Grady and Ben say they're too tired. What about you? You wanna go to the Honky Tonk?"

Conner winced at the memory of his last visit, when he'd sat alone for hours and drunk himself silly. It had hardly been a rip-roaring good time, and he hadn't been back since. "I don't think so. Place was dead when I was there."

"That's because you went in the middle of the week. No one here parties in the middle of the week. We got too much work to do. But it's Friday night, and the Honky Tonk's always packed on Friday night. Come see for yourself."

"I don't know," Conner said. "I should really…" He let his words fade because he wasn't sure *what* he should be doing anymore. Now that the ranch was passing out of his control, almost everything on his "to do" list seemed to have little point.

"Come on," Roy said, adjusting the new hat he wore on social occasions. "It's time you got out."

Conner had never dreamed someone would say that to him—to his grandfather, yes, but not to him.

"Delaney will probably be there," Roy added.

Conner shrugged as though that didn't matter, but she was becoming such a regular fixture at the ranch that he was beginning to feel her absence whenever she was gone. Especially when she went home on the weekends....

But that was only because he couldn't look out for her if she wasn't around, couldn't make sure she was taking care of herself for the baby's sake, he decided.

"So?" Roy demanded.

"Sure," Conner said. "Why not."

"DON'T LOOK NOW, but Conner just walked through the door," Rebecca said, nudging Delaney as they waited at the bar for their drinks.

"Great," Delaney said. "I can't escape him anywhere."

"Why do you think he came? I've never seen him here before."

Delaney frowned and allowed herself a covert glance across the room. She could easily see Roy and Conner cutting through the crowd, making their way to a table. Roy had scrubbed up and was wearing a western shirt and his dress hat, which added a few inches to his height. Conner looked more casual. He wasn't wearing a hat, just the Wranglers that fit him so well and a thick fleece sweatshirt that he probably considered dressing down but went a long way toward accentuating his powerful shoulders and drawing female attention. Sliding a hand in one pocket, he paused to respond to someone who'd spoken to him, and when he shifted, Delaney saw it was Gloria Palmer, an old friend of hers from high school.

"He's probably here for the same reason we are," she said, feeling a stab of possessiveness she told herself she had no right to feel. "Just looking for a little entertainment."

"Ignore him," Rebecca said. "Don't let him ruin your fun."

Delaney accepted the soda water Rebecca handed her and pressed through the crowd until she reached the darts area in the corner, where Billy Joe and Bobby waited for them.

"I just hit a triple bull's-eye," Billy Joe announced, pointing at a red-tailed dart smack in the middle of the board. "See that and weep, ladies."

"It doesn't count," Rebecca said with a shrug. "We haven't started another game yet."

"What do you mean, it doesn't count?" Billy Joe complained. "I knew we were *going* to start another game, so I went first."

"There's your problem," Rebecca told him. "I was supposed to go first."

"What do you think, Laney?" Billy Joe asked.

Only half listening, Delaney returned to the conversation. "What?"

He gestured at the dartboard. "I think I should get to keep that triple bull, don't you? This is our third game, and it's my turn to start."

"You started last time," his brother told him.

"So?" Billy Joe argued. "If Rebecca was marrying *me,* I might let it slide. But she's rejecting us both for some guy in Nebraska, as if anybody would want to live *there.* Anyway, Laney thinks I should get to keep it, don't you, Laney?"

"Sure," she said, "whatever," and threw another glance over her shoulder to see Conner laughing with a small group near the jukebox.

Rebecca rolled her eyes. "Don't listen to her. She lost her ability to reason about five minutes ago."

"No, I didn't," Delaney protested. "What is it you wanted to know?"

Billy Joe cocked an eyebrow at her. "You're not drinkin' now, are ya, honey? Because that's not good for the baby. Even I know that."

She held up her soda water. "I'm not drinking."

"Then, what's wrong?" Bobby asked. "You feelin' sick again?"

"No, not tonight."

"Well, if you're feelin' sad 'cause you wanna give that baby a daddy, darlin', you just let me know," Billy Joe said. "Because you don't want no millionaire's grandson, no siree. You want a real man like me."

Delaney laughed. Thanks to Rebecca, just about everybody she saw knew about Conner and the baby. Billy Joe and Bobby had been teasing her all night, telling her she had to name the baby Billy Bob, after both of them. But she didn't mind the secret being out in this setting. It was the people who decided her job future who worried her. When they learned about her situation, she doubted there'd be too much laughter.

"Your turn," Rebecca said, after throwing her three darts and winding up with a double seventeen.

"Nice start," Delaney said.

"She didn't start, I did," Billy Joe corrected. "And I got a triple bull."

Delaney threw her own darts and landed a bull's-eye on her first, and a twenty on her third. But she was having a tough time concentrating with Conner Armstrong only half a room away and every available woman in the place—and some who weren't so available—fanning herself at the sight of him.

"He's not *that* handsome," she muttered, but even Rebecca seemed to disagree.

"Laney, you can call that man a lot of things, but un-handsome isn't one of them."

"Whose side are you on?" Delaney asked, looking over her shoulder yet again. Only, this time she found Conner staring right back at her and nearly dropped her drink. Immediately glancing away, she set her glass on the small round table where they kept their darts, grabbed Billy Joe's arm and demanded he dance with her. He seemed a little befuddled by the sudden move, but he obliged, and a few minutes later, his brother and Rebecca joined them on the floor.

"What's up with you girls tonight?" Bobby asked, scratching his head as they all turned slowly in a circle to Lee Ann Womack's "I Hope You Dance."

"Conner's here," Rebecca explained.

"The millionaire's grandson?"

Rebecca nodded. "That's him."

Billy Joe smiled. "Where?"

"Don't look now," Delaney cried. "He might be watching us."

"Then, let's give him a show, darlin'." Pulling her into a much tighter embrace, he buried his face in her neck and clung to her as though they were lovers.

"I think you've had too much to drink," Delaney said, squirming until she could maneuver them into a position that was a little more respectable. But he only laughed and dropped a quick kiss on her lips.

"Let's see how he likes that," he said, but Rebecca and Bobby weren't laughing with him, and the moment Delaney looked up, she saw why. Conner was charging through the dancers, practically shoving them to one side. And he was coming straight for her.

She gazed up at Billy Joe. "I don't think he liked it."

"I don't think so, either," he said, sobering.

Delaney didn't have a chance to say any more before Conner took hold of her arm.

"I believe this is my dance," he said.

Billy Joe hesitated, but after a moment, he stepped back. "Sure. I was just congratulating her on the baby."

"Fine," Conner said. "We appreciate it." But his body language said he didn't appreciate Billy Joe at all, and Billy Joe knew enough to clear out.

"What do you think you're doing?" Delaney asked, as Conner slipped his arms around her waist.

"Dancing."

She tilted back her head to see his face. "You had no right to break in."

"You're carrying my baby. I think that gives me some rights."

Delaney tried to stop dancing, but he pressed his hand against the small of her back and kept her swaying with him to the music.

"Don't you agree?"

"That would depend on what kind of rights you mean," she said. "You're acting as though you have some say over what I do."

"What's wrong?" he asked. "You already got what you want from me and now you're not interested in any more?"

Not interested in any more? Delaney could feel his body only a heartbeat away, and remembered how he'd made love to her. He'd used his hands and his mouth to relax and excite her in ways she'd never imagined, then struck a rhythm that carried her with him, swiftly and easily, until she forgot all self-consciousness and everything else—except him. He'd been part of every thought, every sensation, and was now so inextricably connected to her ideal of the perfect lover that she wondered if anyone else would ever compare.

"I don't know what you want me to say." She glanced

at the people around them as if the sight of the familiar might take her mind off being in Conner's arms again. "I can't undo what happened in Boise."

Rebecca touched her shoulder from behind. "Laney, we'll be over at the darts."

"Great. I'll go with you," she said, and started to step away, but Conner locked his hands behind her back.

"She'll meet you later," he told Rebecca.

Rebecca looked at Delaney, obviously trying to determine whether or not she should get involved, and Delaney waved her on. "Don't worry," she said. "I'll be over in a minute."

Rebecca hesitated another second, but finally nodded and left, and Delaney watched Conner's eyes follow her friend across the floor.

"Your partner in crime," he said.

"She means well."

"And what about you, Laney? Do you mean well?"

Delaney could smell his cologne, feel his breath on her face. His hands gently massaged her back and held her closer, making her wonder where he was going with all this. Was he still trying to punish her in some way? His anger obviously hadn't cooled. Delaney wasn't sure he'd ever be able to forgive her. So why was he dancing with her now?

"Do you want to hear another apology? Is that what you want?" she asked, letting her confusion show in her voice.

He frowned at her, then shook his head and suddenly released her. "I don't know what I want," he said, and walked off, leaving her standing on the dance floor staring after him.

CONNER DOWNED the contents of his glass, hoping the alcohol would calm the conflicting emotions inside him. He was angry—but that was okay. Considering the circumstances, anger was a reasonable reaction. What wasn't so reasonable was the jealousy that twisted inside him every time he saw Delaney dancing or laughing with someone else. The child she carried belonged to him. But *she* didn't. As she'd informed him, he had no say over what she did, and he couldn't figure out why her freedom to interact with other men bothered him so much.

Except she owed him something, didn't she?

He couldn't decide. What had happened in Boise was simply a one-night stand. He'd had brief encounters with other women, women from whom he wouldn't have accepted any claims later on. But this time there was a baby involved, and a baby was a tie that could never be broken. That meant they owed each other *something*. In his mind, Delaney had no business milling about the singles' scene.

Only she *was* still single. And he was here tonight, wasn't he? If she shouldn't be acting as though she was available, did that mean he shouldn't, either?

"Looks like you're having a great time. I'm glad I brought you," Roy said, turning back from a conversation he'd been having with a small group of men at the table next to them.

"I'm having a blast," Conner replied, just as sarcastically, but before he could say more he noticed the tall blond cowboy he'd once met at the feed store approaching their table.

"Hey, Josh," Roy said. "How's the horse-breeding business?"

Josh nodded at him. "Roy. Can't complain. How's things at the Running Y?"

Roy shook his head. "Could be better. You remember Conner Armstrong, don't you?"

"I do." Josh reached out to shake his hand, which forced

Conner to turn his thoughts away from Delaney for a few seconds.

"Good to see you again," Conner said. "Want to sit down?"

"Sure." Josh pulled up a chair, stretched his legs out in front of him and hooked an arm over the wooden back. "I'll have a Heineken," he told the waitress, who'd hurried over the moment she saw him and was smiling eagerly at them both.

"I'll have one, too," Conner said.

She looked expectantly at Roy, who shook his head, then told them she'd be right back.

Josh scooted his chair around so he was half facing the dance floor. "I hear you've put the place up for sale," he said.

Roy's scowl left no question as to how he felt about that, so Conner answered. "Yeah."

"How much you askin'?"

"You in the market?"

"Possibly. My brother and I've been looking for some long-term investments and we think the land will be worth quite a bit someday, when the economy improves." He shrugged. "In the meantime, we can always use the acreage to expand our business."

Conner thought about how his grandfather had started out—as a poor country boy who'd borrowed every dime he needed to buy land and stock his first year. Somehow Clive had managed to make good, to build something out of nothing. The last thing Conner wanted was to let the symbol of that legacy slip through his fingers.

But all the nostalgia in the world couldn't save a failing ranch. "I'll send you a sales packet," he said.

Josh gave him a friendly smile. "Roy knows where to find me."

The waitress returned with their beers, and Conner insisted on buying. Josh said he'd grab the next round, but the way he kept glancing at the corner where Delaney and her friends were playing darts bothered Conner. He wasn't sure there'd be a next round.

"You see something you like?" Conner finally asked.

"What?"

Conner indicated Delaney and her group with a nod.

Josh grimaced and brought his chair around. "No, Rebecca's engaged. And I'm going out with someone else."

So it was Rebecca who kept drawing his eye, not Delaney. Conner couldn't understand any man being attracted to Rebecca over Delaney, but in that instant, he decided he liked Josh Hill, after all.

Roy chuckled. "Josh would never get involved with Rebecca, anyway. They can't even say hello without an argument. Ain't that right, Josh?"

"Right. I'm not a glutton for punishment," he said, but something about the way he said it made Conner wonder whom the man was trying to convince.

"Remember that time when you two were still in high school and she wrote 'Josh sucks' with bleach on your lawn?" Roy asked.

"How could I forget?" Josh laughed and shook his head. "My father was furious. It took all summer to restore the grass."

"What did you do to set her off?" Conner asked.

"Stole some panties from her gym locker and ran them up the flagpole," Josh said with a grin. "Which was probably bad enough. Only Rebecca doesn't wear just any panties. These were more like a thong, so she was pretty embarrassed."

"But he didn't have to *do* anything to provoke her," Roy explained. "For some reason, she's always had it in for him."

Josh glanced over at Rebecca again. "Yeah, it's a good thing she's marrying and settling down."

The wistfulness in his voice told Conner he wasn't very convinced of that, either, but before the conversation could go any further, a tiny brunette—probably only five feet flat and a hundred pounds—marched up, wearing a pair of tight jeans and an even tighter sweater, and helped herself to Josh's beer.

"There you are," she said to him. "I've been looking all over for you."

"This is Mary," Josh said. He took a drink from his beer bottle, since she had his glass, then tipped the mouth of it at a slight angle toward Conner. "Mary, have you met Clive Armstrong's grandson?"

She shook her head, her smile bright. "This is Conner? I haven't met him, but I've heard a *lot* about him."

Conner could only imagine what.

"Congratulations on the coming baby, by the way," she said. "I didn't realize you and Delaney even knew each other before you moved to town."

We didn't, Conner thought, but he wouldn't say it. He sensed Mary was probing, and whether Delaney deserved to have the truth catch up with her or not, he refused to leave her vulnerable to the ridicule of this woman or anyone else. "We once met in Boise," he said, making it sound as though it was some time ago.

"That must have been a memorable meeting," she said.

Conner smiled. "It was."

Too memorable, he added mentally.

"WHAT DO YOU THINK they're talking about?" Rebecca asked, covertly eyeing Conner and Josh when Billy Joe and Bobby went to the bar to get another drink.

Delaney set down her darts and took a stool, firmly keeping her back to Conner so she wouldn't be tempted to stare. "Us. They keep glancing over here." She knew because she caught Conner looking at her whenever she looked at him.

Rebecca bit her lip, and Delaney knew she wanted to smoke, just as she knew Rebecca would never let herself do it while Josh Hill was in the bar.

"I haven't seen Josh for months and now I seem to run into him everywhere," she complained.

"Maybe he's trying to warn Conner about us," Delaney said.

"No one's ever warned anyone about *you.*"

"He's too late, anyway."

Rebecca didn't seem to be listening. "And where there's Josh, there's Mary," she added.

"Beck, you're really scaring me. You're getting married in a month, and yet I'm beginning to suspect you have some sort of interest in Josh."

"Interest?" Rebecca cried. "I have no interest in Josh Hill. I've never even liked him. He's the last person on earth I'd ever get with. I—I don't even find him attractive."

Delaney narrowed her eyes. "Okay, I know *that's* a big lie."

Rebecca glowered at her for a moment before answering. "All right, so six feet two inches of lean muscle, a calendar smile and golden-brown skin would be attractive to anyone. But the only feelings I have for him are bad feelings."

"I don't know, Beck. Methinks thou dost protest too much."

"When I was eight, he made me wreck my bicycle and skin both my knees," she said, as if this unfortunate incident was somehow relevant today.

"So? You paid him back by giving him a fat lip. Besides, that was twenty-three years ago. What's your point?"

"That I don't like him any more now than I did then."

Delaney scrutinized Rebecca's face. She knew her best friend too well to believe what she was saying, and yet Rebecca was so emphatic about it that Delaney could do nothing but accept her words at face value. "You're sure, then? About Buddy, I mean?"

Rebecca waved her concern away. "Of course I'm sure."

"*How* are you sure?" Delaney pressed.

"What do you mean?" Rebecca picked up her darts and threw a perfect bull's-eye. "He loves me for who I am. And he...I don't know." She threw another dart and hit a ten, which didn't count for anything. "There's no pressure. It's nice."

"And Josh?" Delaney asked.

Rebecca threw her third dart, which missed the board entirely, bounced off the wall and hit the floor. The two groups playing on either side of them looked up in surprise. Rebecca gave them a glare that told them to mind their own business, and they went back to their respective games. "He and Mary are meant for each other," she said. "Golden boy marries golden girl. High school quarterback marries high school cheerleader."

Delaney scooped up her own darts, waited for Rebecca to remove hers from the board, then began to throw. "I hope you're right—about Buddy, about Josh, about everything," she said. "Because I've got to tell you, I've never met anybody as unlucky in love as we are."

"Did someone say they want to get lucky?" Billy Joe piped up as he and his brother returned, coming in on the end of the conversation.

Bobby wiggled his brows at them. "Ladies, look no farther," he said, but before Delaney and Rebecca could tell them both to quit dreaming, another man interrupted. A man who hadn't previously been part of their group.

"Not tonight," he said, and the sound of his voice made Delaney's final throw veer off and nearly stab Rebecca. It was Conner. He was standing at their table, holding her coat, which she'd slung over a stool. "Come on, Delaney," he said. "It's time to go."

CHAPTER FIFTEEN

DELANEY BLINKED. "Did we have plans to leave together?" she asked.

For a moment Conner looked a little uncomfortable. "No, but it's getting late and you need your rest."

Delaney wasn't ready to go. She was having fun for the first time in weeks. "But I'm not going back to the ranch," she said, trying to understand why he was being so insistent. "I'm off for the weekend, remember?"

"I know," he said. "I'll give you a ride home."

An assertive person stands up for her tastes, desires, values and opinions, Delaney told herself. An assertive person does not give in to the domination of others.

But an assertive person also recognizes the validity of others' views. So she didn't see any harm in standing up to Conner *without* making a scene.

"Will you excuse us for a moment?" she asked Rebecca, Billy Joe and Bobby, who were staring at them in surprise.

"Remember what I did to Josh when he skinned my knees?" Rebecca muttered. "All it takes is one punch."

Delaney feared it wasn't going to be as easy as one punch. "I'll be right back," she said, and took her coat from Conner.

"You tell him, Laney!" she heard Billy Joe call as they made their way out.

The cold air felt good after the overcrowded, smoky atmosphere of the Honky Tonk. The night was clear, the stars bright. Delaney leaned against the outside wall and opened her mouth to tell Conner exactly what she thought, but then Josh and Mary came out and she said good-night to them instead.

"What's the matter?" she asked Conner once they were gone.

The light from the windows of the Honky Tonk was too dim to read much of his expression, but Conner didn't look happy.

"Nothing," he said. "Everything's fine. It's just getting late."

"Late? It's not even midnight. The Honky Tonk doesn't close until two."

"I'm ready to leave," he said.

"I'm not."

Shoving his hands in his pockets, he walked to the edge of the porch, pivoted and came back. "Well, you shouldn't be drinking. It's not good for the baby," he said.

"I'm not drinking. I've only had soda water. I'd never do anything to endanger this baby."

He hesitated. "Secondhand smoke isn't good for the baby, either."

Where was he going with this? "Conner, Rebecca always smokes outside the house. So the only time I'm around secondhand smoke, even hers, is here, and I come maybe twice a month. I don't think that puts me in a high-risk category."

"Why do you want to stay here, anyway?" he suddenly demanded. "So you can dance with Curly and Moe in there?"

"That's Billy Joe and Bobby, and they happen to be friends of mine." She pushed away from the wall and went to sit on the bench that seated the Honky Tonk's overflow on warm summer nights. "And I'm having fun. You don't have a problem with that, do you? Because I'm finding your reaction a little strange. You're my *employer*.''

''I'm also the father of your baby.''

''What does that mean?''

''That's what I want to know!'' He leaned on the railing facing her, but where they were was even more shadowed than by the door, and she had a hard time figuring out what he was feeling. He seemed upset, frustrated, but when she'd left him at the ranch he'd been fine. Why the change?

''I can tell you what it doesn't mean,'' she said. ''It doesn't mean you can order me around or decide where I go or when I leave.''

''This is crazy,'' he said. ''I have no rights where you're concerned. If you want to dance with someone else, you're free to do so. If you want to go home with someone else, you're free to do so. Yet you're walking around with *my* baby inside you.''

''I already told you, I'm not going to do anything to endanger this baby! I'm amazed you care so much about it. You've been angry ever since you found out.''

''It's not just the baby,'' he said.

''Then, what?''

He frowned. ''It just doesn't seem right that you can take off with any guy you want.''

''You have the same freedom I do,'' she argued.

''Maybe I don't want it,'' he said, then straightened as though he was surprised by what had come out of his mouth. He tried to correct himself. ''I mean, of course I want my freedom. I just…''

''Don't want me to have any?'' Delaney supplied.

''No, that's not it. I realize that wouldn't be fair. But—'' he paused, grimacing ''—oh, I don't know. If you stay, what are you planning to do?''

''Nothing!''

"Then what's the big deal about leaving?"

"*You're* the one who's having a problem." She thought about going home just to please him. He was obviously worked up about her staying. And she'd brought this whole baby thing on herself. But she couldn't see any point in giving him that kind of power over her, didn't like where it could lead. Whether she stayed at the Honky Tonk or went home shouldn't matter to him. She'd just gone through three of the most miserable months of her life, and tonight, for a change, she wasn't sick. She wanted to be with her old friends and pretend she hadn't destroyed the life she knew—before Rebecca got married and moved away and everything became irretrievably different.

"This conversation isn't making sense," she said.

He closed his eyes and pinched the bridge of his nose, and after another pause, said, "You're right. I don't know what I'm saying. Go inside and have a great time." Then he strode off into the darkness.

Delaney heard his truck start, watched his headlights swing around as he drove out of the lot, and wondered why going back inside suddenly seemed so much less important than it had five minutes earlier.

DELANEY SAT AT THE TABLE, no longer interested in playing darts or dancing or anything else. Rebecca and Billy Joe and Bobby badgered her about her abrupt change in mood for the first half hour or so, but Delaney couldn't forget the frustration on Conner's face, couldn't release herself from feeling responsible for his confusion and anger.

Eventually Billy Joe took a bathroom break and Bobby wandered off to play some pool, leaving Delaney and Rebecca alone at the table. "Delaney, he was in the wrong, so forget about it, okay?" Rebecca said.

Delaney rested her chin on her fist. "I'm the one who started all this, Beck. I feel terrible."

"I told him he can walk away if he wants to, that you *want* him to walk away."

"I don't *want* him to walk away."

"Then, what *do* you want?"

At this point, she wasn't sure. She'd altered her life and Conner's, and even Aunt Millie's and Uncle Ralph's, with one night's irresponsible behavior. But there was no changing things now. And sometimes, when she thought about the baby, she knew she wouldn't go back even if she could.

"I want to go home," she said. "Can you get a ride?"

IT FELT GOOD TO BE HOME in her own bed, in her own room, and yet Delaney couldn't stop thinking about the ranch. Rebecca had stayed at the Honky Tonk, promising to catch a ride with someone sober, but she wasn't home yet, and Delaney found it odd to be completely alone. She was so used to Conner being somewhere in the house, just a few rooms away. She thought about the times she saw him throughout the day—when he was freshly showered in the morning, with his hair wet and curling slightly around his ears; when he was heading out to work, wearing his jeans, boots and cowboy hat; when he came in for dinner, looking tired and dirty but still appealing, always appealing; at night, when he buried himself in his office and his jaw was just beginning to show dark stubble after a long day. The moment she'd realized Conner was Clive's grandson, she'd expected him to be lazy or incapable of doing the work required of a cowboy. But from what she'd observed, he cared about the ranch, worked hard and was quickly gaining the respect of the other ranch hands. Even Roy, who hadn't been the least bit happy to have Conner at the Running Y, now seemed to admire him more than anyone else did. Except, perhaps, some of the ladies who'd seen him at the Honky Tonk tonight.

Delaney remembered the heads he'd turned and wondered how she would've felt if he'd shown any interest in those women. It would've bothered her to see him on the dance floor with someone else, to think he wanted to take someone home with him. Billy Joe and Bobby weren't any threat to Conner or anyone else, so she had difficulty seeing them in the same light. But Conner didn't know them or her habits. Maybe the way he'd behaved tonight hadn't been so strange, after all.

Rolling over, she eyed the phone, wanting to call him. But it was nearly one o'clock. Conner was probably asleep; he'd left the Honky Tonk before midnight.

When she went back to work on Monday, she'd tell him she understood how he felt and see if they could work out something they could both live with until the baby was born. The front door opened and closed, and Rebecca made her way noisily through the living room and down the hall.

"Buddy called," Delaney said, when Rebecca passed her door.

"What'd he say?"

"He wants you to call him tomorrow."

"Okay. Want to go out for breakfast in the morning?"

"Sure," Delaney said. "Just don't wake me up too early."

"No chance of that. But aren't you going to get up and bake pies this weekend like usual?"

"I'm not going to bake any pies for the next few months. I'm sick of baking pies."

"Jeez, Laney. You get yourself pregnant *and* give up baking." Rebecca yawned. "The world must be coming to an end."

"The world as I know it already has."

"So what do you think?" Conner asked, eyeing Roy closely.

Roy bent toward the magazine Conner had spread out on the desk. "You dragged my butt out of bed to show me an article in a magazine from—" he flipped to the front cover "—two years ago?"

"Yeah."

"This couldn't wait? It's six o'clock in the morning."

Ever since Conner had learned that Josh Hill and his brother had money to invest, something had been niggling at the back of his mind. Once he'd gotten home and been able to think beyond Delaney, it had come to him. He'd been up half the night searching through every magazine he'd ever read and had just found what he was looking for. "Don't you know what this is?"

"It's a golf course," Roy said, as though he wasn't particularly impressed.

"It's more than a golf course. It's our answer."

Roy picked up the magazine and read the caption. "'Visitors travel from as far away as Europe and China to play eighteen holes on this unique and difficult course.'"

"See? Golf is huge," Conner said. "People pay green fees of over $200 per game to play on this course."

"That might be true. But golf courses take a lot of money to build and maintain. You're not thinking of putting one out here on the ranch, are you?"

"Not just a golf course," Conner said. "Look at this." He pulled out another magazine and slapped it on top of the first. On one side was a picture of a large, rustic-looking lodge. On the other was an article with the headline "Last Bastion of the West?"

"I don't get the connection," Roy said.

"I'm thinking of turning a section of the ranch into a resort. We could have hunting and fishing, horseback riding, songs around the campfire, you name it. We could get into one of these vacation magazines and draw people from all over the world with the promise of a truly western experience. And we could hedge our bets by having one of the best golf courses in America.''

''Are you still drunk from last night?'' Roy asked.

''I was never drunk last night. Listen to me. All it takes is money.''

''That's what we don't have, Conner. Your grandfather's not going to spend any more money on the ranch. He's selling, remember? He'd never go for something like this.''

Conner tapped the magazine. ''I don't think my grandfather will like the idea, either, which is why I've never really considered it until now. But didn't you hear what Josh Hill said last night?''

''Yeah, he's looking for some long-term investments. But this is...'' Roy shook his head as he gazed down at the two magazines, then at the others strewn across the floor and around the desk. ''This is crazy. For Josh, this wouldn't be as simple as buying a piece of land, Con. This would be spending millions of dollars to change the use of the land.''

''Not completely. That's the beauty of it. It would still be a ranch.''

''Josh is just a homegrown horse-breeder. He's done well, but I doubt he has as much as this will require. On top of everything else, he already has a business to run. Why would he want to branch out into an area he doesn't know anything about?''

''Because it's smart not to have all your eggs in one basket,'' Conner said. ''And we'd be giving him the chance to be part of the biggest thing ever to hit Dundee. We'd run it. He'd just lend us the money.''

''But your grandfather's already listed the ranch, which means he has to follow through with selling it if a buyer comes along. Someone could buy it right out from under us.''

''Only if that buyer meets all the terms and criteria of the listing agreement. If the Realtor procures an offer that's even a penny short, we can reject it.''

''*We?* We don't have anything to say about it. And you know how gung ho your uncles are to get rid of the place. I tried telling them about the campsites we've cleared, but they didn't want to hear it.''

''So you're giving up?'' Conner said, mimicking him.

Roy rubbed his whiskery chin. ''You're serious about this?''

''I think so,'' Conner said. ''It would mean I need to figure out a way to buy the ranch myself as soon as possible, which is definitely risky. But it's going to take something big to save the Running Y.''

The telephone rang, and Roy answered it because Conner was too excited to bother. What if he could do it? What if he could pull it off? He'd be able to keep the ranch in the family and start something of his own at the same time. He'd be able to provide for his child, put down some roots, *belong.* Best of all, he'd be a father his child could be proud of. And a resort would be good for the community, too. It would bring in thousands of tourists who'd spend their money right here in Dundee without destroying the country setting he'd come to love....

''Con?''

The somber note in Roy's voice finally pierced Conner's preoccupation. ''What?'' he said.

Roy handed him the phone. ''It's your mother. Clive's had a heart attack.''

IT WAS TOO SOON. His day of reckoning had come too soon.

Conner sat on the plane, staring out the window at nothing but sky. After his mother's call, he'd packed, headed straight to the airport in Boise and gotten on the first flight to California. They'd be landing in San Francisco, where his mother would meet him, in just another twenty minutes, but he still felt numb from the news—numb and afraid. He'd known his grandfather couldn't live forever, that he'd die sometime. But the old "it could never happen to me" mentality had lulled him into thinking it would be later, always later.

What if the old guy didn't make it?

Conner thought of his life and how he'd wasted so much time in empty pursuits, and was suddenly more ashamed than he'd ever been. He'd persuaded himself that he was fighting his uncles, somehow besting them by proving he could live fast and loose and get away with it, that he didn't care about anything. But he was only playing into their hands. And now, when the important things in life seemed so apparent, he felt like a fool because he did care, deeply.

I'm coming, Grandpa. Hang on, he thought. Then he took out the magazines he'd shown Roy and stared down at them. The idea of turning part of the ranch into a resort seemed even more grandiose now. It would take millions of dollars. It would also require total control of the ranch and at least a couple of years. But Conner believed his plan could work. And he promised himself that he'd save the Running Y for his grandfather—and his baby. He'd link the past to the future if it was the last thing he did.

CONNER WAS SITTING in the breakfast room at the Napa house with his mother when he saw Stephen for the first time. They'd stopped by the hospital the night before, just after Conner had flown in, and spent several hours at Clive's bedside. His grandfather had been in good spirits, and looked better than he'd expected, which gave Conner hope that he'd recover, but the doctors said he had a bad valve and would need surgery before they released him. Stephen had been in San José on business and hadn't returned until late at night. To Conner's knowledge, he hadn't even been over to the hospital yet.

"Yee-haw! Well, if it ain't the cowboy in the family," Stephen said, lowering the newspaper he'd been reading as he walked.

Conner glanced down at his apparel, which was exactly what he would've worn out on the range, minus the heavy jacket and hat, and grinned. "That's right."

"Well, don't get too comfortable in those boots. The Realtor said we should be expecting an offer on the ranch this week," he said, and took the seat across from Vivian, where he immediately began to spread out the business section of the paper.

"That's all you have to say?" Conner asked over the crackle. "Aren't you going to ask about Grandfather? You know he had a heart attack yesterday."

Stephen didn't look up as he poured himself a cup of coffee. "Marjorie's been there."

Stephen's tennis-playing, social-climbing wife. "Now you have a delegate handling your familial obligations?"

"Conner, let's not start," his mother warned, wrapping her long fingers more tightly around her own coffee cup. But Conner wasn't interested in backing down now. He stretched out in his chair, crossed his arms and waited for Stephen's response.

"I'm doing what my father would want me to do," Stephen said, setting his cup in its saucer with a *clink*. "Which is more than can be said for you most of the time."

"Forever the dutiful son. Tell me, have you and your brothers broken out the will yet?"

"Conner!" Vivian said.

Stephen dropped the spoon he'd been using to dump sugar in his coffee and narrowed his eyes. "Funny you should bring up the will, since you're the only one in danger of being cut out of it."

Conner made a tsking noise. "And Grandfather hasn't taken care of that yet? I can certainly see how this little heart attack would give you and your brothers a scare. What a relief to think there's still time."

Stephen clenched his fists as he stood, and his face went splotchy with anger. "You little bastard," he said. "How dare you come into my house and—"

"Whoa, slow down. Grandfather's not dead yet," Conner said, but he didn't bother to stand because Stephen suddenly seemed too pathetic to be considered a threat. "This house still belongs to him, and I'm still welcome in it."

"Once we sell that ranch, you won't be welcome anywhere," Stephen promised.

"We'll see about the ranch," Conner said, and for the first time in years, he thought he detected a glimmer of fear in Stephen's eyes.

"Why do you say that?" Stephen asked. "What's changed?"

Conner smiled. "I have."

CHAPTER SIXTEEN

DELANEY LOOKED DOWN at the notes she'd taken in her assertiveness training classes, wondering if any of the techniques she'd been taught might help her now. She needed to tell Aunt Millie and Uncle Ralph that Conner was the father of her baby before they heard it somewhere else. But they were still adjusting to the idea of her having a baby at all. She hated to rock the boat again so soon. Especially because she knew they'd want some definite answers—what role, exactly, did Conner plan to play in the child's life? Would he help out financially? Take partial custody? Delaney couldn't give them those answers because she didn't know them herself. She wasn't sure Conner even knew what he was going to do once the baby arrived. The ranch was up for sale. Once it left the family, would he stay in Idaho? Move back to California? She had nothing but questions, and now that Clive Armstrong had had a heart attack and open-heart surgery, things were even more up in the air.

She flipped the pancakes she was cooking for the cowboys' breakfast, then returned to the kitchen table to read the definition of self-disclosure again, this time focusing on the last line. "A key element of successful assertiveness is the development of rejection tolerance, so that disclosure of one's self is not as threatening as it is to someone preoccupied with the thought 'But what will they think if I say that?'"

"Morning," Roy said as he entered the kitchen.

"Morning," Delaney replied.

"You studying somethin'?" he asked, helping himself to a cup of coffee.

Delaney covered her papers. "Nothing important. Have you heard from Conner? How's his grandfather doing since the surgery?"

"I talked to him last night. Clive's doing good." He shook his head. "He's a tough customer."

"When's Conner coming home?"

Roy considered her over the rim of his coffee cup, and she realized she'd sounded a bit too eager.

"I don't know. Is someone missing him?"

She went back to the griddle to scoop the pancakes onto a plate and to pour another batch. "I was just curious."

"Yup," he said, and flashed one of his rare smiles that told her he saw right through her.

"Josh Hill called for him early this morning," she said, suddenly eager to change the subject.

Roy instantly sobered. "He did? What'd he say?"

"Just wanted to talk to Conner. He said he had another number he'd try."

Roy didn't answer.

"Did you hear me?" she asked.

He nodded. "Yeah, I heard."

CONNER WAITED until the nurse had finished checking his grandfather's blood pressure before slipping around her to take the seat he used every visit.

"How're you doing today, Grandpa?" he asked, as she returned the blood pressure cuff to its rack on the wall, patted Clive's arm and left the sterile white room.

Clive nodded. Propped up in bed, he still looked paler

than usual, but more like himself than he had since the surgery.

"A little better. You?"

"Good."

"You still heading back to the ranch today?"

"I am." Conner glanced up as Vivian entered the room, carrying a bunch of fresh flowers she'd no doubt cut from the garden at the Napa house. Her perfume and the fragrance of the flowers instantly overcame the slight antiseptic odor that generally predominated in the hospital. "Hi, Mom."

She cleared a spot on the rolling table between the window and Clive's bed and placed her arrangement next to several other bouquets he'd received over the past few days. "Hi, Con. Why didn't you wake me this morning? I would've ridden over with you."

Conner had been up since before dawn, using the Napa house's library as a makeshift office to talk on the phone with Josh and Mike Hill, take notes, make plans. The Hill brothers were definitely interested in his idea and sounded as though they were going to get behind him. But that meant his work had just begun. He still had to draw up a partnership agreement, create a proposal for investors, construct an offer to buy the ranch and find a general contractor who was familiar with this type of project and capable of handling its scope—all details that were difficult to control from afar. Now that his grandfather was on the mend, he needed to get home.

Home? He chuckled at his own thoughts. Only a few months ago, he'd considered Idaho no better than Siberia. Now he was calling it home. How that had happened he wasn't quite sure, but as he pictured the snow-capped mountains, the quaint town with its diner, small-time grocery store and single high school, and imagined the crisp, clean air, he felt more eager than ever to get back.

"I wanted to let you sleep," he told his mother. "You've been so worried about Grandpa, I figured you could use the extra rest."

"But this is your last day. And I'm feeling fine."

As long as his grandfather was doing well, Conner knew his mother would be okay, too. She loved and admired the man who'd adopted her, almost to the point of hero-worship.

Bending, Vivian kissed her father on the cheek and greeted her son in the same way before taking the only other seat in the room. "Hasn't it been great to have Conner home, Dad?" she said, crossing her legs at the ankle as elegantly as she did everything else. "I hate that he's leaving."

Conner had actually enjoyed his visit. Before leaving for Dundee, he'd purposely spent very little time with his family, but this stay had been different. He'd spent many hours at the hospital, of course, but even when he wasn't here, he was content to visit with his mother, help her with grocery shopping, meals or other household activities.

"It has been good," Clive said. "He seems to have grown up. The ranch has made a man out of him, just like I knew it would."

"The ranch has made a man out of who?" Stephen asked, surprising them all with his sudden appearance. He'd visited the hospital a few times over the past week, but he generally claimed to be too busy. His preoccupation with business was definitely reminiscent of the hours Clive had always kept. But as far as Conner was concerned, the similarities between father and son ended there.

"We're talking about Conner," Vivian said. "He's done so well in Dundee, don't you think?"

Stephen laughed outright, even though Clive was in the room, which gave Conner his first indication that something was different. "Conner?" he scoffed. "Come on. He's a lost cause. When are you two going to give up on him?"

His grandfather's brows puckered. "I don't appreciate you trying to start trouble when—"

"When what?" Stephen interrupted. "When he's snowed you into believing he's actually cleaning up his act?"

"You've never liked him," his mother said. "You've always done everything in your power to make him look bad."

"Mom, I don't need you to stand up for me," Conner said.

"I haven't had to do anything to make him look bad," Stephen continued. "He takes care of that all on his own. I just talked to Dave Small, who's on the Dundee city council—"

"Called you, did he, Stephen?" Conner interrupted, knowing perfectly well that Stephen had been rooting around and checking up on him in the hope of turning the tide against Conner. But Stephen was already too involved in his tattling to acknowledge his words.

"He had a few things to say about the new and improved Conner," he went on.

"What does Dave Small have to do with Conner or the ranch or anything else?" his grandfather asked.

"He doesn't have anything to do with the ranch," Stephen said. "But he knows plenty about the scandal Conner's caused."

"Scandal?" Clive asked sharply.

Stephen leaned an elbow on the counter as though delighted with the attention he was receiving—and the bomb he was about to drop. "You know Millie and Ralph Lawson, right?"

Conner felt his stomach tense. *Here it comes...*

"Sure, I know 'em. Known 'em for years," Clive said. "They're good folks."

"Well, you may be hearing from them real soon. Conner's knocked up Dundee's librarian, who also happens to be their daughter. The whole town's buzzing with the news." Stephen's mouth twisted into a self-satisfied smile. "Seems Delaney Lawson was a bit of a saint before she ran into *him.*"

Clive's eyes shifted to Conner, and the spark of pride that had flickered in their depths only seconds before disappeared. "That's not true, is it, Con?" he asked. "You haven't left Millie and Ralph's daughter, or any other young lady, holding the bag, have you?"

Conner stood. Stephen had laid it all on the line; his secret was out. For a moment, he thought of explaining how it had happened, how Delaney had asked him to dispense with her virginity and he'd innocently obliged. But he knew, with his past, how hollow any excuse would sound. And he wasn't willing to save himself at Delaney's expense. He had to take full responsibility and make it right—or he'd disappoint his grandfather again.

He forced a bright smile even though the resentment he felt toward Delaney suddenly spiked. "Thanks for ruining my surprise, Stephen," he said. "And just when I was about to make the big announcement."

"The big announcement?" Stephen scoffed, still smug.

"Yeah. I have good news, but I wanted to save it for the right moment, which I guess is now, thanks to you."

Stephen's expression finally showed a touch of uncertainty. "What do you mean?"

Taking a deep breath, Conner replied with as much excitement as he could manage. "I'm getting married."

His mother briefly covered her mouth with one hand. His grandfather pushed the button that raised his bed.

"You're marrying this woman who's pregnant with your child?" his mother asked.

"It's true that Delaney and I are expecting a baby. But I'm happy about it," he lied.

Stephen looked stricken, but his grandfather was obviously pleased. "I can't think of anything better for you, son," he said. "The people of Dundee are good people, salt of the earth, and it's high time you settled down."

Conner had a momentary vision of Delaney lying to him in the lobby of the Bellemont, lying to him in his hotel room, and wanted to throttle her. If not for her, he wouldn't be in this position.

At least the shock on Stephen's face was gratifying. "That's what I've been thinking," he murmured.

"But you haven't even mentioned her," his mother said. "When did you two meet?"

Conner focused on Stephen and kept his smile firmly in place. For the moment, he'd outmaneuvered him, but it was going to be a costly move. Marriage? Now? "Almost the minute I arrived in Idaho."

"He's lying," Stephen said. "He just came up with this. I can tell."

But everyone ignored him.

"A wedding. Isn't that wonderful, Dad?" Vivian gushed. "Conner's getting married and starting a family. I can't wait to meet the lucky bride. When's the wedding?"

"Uh…we haven't set a date yet. But soon," he said. "You'll be the first to know." *Right behind Delaney.*

"So when we see you next, it'll be in Dundee? Is that where you're having the wedding?"

"Yeah."

"Isn't that wonderful?" Vivian said again.

Thrilling, Conner thought. Now all he had to do was convince Delaney. He doubted she'd be too happy about it, but she was the one who'd gotten him into this. And she was going to be the one who'd get him out.

IT WAS LATE BY THE TIME Conner's plane touched down in Boise. He rented a car because he hadn't arranged for anyone to pick him up, and headed out onto the open road, eager for a couple of hours to think before he confronted Delaney. How was he going to get her to marry him? He couldn't exactly force her, which meant he had to enlist her cooperation. But how? They didn't know each other very well, and he hadn't been particularly nice in the time they'd been acquainted; he'd been too angry for that. He didn't have a lot to offer as far as stability went, considering the risk he was about to take, and she'd made it abundantly clear that she didn't want anything from him. None of which stacked the odds in his favor. Besides, he couldn't help balking at having his hand forced like this, which made winning her heart completely out of the question.

So what other weapon did he have?

Logic, he decided. Marriage would solve a myriad of problems. It would give their baby his name, save Delaney's reputation, relieve her of at least part of the financial burden, protect his grandfather from further shame and reduce his uncles' power over him. It also gave Conner some claim on Delaney. If they were married, she wouldn't be slow-dancing with other men at the Honky Tonk as though she were single, he told himself. She'd make a commitment to him, he'd make a commitment to her, and they'd both be committed to their baby. That was the way it was supposed to be, and she was the one who'd chosen this path back in Boise, right?

By the time Conner passed beneath the wrought-iron arch leading to the ranch, he'd made his decision. He'd approach her in the morning, lay it all out and they'd set a date. How hard could it be? Then he'd get back to all the other things he had to do, like buy a nine-million-dollar ranch without any money of his own. And buy it, moreover, from his uncles, who would certainly fight him if they thought he had half a chance of succeeding.

He was the black sheep of the family, the one who wasn't supposed to be able to do anything right. But now he was getting married, having a child, buying a ranch and building a huge resort. Was he crazy? Probably. But he wasn't about to change course.

With a sigh, Conner parked as close to the door as he could manage with all the other vehicles already clogging the drive. He grabbed his bag and hopped out. He'd told Roy to let Delaney know he'd be home tonight, but he hoped she hadn't waited up. He was tired and overwhelmed and figured tomorrow would be soon enough to set everything straight. Yet, when he let himself inside and found the whole place dark, he was strangely disappointed.

Evidently she wasn't very excited about seeing him. Was she asleep? Or had she gone home for the night?

He set his bag in the living room and paused at the end of the hall instead of going immediately to bed. The house smelled of fresh-ground coffee and wood smoke, but there was a hint of Delaney here, too—her perfume, perhaps— and it caught him by the throat. He wanted to see her, he realized. He wanted to see her now.

Only because they had unfinished business, he told himself, but it was enough of an excuse to get him moving quietly down the hall toward her room. He stood on the other side of her door, listening for any sound, but he couldn't hear anything. Dare he barge in? She hadn't worried about changing his entire life that night in Boise. Why should he care about courtesy now?

He lifted a hand to knock, then hesitated and quietly opened the door. Delaney was sleeping in the middle of the bed. The blinds, only half-drawn, let in sufficient moonlight to reveal the fan of hair on her pillow, the delicate profile of her face, a bare arm thrown over the blankets.

The sight of her sleeping so peacefully soothed Conner's anger, but it did nothing to make him feel like going to his room. Shoving his hands in his pockets, he slipped inside and stood by the edge of her bed, gazing down at her. She was beautiful. Regardless of what she'd done to him, regardless of what might happen between them, he had to give her that. When he imagined her growing big with his child, he felt an inexplicable sense of pride. And when he lay in his bed at night, he sometimes thought about the coming months and visualized her taking his hand and guiding it to her swollen abdomen to let him feel his baby kick.

From there, it wasn't hard to fantasize about her taking his hands and guiding them someplace even more exciting. He remembered her hesitancy the first time he'd made love to her, the slow yet trusting way she'd eventually opened up to him, and wondered what it would be like to make love to her a second time. Here. Now.

Arousal swept through him as he imagined her waking up and pulling back the blankets in a silent invitation, pictured himself eliciting from her the same desire he felt, then taking her hard and fast until she cried his name. He wanted to hear her say she wasn't content with being alone. That she wanted more than his baby. That she wanted *him*.

But he knew better. She already had what she wanted.

She'd told him that, and her indifference at the Honky Tonk only confirmed it.

Raking a hand through his hair, he started to go, but her voice stopped him.

"Conner? Is that you?"

He turned, his heart in his throat. "Yeah, it's me."

"What are you doing here?"

What *was* he doing here? Why had he complicated his emotions by acknowledging the desire she evoked? He had no idea. "Just checking on you. I thought maybe you'd gone home for the night."

She didn't answer right away. "Do you need something?" she said at last.

"I need to talk to you, but we'll do it in the morning."

"Are you sure?"

"Yeah."

"Is your grandfather going to be okay?"

"I think so."

"That's good."

"Yeah, that's good," he said, but he wasn't thinking about what he was saying, he was thinking about touching her again, and he knew that if he didn't get out of her quiet, dark room, he'd try. "It's late. I'll see you in the morning."

"Conner?" she called as he left.

He didn't dare stop. He forced his feet to carry him at a quick and decisive pace to his room.

CHAPTER SEVENTEEN

CONNER DIDN'T COME to breakfast or go out on the range with the other cowboys. Delaney had assumed he was sleeping after getting in so late, but she found him in his office, looking as though he'd been up all night, judging by his rumpled clothes and the stubble on his chin.

"Are you hungry?" she asked, pausing in the doorway and wondering at the change in him. Something was different. She could sense it. She'd felt it last night when he came to her room, and she felt it now, the second his eyes flicked in her direction. He was rather morose, for one thing, which Delaney didn't really understand. But it wasn't just his dark mood. He was also more focused, more driven. Why? "I've brought you some bacon and eggs."

"Set it here, please." He shoved some papers to the side and went right back to his computer.

Delaney deposited the plate on his desk. She knew he expected her to leave, but she'd been waiting for more than a week to talk to him. She wanted to discuss what they could both expect in the months to come, and felt it was time they made some decisions. So she waited, clearing her throat when he didn't immediately look up, and finally managed to capture his attention.

"Is there something else?" he asked.

"Last night you said you wanted to talk to me. And I've

actually been wanting to talk to you, too. So I was hoping this might be a good time."

He kept typing. "Why don't you go first?"

"Okay." She waited for him to turn toward her, but he didn't. "Are you going to stop that?"

He checked his watch, then glanced reluctantly at his computer screen. "I can only spare a few minutes."

"Then, maybe we should postpone this until—"

"No, go ahead." He swiveled to face her. "We need to get it handled. That'll put at least one hurdle behind me."

Hurdle? Delaney rubbed her palms on her jeans. "I wanted to talk about what happened at the Honky Tonk before you left for California."

"You don't have to worry about that," he said.

"Why not?"

He shrugged. "Because it won't happen again."

"It won't?"

"No."

"How can you be sure?"

"Because you won't be going there in the future."

The hairs on the back of Delaney's neck stood on end, and she took a step closer, coming to the edge of his desk. "Excuse me?"

"The place is a singles hangout," he said, as though that explained everything.

"Not really, but sort of, I guess. Anyway, I *am* single."

"You're also pregnant."

"Which is why I'm willing to compromise. Maybe while I'm carrying the baby, we can agree to—"

"A compromise won't be necessary," he said.

"Why not?"

"Because I have a better solution."

Delaney was almost afraid to hear what it might be. "And that is…"

"I think we should get married."

Her knees buckled, and she quickly put both hands on the edge of the desk to support herself. "Did you just say what I thought you said?"

"You heard me." He turned back to his computer. "Think about it and you'll see that it's the only answer."

Bald. Matter-of-fact. Emotionless. Delaney cringed. "I don't think it's the only answer."

His eyes met hers. "This is what's best for the baby. It gives the baby a name, saves your reputation—"

"No."

That made an impact. "What?" he said, apparently forgetting the computer.

"I said no. I'm not going to marry you."

He scowled fiercely. "You haven't heard all the reasons. I'm sure once—"

"I know all the reasons."

"Then, why are you saying no?"

"After such a romantic proposal, I can't *imagine*." She started out of the room, but he stood and rounded the desk so quickly that he caught her by the wrist before she could reach the door.

"What's the matter, Laney? You landed us in this mess and now you're not happy that there's no wine and roses?"

Delaney could feel the strength in his hand and wanted to twist away. At the same time, she wanted to strike out at him. But most of all, she wanted to kick herself for causing this disaster in the first place. He was right: it *was* her fault. How could she have been so foolish? "I should never have told you," she said.

"You should never have done it!"

"Okay! I agree, but I can't change that now. I regret what I've done, but I can't fix it, Conner. I did everything I could do when I told you the truth."

Nostrils flaring, he stared down at her, his lips set in an angry line. Suddenly, inexplicably, she had a momentary vision of his mouth descending on hers. They hadn't been quite this close since that first night, not even when they were dancing. His breath fanned her face, his heart beat above her own, and for some reason she didn't understand, desire swirled through her. All her feelings seemed to spin together so fast that she could no longer separate one from another.

Conner must have experienced something similar, because she sensed a subtle change in him right before he pulled her into his arms and made the kiss she'd just imagined real.

As hard and hungry as his kiss was, it answered everything Delaney needed in that moment. They were caught in a web of blame and frustration, anger and regret, from which there was no escape, yet something very elemental kept them clinging to each other now. Her hands delved into his hair, urging him even closer as she opened her mouth to meet his tongue and simply let herself feel what he'd made her feel in Boise. Only better. This was somehow more poignant, more meaningful. She *knew* him. She knew she wanted him. But she also knew he'd never be able to forgive her.

"Marry me," he murmured against her lips, still taking and tasting, giving, touching.

But passion wasn't enough. Eventually his resentment would take over, and she couldn't live with that. For her baby's sake, she wouldn't follow one mistake with another.

"No," she said, and, finally breaking away, she ran from the room.

WHEN DELANEY REACHED her bedroom, she stood at the window for several minutes, trying to calm down. Somewhere in the house she heard a door open and close and Roy telling Conner they had to hurry or they'd miss Josh Hill. Then the front door banged, and the truck started and drove off. As silence fell, Delaney dialed the beauty shop.

Katie answered the phone. "Hello?"

"Is Rebecca there?" Delaney asked.

"Rebecca! Laney's on the phone!" Katie's scream blasted across the line, then there was a long pause during which Delaney could hear the dryers, the cash register and a few voices before Rebecca picked up.

"Laney?"

"Yeah, it's me." Until that moment Delaney had been able to hold her tears at bay. But it only took the sound of her friend's voice to make them spring to her eyes.

Rebecca immediately recognized her distress. "What's wrong, Laney?"

"I should never have let Conner blackmail me into working here."

"Why not? I thought it was going okay."

"It's not okay."

"Why?"

Delaney sniffed. "I think...I think I'm falling in love with him."

Silence. Then Rebecca whispered, "Oh boy, Laney. Tell me he feels the same way."

"Do you think I'd be crying if he did?" she said. "He hates me."

"Well, I wouldn't tell Conner how you feel, not if he hates you."

Delaney groaned. "Gee, that's a valuable piece of advice."

"You're the type to spill your guts. I thought it was worth mentioning. What *are* you going to do?"

"Quit this job so I don't have to be around him anymore."

"Okay. What are you waiting for?"

"He's gone. He and Roy went to meet Josh Hill."

The tone of Rebecca's voice changed completely, grew a little possessive. "What's he doing with Josh?"

"Business of some sort."

"Oh." A pause. "So are you going to tell him you're out of there as soon as he gets back?"

"Yeah."

"Great. Maybe you'll be home in time to go to the Honky Tonk."

"Your sympathy overwhelms me, Beck."

"Just kidding. Who's going to take over Dottie's position for you, then?"

Delaney buried her head beneath the pillow. "Don't ask me questions like that."

"Why? Look, Mrs. Peters is waiting for a perm, so I have to get to the bottom line here."

"What is the bottom line?"

"The bottom line is, you can't quit because Dottie's not there, and you would never leave Conner and the other cowboys without a replacement. So, what are you *really* going to do?"

"I don't know. Crying feels pretty good."

"Then, have a—"

"He asked me to marry him," Delaney told her.

Surprised silence. "And you said—"

"No! I said no, of course."

"Why? You just told me you love him."

Delaney sat up. "Beck, can everyone in the salon hear you?"

"Only the bigger gossips. Why?"

"Wouldn't want them to miss anything, that's all. Tell them I can't marry a man who doesn't love me."

"If he doesn't at least like you, why'd he ask you to marry him?" Rebecca asked.

"Because it's best for the baby. That's what he said."

"But he's never brought up the *M* word before. Why the change of heart?"

"I don't know."

"He's got a point, though, about it being good for the baby."

"You're not helping," Delaney said.

"I'm sorry. I'll have to give you a condensed version of my counseling—"

"I know, Mrs. Peters is waiting. Go take care of her."

"I'll call you back," Rebecca promised.

"Don't bother. Just meet me and Aunt Millie and Uncle Ralph at the diner tonight. I said I'd take them out for their anniversary."

"And they want *me* there?"

"No, *I* want you there. The way I'm feeling, I need a buffer, and you're good at drawing attention."

"I think that's a compliment."

"See you at six."

"WHY DIDN'T YOU TELL US?" Aunt Millie demanded, as soon as the waitress led her and Uncle Ralph to the table where Delaney and Rebecca were already waiting.

"Tell you what?" Delaney asked, as foreboding settled in the pit of her stomach. After what had happened with Conner in his office this morning, she didn't need another confrontation. She hadn't been able to forget the intensity of his kiss or the head-over-heels, free-falling sensation that said her heart was no longer her own.

Uncle Ralph shoved the table toward Delaney and Rebecca so Aunt Millie could fit inside the red vinyl booth. "About Clive Armstrong's grandson being the father of your baby."

Morning sickness hadn't bothered Delaney for over two weeks, but she felt ill now. "How did you hear?" she asked in resignation.

"Bertha Young told Ralph at the grocery store. Can you imagine his embarrassment, having to hear that way?" Aunt Millie said.

Uncle Ralph nodded to confirm that the way he'd learned the truth had been treacherous indeed and Delaney shot Rebecca a furious look. "Thanks," she muttered. "You just had to set everybody straight."

"They were bound to find out sometime," Rebecca said.

"I don't understand why it was a secret to begin with," Aunt Millie put in, clearly unhappy. "Especially from us. Conner Armstrong needs to own up to his responsibilities. It's not right for a man to get a woman pregnant and just walk away. And we thought he was so nice."

Delaney sighed. Now she had to tell them *how* she'd gotten pregnant. She couldn't have them going around blaming Conner for something that was entirely her fault. Soon the whole town would be giving him dirty looks and muttering disparaging remarks behind his back. She opened her mouth to explain, but Rebecca silenced her with an elbow and started right in herself.

"These days, things are a little different than they used to be," she said, treating them all to a sample of what she thought Delaney should say. But Delaney already knew it wasn't going to help. Aunt Millie and Uncle Ralph saw things one way, and after seventy-five years, that was the only way they were going to see them.

"Women think for themselves now," Rebecca went on, "make their own decisions—independent of their parents or a man, I might add—and women have babies on their own all the time. Especially women Delaney's age."

"That might be what you think, missy," Aunt Millie snapped before Rebecca could really warm to her subject. "But we all know how loose *your* morals are."

"The point is, you don't have the right to meddle in Delaney's life anymore."

"Meddle! Did you hear that?" Millie cried to the table at large. "We're family! We have every right to meddle, if that's what you want to call it. We're talking about our daughter and our grandbaby here. If we don't take care of them, who will? Certainly not you. You're probably the reason Delaney's in this mess to begin with. I've always told her you're a bad influence." She shook her finger at Delaney. "Now you know why, Laney. Just listen to the way she speaks to me!"

Rebecca's eyes narrowed, which wasn't a good sign, so Delaney tried to calm everyone before Rebecca turned into a heat-seeking missile and Aunt Millie started brandishing her cane. "What Rebecca's trying to say is—"

"We weren't born yesterday," Uncle Ralph broke in. "We know what Rebecca's trying to say. She thinks we're too old-fashioned. But right is still right and wrong is still wrong. Conner has a responsibility to this baby, and I'm going to make sure he lives up to it."

"No! You can't get involved," Delaney cried. "You need to let me handle the situation. I mean it. I don't want anything from Conner. He isn't to blame for this—"

Rebecca nudged her again and pointed toward the entrance, and Delaney's words fell away. There was Conner Armstrong striding across the lobby, heading straight for their table.

"Oh, no. You've already called him, haven't you."

Aunt Millie nodded smugly. "You don't have anything to worry about. He said he'd meet with us. And I didn't even have to call his grandfather."

Rebecca made a sound of disbelief, and Delaney dropped her head in her hands. "Only in Dundee," she moaned. "Only in Dundee."

"WHAT? NO SHOTGUN?" Conner said.

Pulling up a chair, he sat in the aisle, angling the lower half of his body so he could cross his legs as well as his arms while he waited to hear what the old couple had to say. Whatever it was, he still didn't understand why they couldn't have said it over the phone. Delaney looked as though she wanted to disappear, but that hardly made Conner feel better. He'd asked her to marry him. She'd turned him down. Then Millie had called, spouting off about his "responsibility to the baby."

If only he'd said no to Delaney at the Bellemont…

"I appreciate the fact that you're here," Millie said, nodding stiffly like an old schoolteacher about to rap his knuckles with a ruler. "We thought it would be prudent to discuss what should be done about this situation."

"I told them it's none of their business, but they won't listen to me," Rebecca piped up.

Delaney was moaning something about living in a small

town and how maybe she should've grown up a ward of the state, but Millie was clearly too provoked by Rebecca's challenging tone to pay Delaney much attention.

"This baby is my grandchild, which definitely makes what happens here my business."

The waitress delivered some chips and salsa, and Rebecca began eating, but no one else seemed interested. Delaney stopped muttering, but she looked too ill to eat, and too tired to deal with a conversation as potentially upsetting as this one. Conner felt a sudden impulse to tell them all that she needed to go home and rest, that they could handle this later. But then he reminded himself that she was the reason they were all here in the first place—and that maybe he could use Millie and Ralph's help.

"So, what do you have to say?" he asked, directing his question to Millie. It was Delaney who answered. "Nothing. She has nothing to say. Aunt Millie and Uncle Ralph are just… To understand what they're doing, you'd have to know them. They mean well. Just keep telling yourself they mean well. It'll help."

"We're trying to make sure you do the right thing," Aunt Millie said.

"And what is that?" Rebecca muttered between chips. "You think he should marry her even though he doesn't like her?"

"A child needs a mother and a father," Ralph said. "What's wrong with the younger generation, anyway?" he asked Millie.

"I'm not that young. I'm thirty years old," Delaney said. No one responded.

"Marriage might sound like a great solution, but it'll never work," Rebecca argued.

"Is anyone listening to me?" Delaney cried.

"Then, they should've thought of that before they—" Ralph glanced at Millie "—before."

Delaney sat up taller. "This is my life and my baby."

Rebecca leaned forward, crunching chips as she talked. "Don't you think putting a child through a painful divorce would be more harmful than never giving that child a father to begin with, Ralph?"

"My baby will have its father," Conner stated in no uncertain terms.

"See?" Rebecca drew the salsa closer to her. "Problem solved. He's going to be a father to the baby."

Millie levered her upper body halfway across the table, coming almost nose to nose with Rebecca. "Why don't you just stay out of this?"

"Why don't you let Delaney—"

Delaney stood up, the decisiveness of her movements finally catching everyone's attention. "Time out," she said. "That's it. Conner and I are leaving."

Millie and Ralph blinked up at her. Even Rebecca looked mildly surprised. "What is it, dear?" Millie asked.

"This is between Conner and me. We'll decide what's going to happen with our baby and what isn't. Then we'll let you know."

Our baby. The words alone felt like someone had just dumped a bucket of ice water over his head. And here he was trying to make matters worse by adding a wife!

Millie wore an injured expression, but Delaney gathered her purse and slipped out of the booth.

"I'm going with you," Rebecca said, sounding equally indignant.

Delaney shook her head. "No, like I said, this is between Conner and me. We'll talk, then I'll call you all later."

Rebecca assumed the same injured expression Millie

wore, but Delaney ignored it and turned to him. "Are you coming with me or not?"

He watched her staring down at him, her dark hair pulled back, her face scrubbed clean of makeup, and wondered, for the first time, if marriage, even a *convenient* marriage like this, would really be so bad. He wanted more for his child than what he'd experienced in his own life. He wanted legitimacy, a conventional home, a strong marriage, a complete family. It was all just a little premature.

And he wasn't sure he could get there working backward....

CHAPTER EIGHTEEN

DELANEY SAT in the old white pickup, refusing to look at Conner as he drove, even when he pulled off the main highway onto a side street that ended in a cul-de-sac of unfinished lots.

"This okay?" he asked, stopping in front of a mustard-yellow subdivision map that announced the sale of five quarter-acre lots.

She nodded. He shifted into park and let the truck idle, and she turned to face him, wondering what in the world they were going to say to each other after this morning.

At first they said nothing. They sat staring at each other as though the silence was too profound to break.

"You're still not gaining any weight," Conner finally said.

"Not yet," she responded. "But I will."

"When?"

She shrugged. "Soon."

"What happens if you don't?"

"I could miscarry. Then all your problems would be solved, right?"

He slung one arm over the steering wheel and squinted into the distance, toward the mountains. "I'm not hoping you'll miscarry," he said gruffly.

"Then, what are you hoping for? We can't go back in time."

He didn't answer her question, but he asked one of his

own. "Why did you go to Boise in the first place? What happened to falling in love before making a baby? You're a beautiful woman with a—" he hesitated "—great body. You're well-liked around here. What were you thinking?"

Uncomfortable with his scrutiny, she turned back to the window, which overlooked green, waving grass and, farther off, a stand of shady trees. "I'm thirty years old and I haven't met anyone special. I wanted a baby before it was too late, and I was afraid it would never happen." She looked at him again. "Haven't you ever done anything wrong, not out of some diabolical urge to hurt and destroy, but simply because you wanted something so badly?"

He sighed. "Actually, I've done plenty of things wrong, but I've always erred on the side of giving up too soon. I've never really fought for anything—until now."

"Until now? What does that mean?"

He studied her. "I'm going to fight for this, Delaney."

"This?"

"The ranch. The baby."

Fear trickled down Delaney's spine, but she couldn't bear to ask him, just yet, how he meant to fight for the baby. "I thought your grandfather was putting the ranch up for sale."

"I'm going to buy it. Then I'm going to turn the ranch around, make it work."

"So that means you're staying here in Dundee."

"Exactly."

She digested this information, unsure whether she was happy about it or not. "And the baby? Are you willing to settle for joint custody?"

"No. I want you to marry me."

Marry him... They were back to that. "Marriage is more than having a baby together," she said. "What about love?"

"A lot of people who are in love get married, and their marriages end in divorce. Love is no safety net."

"But we wouldn't even start with that much. What happens if—" she ran a hand through her hair "—if one of us has an obnoxious habit the other can't tolerate? Or what if one of us meets Mr. or Ms. Right and regrets our...our arrangement?"

"We'll agree now, that if it ever comes to that, we'll split amicably and settle for equal custody of our child. As far as assets go, we're starting with practically nothing, so whatever we accumulate together we'll split. The baby will have my name, you'll have whatever financial support I can provide, and I won't shame my grandfather in front of the people he most respects, people he's known his whole life."

So that was it. He was doing it for his grandfather. "Will he cut you out of his will if you don't make good?" she asked.

"It's not about money."

Then, it was something deeper. She'd put Conner in a bad position, and he was doing his best to rectify things. How could she stand in his way?

Fidgeting with the strap of her purse, Delaney thought about being married to him, taking his name, making love with him, living with him on a full-time basis—and felt her heart beat faster. Part of her wanted nothing more. The other part showed her a picture of a miserable future with a husband who resented her. Could she live with a man who didn't love her, for anyone's sake? "If either one of us is miserable, we just agree to split amicably. Isn't that the gist of what you said?"

He nodded.

"And a traditional upbringing would definitely be better for the baby. I know that."

"Definitely."

She took a deep breath to ease the tension knotting her stomach. "Okay."

"Okay what?"

"Let's get married."

He almost smiled, then seemed to catch himself. "When do you want to do it?"

"As soon as possible."

"You want a church wedding?"

"I'm sure that's what Aunt Millie would prefer."

"What would *you* like?"

"That's what I want, too."

CHAPTER NINETEEN

THE FOLLOWING DAY, Conner checked his watch to make sure it wasn't still too early, then called his mother from the office.

"We've set a date," he said as soon as she answered.

"When?"

"In three weeks. Can you come?"

"Of course. I'll book my flight right away."

He could hear the smile in her voice, but it didn't bring him the pleasure it normally would have.

"I can't believe some lucky girl has finally stolen your heart," she said.

Delaney had actually stolen something a little farther south than his heart, but saying so would only prejudice his family against her, and Conner was approaching this marriage the way he was approaching the ranch—with the intention of making it work. So he changed the subject.

"Do you think Grandfather will be up to the trip by then?"

"He's out of the hospital and already trying to work. It's all I can do to slow him down. I'm sure he'll be able to come."

"Good."

"You do love this woman, right, Conner?" she asked. "You're positive you're doing the right thing?"

Conner dodged her first question by answering her second. "I don't think there's any way to be a hundred percent positive, is there, Mom?"

"No, I guess when we get married, we all take a risk. But love is worth the risk. And if you've chosen her, I'm sure I'll love her, too."

Conner shifted uncomfortably. "I hope so."

"That real estate offer you asked me to look for came in, by the way," she said. "I was planning to call you, but I was waiting to see how Dad's going to respond."

"Is it a good offer?"

"Stephen didn't seem too excited about it. I think they'll submit a counteroffer."

"Well, mine's on its way," Conner said.

"Your what?"

"My offer."

"I'm sorry, I don't know what you're talking about."

"I want to purchase the ranch."

"Conner, I'm not sure I know you anymore," she said after a silence.

Conner couldn't help chuckling. "You want me to go back to my old ways?"

"Definitely not. But I do want you to explain a few things to me. How are you going to buy the ranch? You don't have that kind of money."

"People buy property without money all the time. That's how Grandfather bought this place to begin with. He borrowed every dime."

"But you have to have a down payment to get a loan—"

"I'm asking Grandfather to carry the paper for five years. But I'm giving him his purchase price, which is more than fair, and I'm paying a good rate of interest."

"What about operating expenses?" she asked.

"I think I've got that covered."

"How?"

The Hill brothers were his ace in the hole, but Conner wasn't willing to reveal that information yet. He knew his mother meant well, but he couldn't afford to have anything slip out in front of Stephen, Dwight or Jonathan. Not when his uncles' opposition would increase with his chances of success.

"You'll see," he said. "Just make sure Grandfather looks at my offer before Stephen can deep-six it."

WHERE WAS DELANEY?

Conner sat at the kitchen table, eating the chicken and polenta salad she'd made them for dinner, pretending to be completely absorbed by the simple act of lifting his fork to his mouth. But he kept listening for movement elsewhere in the house, kept expecting Delaney to return to the kitchen and start cleaning up while they ate, like she usually did. When she didn't come, he wondered if she'd gotten sick again. She seemed to be doing so much better, but—

"What's on your mind?" Roy asked.

Conner shook his head.

"Come on, what is it?"

"It's nothing," Conner said to stop Roy from jumping to the conclusion that the Hills had backed out of the deal or something. Though they still had a lot to do before the resort became a reality, everything was on track.

What was bothering Conner had nothing to do with business. This was personal. He'd asked Delaney to marry him, and she'd agreed, but they'd barely spoken in the past week. He couldn't help looking for some indication that she wasn't actually dreading the prospect of becoming Mrs. Conner Armstrong.

He continued eating, trying to wait long enough that no one would connect his question with Roy's expression of concern. Then he asked, "Anyone know where Delaney went? Is she sick?"

"No, she's gone." It was Isaiah, her not-so-secret admirer.

"Where?" Conner asked.

"Millie and Rebecca are giving her a bridal shower."

"They are?"

Isaiah glanced up from his plate. "Yeah. Didn't you know?"

Conner didn't answer. He hadn't known. And it irritated him that Isaiah did. "She's engaged," he said, suddenly losing his appetite.

"That's why I thought you'd know."

There was something challenging in Isaiah's words, and his stare accused Conner of not treating Delaney right, which bothered him, too. Maybe because he felt a little guilty. He hadn't done anything unkind to Delaney; that was how he'd justified his behavior. But he certainly hadn't gone out of his way to speak to her, either.

"Mind your own business," he growled, and headed back to his office. But even as he worked, he kept one ear trained for the sound of a car pulling into the drive. When he didn't hear anything for over an hour, he returned to the kitchen to find Isaiah wiping off the kitchen table.

"What are you doing?" he asked.

"Cleaning up so Delaney won't have to come home to dishes," he said. "I guess that never occurred to you."

It hadn't. Conner had been too preoccupied with listening for her car and wondering if a bridal shower resembled a bachelor party—or whether Delaney's shower might include a finale at the Honky Tonk. But Isaiah didn't know anything. Conner opened his mouth to tell him so, to tell him that Delaney had wronged Conner, not the other way around. But then he realized Isaiah was probably smarter than he'd thought, which didn't make him feel any better, so he trudged back to his office and slouched behind his desk. If he'd been nicer to Delaney, she might've told him that her friends were giving her a bridal shower....

An hour later, the crunch of gravel on the drive told him she was home. Dropping the pencil he'd been twirling in agitation, he hurried to the front door, but she barely looked up when she came in. Buried beneath the boxes and gift bags she carried in her arms, she brushed right by him and started down the hall.

"How was it?" he asked, rushing to catch up with her.

"Great," she muttered. "Everyone's excited but us."

Her words felt amazingly like a left hook. "Nice one," he said, rubbing his jaw.

"What?"

"Never mind. Want some help?" he asked, trying again.

"No, thanks."

"What'd you ladies do?"

She cast him a glance over her shoulder. "Nothing much."

"It doesn't look like nothing much." They'd reached her bedroom, and he flipped on the light. "What'd you get?"

"Stuff."

He needed to ask her a question she had to answer with more than one or two words, he thought as she dropped everything on her dresser.

"I'll get to the dishes in a minute," she said, obviously misunderstanding his reason for bothering her.

Conner felt a twinge of guilt. "Uh, they're done."

"They are?"

"Yeah."

"Who... Oh, Isaiah! Did he do them for me?"

She'd known immediately that it wasn't him. Conner frowned. "Yeah. Isn't he *sweet?*"

She ignored his sarcasm.

"If you see him on your way out, would you tell him I brought him a piece of cake? It's still in the car."

Her words sounded a lot like a dismissal, but Conner wasn't ready to leave. "Is there a piece of cake in the car for me?" he asked.

She blinked up at him. "*You* want cake?"

"Yeah, I like cake. Everybody likes cake."

"Sorry," she said. "I figured you'd be busy—working in your office."

He'd spent a lot of time there lately. But he had big plans. She knew that.

The telephone rang. She waited for a minute, as though she wanted to shoo him out before she answered it, but there wasn't time to do it politely, and one thing he'd learned about Delaney was that she was almost always polite. Turning at the last second, she grabbed the receiver.

"Hi, Beck," she said, facing away from him.

That left him free to poke through the presents. If they were bridal shower gifts, they were ultimately for him, too, right?

Massage cream...bath soaps...edible underwear—*edible underwear?* Who gave her that? Probably Rebecca...

"I did?" she was saying. "Okay, I'll pick it up this weekend. Yeah, it was fun and I got a lot of great stuff, but what I really wanted was one of those bunnies Hal over at the feed store has leftover from Easter.... So? I could get Isaiah to build me a cage out by the chicken coop..."

Conner frowned. *Isaiah again.*

"Maybe I should buy one myself." She gave a quick shrug. "Nah, there's too much going on right now. Maybe next year... What?...I think so, too. Wasn't that awkward with Aunt Millie there? Who thought of the...the you-know."

She turned and saw him going through her gifts and her eyes widened meaningfully as she waved him away.

"The what?" he asked. Ignoring her unspoken directive to leave the presents alone, he rifled through some red tissue paper to get to the perfume beneath.

She covered the phone. "This is a private conversation. And that belongs to me."

She whipped the bottle from his grasp before he could even open it.

"It's not as though these things belong *exclusively* to you," he said. "You only got them because you're getting married. And you're marrying me." He pulled out a black bustier, imagined Delaney in it and grinned. Maybe this marriage stuff wasn't so bad, after all.

"Rebecca, I gotta go," Delaney said. "No, nothing's wrong... What?"

Conner's fingers encountered something voluminous and soft, fabric that felt as sheer as the bustier but much more flowing. Removing it from its box, he held up a diaphanous ivory negligee that was probably the most elegant piece of lingerie he'd ever seen. What struck him as even more significant was that it looked exactly like something Delaney might choose.

"This is beautiful," he started to say, but she slammed the phone down, ripped the nightgown from his hands and shoved it back in the box.

"Don't," she said. "I'm returning it."

"Why?" he asked, but he already knew the answer. She didn't want to wear it for him. It wasn't that kind of wedding.

"There's no need to pretend."

"Pretend. Right." Somehow his interest in the presents disappeared just that quickly, and he wondered what he'd been doing following her around, digging through her things. "Sorry to intrude," he said. "I'll tell Isaiah about his cake."

DELANEY SIGHED when she heard Conner's steps retreat. She knew she'd hurt him in some way, but she didn't know what to do about it. She'd come home overwhelmed by the attention she'd received at the shower, already embarrassed because everyone in town seemed to think she'd met her prince charming—and yet she and Conner were barely speaking to each other. She was marrying him to make amends, as far as she could, for what she'd done, but she wasn't sure marriage was very wise in the long run, for either one of them. And just when all these thoughts and feelings seemed to be colliding inside her, he appeared out of nowhere and began examining these stupid gifts, things that felt too personal to share with him. And she'd... Well, she hadn't reacted in the best manner.

She slumped down on her bed, started to call Rebecca back, then hung up. She'd talk to Conner instead, open communications between them, try to gain some understanding of his confusing behavior.

Leaving her presents behind, including the embarrassing memory of unwrapping edible underwear in front of Aunt Millie—thanks to Katie, another stylist at the salon—she walked silently to the other side of the house. But Conner's office was, for once, dark.

Was he in his bedroom? Continuing around the corner, she came face-to-face with his closed door, hesitated, then raised her hand to knock.

The door opened a second later and Conner stood there, wearing jeans but no shirt. The sight of his bare chest brought their night in Boise back to her—the steam from the shower, the smell of his soap and shampoo, the intimacy of talking to him and getting to know him. She tried to tell herself this wasn't the same man she'd met that night, that this Conner had good reason to hate her, but it was difficult to get beyond a very basic desire to touch him again.

"Is something wrong?" he asked.

Delaney opened her mouth to apologize, to try to explain why she'd behaved the way she had a few minutes ago. But once more, he looked so composed and remote that she couldn't bring herself to do it. She must have imagined the hurt, she decided. Conner didn't care enough about her to feel hurt. "Um…Aunt Millie wanted me to tell you that she thinks you're doing your grandfather proud by taking responsibility for the baby."

He studied her but said nothing.

"And I…" She cleared her throat. "I wanted to thank you for not telling anyone about how I…you know, how we met. I've tried to take as much of the blame as possible, but for the baby's sake, I haven't told the exact truth. I'd rather not have something that could embarrass our child flying around a community this size, because Dundee never forgets, you know? Do you understand?"

Conner nodded. "I understand," he said, and shut the door.

CONNER CAUGHT DELANEY by the arm just as she was about to get out of the Suburban they'd taken to Boise to pick up his mother. According to Conner, Vivian Armstrong had decided to fly in a day before the wedding to have some time to meet Delaney; however, Delaney felt less than excited about this aspect of marrying Conner. She felt as though she'd wronged his mother and the rest of his family as much as she'd wronged him.

"At least pretend to like me," he said. "She's not stupid."

Delaney nodded and tried to calm the butterflies in her stomach. *She's going to hate me. They're going to know I've ruined Conner's life, and they're all going to hate me.* Fortunately she didn't have to meet the entire family today. Conner's grandfather and uncles were flying in tomorrow, just in time for the ceremony, and would stay at the ranch overnight. Then they'd all fly back to California together.

Two days had never sounded so long. How were she and Conner going to keep up appearances for such an extended period? Even the ranch hands knew their engagement wasn't exactly typical.

She put a palm to the small bulge in her stomach, knowing the baby would be a focal point over the next few days, and threw her shoulders back as Conner came around the car.

"Are you feeling sick?" he asked, looking concerned when he saw her.

"No." She let her hand fall and started moving woodenly toward the terminal.

He stopped her. "What's wrong?"

"Nothing."

"Are you scared?"

"No," she lied.

Maybe he could see through her, or maybe he was just practicing their act, because he took her hand, and Delaney was surprised at how much the warmth and strength of that contact helped her.

"She'll think you're lovely," he said as they walked.

"How do you know?" she asked.

He didn't look at her. He was too busy navigating across the loading and unloading zones so they could enter the airport. "Because you are."

Delaney was beginning to think she'd never understand him. One minute he ignored her, the next he was angry, the next he actually seemed to like her. But she didn't have much time to ponder their unusual relationship, because they'd reached the gate and the passengers were already filing into the arrivals lounge.

Delaney curled her fingers more tightly through Conner's and waited. She'd survive the next two days *somehow,* she told herself, just as Conner waved at a tall dark-haired woman dressed in a stylish black pantsuit that highlighted her still-trim figure. At the same time, he raised their clasped hands and kissed Delaney's knuckles, and the action seemed so spontaneous, Delaney almost believed it had come naturally to him.

With that type of acting, even his mother would be convinced.

"There you are," the woman said as soon as they'd threaded their way through the crowd and managed to get close enough to take a good look at each other. "This must be Delaney."

Delaney smiled, but her smile shook, and she'd never felt more vulnerable than she did during the next few seconds when Conner's mother stared into her face, then slowly returned her smile.

"She's beautiful, Con." Tears filled her eyes and she pulled Delaney into her arms. "I'm so happy he's found you," she whispered, and Delaney didn't know what to say. She blinked rapidly to avoid tears of her own and clung to this stranger she immediately knew she'd rather die than disappoint.

"Delaney, this is Vivian," Conner said.

Vivian relaxed her hug a little, looked over at her son, then back at Delaney. "Would you rather call me something other than Vivian?"

Delaney was still fighting back tears and had a difficult time speaking. "I'm happy to call you anything you like."

Vivian smiled and kissed Delaney's temple. "Then, call me Mom, dear."

Oh God! Delaney felt as though she were wearing a scarlet letter *L* on her chest for liar, or a *U* for unworthy. But after Conner kissed his mother's cheek and picked up her carry-on, he slung an arm around Delaney and she thought she heard him murmur, "It's okay."

Vivian kept one hand on her arm as though they'd known each other for years. "I want to take you both out to breakfast," she said. "Where should we go?"

CHAPTER TWENTY

CONNER WAS SO NERVOUS he could hardly breathe. It had been an awkward twenty-four hours with his mother in town, and now he'd reached the point of no return. Already. He was going to be married today to a woman who didn't want to marry him, a woman whom—if he were being completely honest—he had yet to forgive. But that wasn't all. Roy had just picked up his grandfather and uncles from the airport and they were waiting in the office to talk to him about his offer on the ranch. The next fifteen minutes would tell whether his dream had any chance.

Though he'd just gotten dressed, Conner unraveled the bow tie on his tux so it hung limply around his neck and unfastened the top button of his white pleated shirt as he made his way down the hall. He'd spent so many hours in the office that he now thought of it as his own domain and not his grandfather's, but it wasn't a sanctuary for him today.

Wiping a hand across his forehead as though it were ninety degrees in the house instead of a cool seventy, he opened the door and strode across the carpet to greet his grandfather and uncles. His mother wasn't part of this little gathering. Along with Dwight's wife and four children, Jonathan's son and Stephen's wife, she was in the south wing, getting ready for the wedding, which was scheduled to start in less than an hour.

Less than an hour…

"Grandfather," he said.

"Conner." His grandfather nodded and shook his hand, and Conner noticed that the firmness of his grip hadn't changed. Never a large man to begin with, he'd lost weight and looked even smaller since the surgery. But his presence still filled the whole room and commanded respect.

"In spite of everything, you're looking fit," Conner told him. "You must be bouncing right back."

"Fit as a man can look after open-heart surgery at eighty-four," he said with a smile.

The way he greased his hair straight off his forehead was hardly the fashion of the day, but it suited him almost as much as his light blue polyester suit. His cowboy boots had been polished, Conner noticed, but they were the same pair he wore day in and day out, whether he was traveling, meeting with business associates or heading out to the vineyards. There wasn't a pretentious bone in his body. A glance at his uncles told Conner they were wearing Armani suits and Italian leather, and carrying themselves as though they were mighty proud of the fact.

"Thanks for coming," Conner told his grandfather. "I know it's very soon after the surgery, and I know you're busy."

His grandfather sat, a little more gingerly than usual, in the Chippendale chair by the window. "Never too busy to come to my grandson's wedding. I'm looking forward to meeting the bride."

"I appreciate that," Conner said, but he wasn't sure he wanted the kind of familiar closeness that Delaney and his mother already seemed to share. Forcing himself to turn and greet his uncles, he smiled. Stephen and Dwight were lounging on the leather couch, their coats unbuttoned, while Jonathan's huge bulk filled an upholstered chair almost the size of a love seat. "Stephen, Jonathan, Dwight. Good of you to come."

"We wouldn't have missed it for the world," Stephen said.

Conner tipped his head to acknowledge Stephen's mocking smile. "I knew I could rely on that."

"So what's going on? What's this all about?" Dwight asked, cutting to the chase by tossing the offer Conner had faxed to the Napa house onto the coffee table.

"Exactly what it looks like," Conner said.

Jonathan gave up his more comfortable position to lean forward. In the three months since Conner had seen him, he'd lost some hair and gained even more weight. "What it looks like is an offer. But I don't understand why you've signed it as buyer."

"What's confusing about that? I want to purchase the ranch."

Dwight rubbed his jaw and narrowed his eyes. "Problem is, Con, you don't have any money."

"That's why I'm asking for terms. I've seen the appraisal. You padded the price by nearly two-hundred thousand dollars to allow room to negotiate if an offer came in and, in this market, it's going to take a few concessions to get that kind of asking price. Carrying the loan is the concession I need."

"Sounds as though you've actually learned something about real estate since you've been here," Stephen said. "But I'm afraid you don't have much of a track record in business. Three months on this place doesn't make you a rancher. And even if we carry the paper, you don't have the money to keep the ranch functioning."

"I'll manage," Conner said.

"How?"

"That's up to me."

"And in five years?"

"Just like it says in the offer, I'll obtain my own financing and cash you out."

Jonathan rested his beefy elbows on his knees. "You're not going to be able to obtain financing unless you're working in the black, Conner. No bank's going to lend you money on a losing venture."

"I realize that. The Running Y will be in the black by then."

"And what guarantee do we have? Your *word?*" Jonathan looked at his brothers and chuckled.

Conner's grandfather didn't laugh with them. He seemed to be listening, taking it all in.

"If we sold the ranch to you, we'd just end up having to repossess it when you can't make a go of it," Dwight said. "And repossessions can take a long time and get messy. I really don't want to be involved in all that.'

"I understand," Conner said. "Why don't we get around that by including an agreement along with the purchase contract that says I'll simply sign the place over to you if I don't meet my deadline." He propped his hands on his hips, hoping he looked a lot more confident than he felt. "Because it won't come to that. I'm going to make the deadline."

Stephen laughed and began tapping his toe. "I'm afraid chances are much better that you won't," he said. "You're going to need a lot of money to run this place and—"

"I agree," Dwight cut in. "Essentially, you're asking us not to sell at all. You're asking us to give you a guaranteed five years before we liquidate, that's all."

"I'm sorry, Con. There's no way to make it work." Jonathan made a great show of checking his watch. "Now we'd better get moving. Wouldn't want to make you late for your own wedding."

Conner glanced at his watch and cringed at the passing

minutes, but he wasn't about to let his uncles best him quite so easily. "I'm willing to guarantee payment in full after five years against my inheritance, provided I'm still getting one," he said, looking to his grandfather for confirmation.

His grandfather nodded. "You came here and tried to make a go of this place like I asked. It was our decision to sell and had nothing to do with you. I don't see any reason you wouldn't have an equal share with your uncles and your mother."

A muscle jumped in Stephen's jaw, and Conner knew his grandfather had just hit a tender spot. His uncles didn't like the fact that as a grandchild, and an adopted one at that, he was on an equal footing with them.

"If you'll sell me the ranch, I'll walk away from my inheritance entirely," Conner said, facing his uncles. "If I can't pay you off in five years as promised, I'll be written out of the will. I'll make my own way, you'll sell the ranch to someone else, and that will be the end of it."

Stephen and his brothers had gambled on his failure when they sent him to Dundee. Now Conner was calling their bet and raising the stakes by several million. If Conner won, he'd have his portion of the Armstrong estate along with the ranch. And he would've done something for his grandfather they couldn't do. If he lost, he'd have nothing.

Stephen seemed to grasp the "nothing" part of that concept more quickly than his brothers. "You really want to take that kind of risk, Con?"

Conner nodded.

"Fine. I agree."

Dwight's gaze narrowed at Conner for a second, but then he agreed, too. "Sure, I'm willing to give you enough rope to hang yourself."

It was Jonathan's turn. Conner held his breath as he looked

to the man who'd most often tortured him as a child. He seemed a little more hesitant than the others. "Jonathan?" Conner prompted. "You're so certain I won't make good. Are you willing to put your money where your mouth is?"

Malice entered his eyes, the old malice Conner recognized so well, but the challenge worked. "Why not? You'll never do it."

Conner turned and waited for his grandfather's response, but, as usual, Clive took his time. "All four of you want to do this?" he eventually asked. "Because after we leave this room, there'll be no going back."

"Yeah…it's just a matter of time. We'll get it back, anyway," Stephen said, and the uncles exchanged nods and glances to confirm it.

"Conner? Are you sure?"

"I'm sure," he said, even though he wasn't. Everything he stood to gain depended solely on him. But strangely enough, he liked it that way. He felt freer than he'd ever felt in his life—free to succeed or fail on his own, to prove his worth, to *have* some worth.

The old man rubbed his chin, and Conner thought he detected a smile. But when Clive spoke, his voice remained matter-of-fact. "Hand me that offer so I can sign it."

Conner handed him the offer Jonathan had tossed onto the coffee table, and watched, his heart in his throat, as his grandfather scribbled his name on the acceptance line.

"I'll have the rest of the agreement drawn up right away," Stephen said.

Conner nodded, and his uncles left to find their families so they could head into town to the chapel. But his grandfather lagged behind. He circled the room, gazing at the wooden paneling, western prints and worn but sturdy furnishings.

"You miss the ranch, don't you?" Conner asked.

His grandfather's lips curved into a nostalgic smile. "It reminds me of your grandma. Besides, the harder you have to fight for something, the more it means to you. You'll find that out over the next five years, Con."

"I think I'm beginning to understand already." Conner put his hands in his pockets and leaned against the doorway, finally catching on to something he hadn't grasped until that moment. "I was right. Sending me here was a setup, wasn't it. Only, not for the reasons I thought. This is what you wanted for me."

The old man smiled, his eyes twinkling.

"How'd you know I'd rise to the occasion?" Conner asked.

"I didn't. I took a chance on something I love—someone I love. You and your mother have always been special to me." He moved toward the exit and clapped a hand on Conner's shoulder. "Now, let's get out of here before your uncles figure out they just bet against the wrong man."

A warmth filled Conner, a warmth that started from somewhere deep inside him. So much of his future remained uncertain. He wasn't sure his uncles *had* bet against the wrong man. But he knew he was back on the right path. At last.

Shoving off from the wall, he buttoned his shirt and fastened his tie as he said, "You knew Stephen and the others would agree, didn't you."

"I wasn't too worried about it." He winked. "I still had ultimate control of this ranch, and I would've sold it to you with or without their approval. But this is better. They won't have anyone to blame but themselves, and maybe they'll realize what fools they've been. At least, I hope they will." He sighed heavily. "It's hard to believe I could have three sons who think so differently from the way I do."

Conner chuckled. "Maybe blood isn't everything."

"Isn't that the truth? And yet, I can't give up on them, either." His grandfather shook his head, then took hold of Conner's hand and gazed down at the ring his mother had given him. "You get this from Vivian?"

Conner nodded, and his grandfather smiled. "Used to be mine," he said. "Back when I wore such things. Your grandma bought it for me."

"Would you like it back?" Conner asked.

"No, I'd rather you kept it," he said. "She loved you as much as I always have."

CONNER'S SENSE OF RIGHTNESS lasted for a whole fifteen minutes or so, then fell apart as soon as he arrived at the church. Already filled to overflowing, the small New England-style chapel held many faces he recognized, and many he did not. Ralph Lawson hovered near the door at the back, looking a bit lost without Millie, who was probably in some antechamber with Rebecca and Delaney and his mother. The old folks he'd met at the Lawson house a few weeks ago—Ruby, Lula and Vern—occupied the second row on the right, along with a few other seniors, all dressed to the nines and wearing corsages or boutonnieres. And Katie, the young woman he'd seen at the salon the day he'd realized Delaney lived in Dundee, smiled widely when he caught her eye, then nudged the woman sitting next to her.

On the left sat his grandfather and uncles, along with Grady, Ben and Isaiah from the ranch, and Josh and Mike Hill. Dottie had returned from Salt Lake just in time for the wedding. Carrying a stack of photographs of the new baby, which she showed to anyone willing to look, she clucked over his brothers' children, who took up the bench beside her. Only Roy wasn't in the congregation. Conner had made Roy stand up with him. And a sidelong glance told him his foreman wasn't particularly happy about it.

"How much longer before we get this show on the road?" he growled, stretching his neck and yanking on his tie.

Conner swallowed a chuckle. "Should be any minute now."

"And to think I was betting you'd leave town inside of three months," Roy replied. "Good thing I didn't put any money on it."

"You said yourself this ranch is the perfect place to raise a child," Conner reminded him. "I'm taking your advice."

"I wouldn't have said it if I'd known it would land me in a damn monkey suit."

The Reverend Parker, a man Conner had just met, was standing on Conner's other side.

He gave Roy a reproachful look, and Roy quickly apologized. "Sorry for the language, Rev."

"All the more reason to attend services," he responded.

Roy stretched his neck again and looked longingly at the door, mumbling something about changing his ways. "That's probably the right of it, Rev."

"Then, we'll see you on Sunday, will we not?"

"I'll be here," Roy said. He sent Conner an accusing glare, and Conner couldn't help laughing.

"That goes for you, too, Mr. Armstrong," the reverend said, and Conner felt the full weight of the man's will pushing him toward God. But he didn't have time to respond or even feel guilty about his fifteen-year lapse in church attendance. The organ burst into a crescendo behind him, Rebecca hurried forward to take her place on the opposite side of the altar, and Millie and his mother found their seats. Delaney finally appeared at the back of the chapel, pale and almost ethereal in a simple white dress with long sleeves, a straight narrow skirt and no train.

She looked beautiful as she gazed up the aisle. Dignified. Sophisticated. Yet fragile. She nearly stole Conner's breath as their eyes met, but he couldn't help wondering if she was as terrified as he was.

Clasping his hands behind his back, he put an encouraging smile on his face and told himself that everything was going to be fine. So what if marrying and starting a family was completely contrary to anything he'd imagined himself doing in the next five years? So what if he'd just gambled his entire inheritance on a losing ranch? He loved that ranch. And…and he hoped he could grow to love this woman. From the crowded pews, it certainly looked as though he'd be in good company if he did. Even the mayor had come for her wedding. Conner had heard his grandfather greet Mayor Sparks earlier.

Delaney slipped her hand into the crook of Ralph's arm, and he led her up the aisle to the accompaniment of "The Wedding March." *Here comes the bride…here comes the bride…*

With each step, Conner felt his tie growing tighter.

What do you think you're doing? You're not cut out for this. You'll never make her a good husband, never be able to give her and the baby what they need….

Blood isn't everything…

I took a chance on something I love—someone I love….

When life hands you lemons, make lemonade….

And if the ranch isn't profitable in five years? What then?

Then she'd know she shouldn't have bet her future on him.

Conner closed his eyes, took a deep breath and felt Roy nudge him.

"If you back out now, I'll kill ya," he murmured. "I'm not standing here making a spectacle of myself for nothing."

A fleeting glance at Parker revealed that the good reverend was too caught up in the music and the bride's advance to have overheard, but Conner smiled at the memory of first meeting Roy. Who would've thought they'd ever become friends? And who would've thought he'd end up marrying the virgin who'd come to his room that night at the Bellemont?

He briefly recalled the fact that he'd once considered Idaho synonymous with the outer reaches of hell, and his smile widened. If it was hell, he'd just told Satan to turn up the heat.

THE KISS CONNER HAD GIVEN HER at the altar had been light and sweet, but mostly respectful. Delaney had stood in front of all her friends and acquaintances, just about everyone she knew, and imagined they recognized the lack of passion in his kiss as easily as she did. Had he been trying to make some sort of announcement—that he was only marrying her because of the baby?

She was making a terrible mistake, she thought miserably. And yet, whenever she looked up and found Conner watching her, or brushed against him as they cut the cake or posed for a photograph, or heard the deep rumble of his voice, she felt a tingle in her stomach and even a surge of excitement at the thought that, for whatever reason, he belonged to her. Certainly, that was something worth building on....

Rebecca glanced up from her plate and frowned. "What's wrong? This is your wedding luncheon. Aunt Millie and Uncle Ralph have gone to a lot of work to get the yard ready. You're supposed to be having fun."

"It's difficult to have fun when my face hurts from this fake smile, my conscience hurts from all the lies and my pride hurts from the fact that Conner doesn't even want me."

Rebecca shook her head. "You're taking life too seriously. Can I have your cake?"

Delaney shoved her untouched piece of cake over to Rebecca. "And marriage is supposed to be a game?"

"Just relax and celebrate. Hey, Conner's mom is watching you. She looks concerned."

Delaney boosted her smile a few notches and nodded at Vivian. "What's to celebrate? I'm marrying a man who doesn't love me," she muttered to Rebecca, double-checking to be sure her new husband wasn't within earshot. When she saw him several feet away near the rented arbor, deep in conversation with his grandfather, she relaxed. Aunt Millie's small backyard was still crowded, but the wedding luncheon was technically over and the guests were wrapped up in their own conversations. She could hear Aunt Millie gushing to Ruby and some of the neighbors about how she'd waited for this day her entire life, and Delaney felt as though she'd betrayed her. If this was the kind of wedding Aunt Millie had wanted it to be, Delaney and Conner would've left long ago. They would've rushed off before anyone else, eager to start their honeymoon.

But Conner had a ranch to run and had mentioned that he was eager to take care of some business while his grandfather and uncles were in town.

"You're going to have a father for your baby. That's something to celebrate," Rebecca said, polishing off the cake.

Allowing her baby to grow up with his or her father counted for a great deal. But somehow, it couldn't cover everything. Was it too much to ask that he care a little about her, too?

"I just…I don't know," Delaney said. "I feel like I've let everyone down, including myself."

"Conner…"

Delaney heard Vivian's voice, saw her move toward her son and watched their heads bend together for a few moments. Then Conner looked over at her, and Delaney quickly lowered her eyes.

"Oh my gosh. His mother's having to tell him to take me away," she said. "She's feeling sorry for me."

"Somebody should've told him an hour ago," Rebecca said.

Conner walked over, absolutely gorgeous in his tux. Delaney told herself to remember that this was the same man who'd lugged her suitcases into the ranch wearing such an angry expression, the man who'd refused to acknowledge her for weeks, the man who was still treating her indifferently. She had to remember all this, so he'd never have the power to break her heart. But after what she'd done to him, his behavior was all too forgivable, and she ended up thinking instead about the way his hands had felt when they'd touched her that night in Boise.

"You ready to go?" he asked.

"It's about time you got over here," Rebecca said before Delaney could answer.

"Rebecca!" she cried.

Rebecca gave Conner a dirty look and hugged Delaney goodbye. "Well, he should have," she said. "And if he's not good to you, I swear I'm going to—"

"Stop it," Delaney said, but she couldn't help smiling as she led Conner away.

"Rebecca is certainly...her own person," Conner murmured after they'd said their goodbyes to Aunt Millie, Uncle Ralph, his mother and his grandfather, and were heading out to the truck.

"Don't say anything bad about her around me," Delaney said.

Conner laughed. "Calm down. I think I like her. That's the crazy thing. Nothing here in Dundee is turning out the way I thought it would the day I pulled into town."

"I could say the same thing," she said.

CHAPTER TWENTY-ONE

"I SAW MY UNCLE STEPHEN talking to you at the luncheon. What did he say?" Conner asked, keeping his eyes on the road so he wouldn't stare at his lovely bride and swerve into a ditch.

Delaney considered him. "You really want to know?"

Conner shrugged. "I can probably guess, but let me have it."

"He said not to get too comfortable at the ranch, that you never stick with anything."

Quickly masking the anger that flared inside him, Conner told himself not to worry about Stephen. The ranch belonged to him now. At least he had a fighting chance. "Nice of him to wish us well, don't you think?"

"This must be the man you thought had put me up to seducing you in Boise."

"That'd be him."

"He's part of the reason you married me, though, isn't he?"

Conner didn't know what to say. Stephen *had* been part of the reason, but only because he'd insisted on magnifying Conner's flaws. The truth of the matter was that Conner had actually been trying to escape his own reputation. Except, he didn't want to think about that because then he'd have to admit he had some culpability in everything that had happened between them. Delaney might have tried to get pregnant in Boise, but he wouldn't have felt marriage was his only option if he'd led a good life up until that point. In a sense, he'd trapped himself.

"I married you because I thought it would be best," he said.

"Right." She stroked the smooth white satin of her dress, then gazed out the window. Conner allowed himself a quick glance at her. She'd taken off her high heels. Her feet and ankles, covered in sheer white nylons, peeked out from the hem of the gown. He wondered if she wore a garter belt with those nylons—maybe a lacy number that rode low on her hips. The contradiction of his small-town librarian, who'd never known a man until she offered him her virginity just over four months ago, wearing something so wanton made Conner's pulse race.

He opened the window to cool down. "Are you tired?" he asked. They'd talked about a honeymoon and decided to use his family's short stay as an excuse to avoid one, but Conner wasn't so sure he still agreed with that decision. She was his wife. She was carrying his baby. And he wanted to find out about that garter belt...

"I'm not tired," she said.

"How's the morning sickness?"

"It's gone."

The arch at the entrance to the Running Y came up on their right. Conner slowed, but then he remembered that garter belt and the gifts she'd received at the bridal shower and thought maybe he could convince her to share them with him, after all.

"Where are we going?" Delaney asked in surprise when he kept driving.

"There's a string of cabins outside Blackfoot. My mother thought that might be a nice place to take you—"

"Your mother's a wonderful person. And I appreciate

the way she's looking out for me, but I'm fine,'' Delaney said. ''There's no need to change our plans.''

''There's not?''

''No. I knew what I was getting into,'' she said.

''And what exactly is that?''

''An arrangement.''

An arrangement. Conner nodded and tried not to let his disappointment show. ''Okay,'' he said, and turned the truck around.

DELANEY'S SMILE became more and more difficult to maintain. As soon as they returned to the house, they changed out of their bridal wear. Then Conner disappeared into his office with his grandfather and his uncles, leaving Delaney in the living room with Vivian and the two dogs. Delaney suspected Vivian would have joined the men, but she was too protective of Delaney to leave her alone on her wedding day and seemed determined to make up for Conner's neglect.

''What do you think you'll name the baby?'' Vivian asked, glancing surreptitiously down the hall.

''I haven't decided yet. I need to get a book and look at my options,'' Delaney said. But she was thinking about using Vivian's name, if it was a girl. The older woman moved with such grace, such refinement. Delaney already admired her.

''That friend I met—?''

''Rebecca?'' Delaney asked, petting Champ when he came to rest his muzzle in her lap.

''That's the one. She's colorful, isn't she. I liked her right away.''

Delaney smiled. Vivian would. Vivian would see the diamond beneath the rough.

''She said she's getting married,'' Vivian went on.

"She's marrying a computer technician who lives in Nebraska in another month."

"Is her fiancé moving here?"

"No, they'll be living in Nebraska."

"You must hate the thought of her leaving."

Sundance nudged Champ aside and gave a little whine, obviously hoping for his share of her attention. "I do. We grew up down the street from each other. I can't remember a time in my life when Rebecca wasn't there."

Delaney heard her voice wobble and struggled to hold it steady. She might be pregnant and emotional, but she wouldn't feel sorry for herself. She would keep her head high and—

Vivian moved closer to her on the couch and placed a hand over hers as both dogs watched with what seemed like curious eyes. "I know how you feel," she said. "But I don't think Rebecca will go anywhere. She's obviously taken with that other man at the reception. What was his name? Josh Something?"

The surprise that jolted Delaney eased the lump in her throat. "You noticed? You're a complete stranger, and you noticed?"

Vivian raised her eyebrows. "I noticed that he was looking at her, too, and I found the chemistry between them pretty hard to ignore. I thought maybe they had a history."

"They have a history, all right. That's part of the problem."

Conner's mother turned to check the hallway again, as though she didn't want anyone to come in on them unawares. "Delaney, I know that Conner's not an easy man to get along with. I know he's probably not as sensitive and open as he should be. And I—" she hesitated "—I know that your relationship is none of my business. I won't intrude other than to say I hope you won't give up on him too easily."

"Viv— Mom, maybe there's something you should know," Delaney started to say, ready to spill everything, but Vivian squeezed her hand.

"I don't want to know," she said. "I can tell you love him. And that's all that matters to me. The rest will work itself out. Now let's get the others and open all these lovely wedding gifts."

QUILTS PULLED TO HER CHIN, Delaney sat propped up in bed, staring miserably at the digital clock on her nightstand. She'd watched the numbers slowly flip from one to the next for more than two hours. Now it was midnight, and the lack of noise in the house told her everyone had finally retired. So where was Conner?

He must have gone to bed in his own room, she decided. He certainly hadn't come to hers. After they'd opened their wedding gifts, he'd returned to his study. His mother had helped her address thank-you cards until bedtime, and then they'd said good-night. But the book Delaney had been reading now lay discarded on her nightstand next to the blasted clock. Nothing, not even a gripping thriller, had the power to engross her tonight. It was her wedding night, and from the look of things, her new husband wasn't sufficiently interested in her to come and say good-night.

With a heartfelt sigh, she mashed down her pillows and told herself to quit worrying and get some sleep. But she kept thinking about her old life; she missed Rebecca and their house and her job and her good reputation. So much had changed—nothing would ever be the same again. And she'd brought it on herself.

A tear slipped from the corner of her eye as she called herself a fool for believing she could have a baby on her own without destroying her life and everyone else's, but then a small knock sounded on her door.

"Delaney? You awake?"

Conner! Delaney tensed and wiped the tears away as the door cracked open. He stepped into the room, his profile revealed in the moonlight filtering through the blinds on her window, but Delaney would have known him even with her eyes closed. After working for him for almost two months, she could easily single out his footfalls from the others, easily identify his outdoorsy scent, his breathing, his aura. His proximity never failed to make her more aware of everything around her.

"Delaney?"

She didn't answer. Squeezing her eyes shut, she pretended to sleep, hoping he'd go away and at the same time she was hoping he'd stay. She didn't want him coming to her out of the sense of obligation that had led him to marry her in the first place. She didn't want him coming to her because his mother had shamed him into it. Which was why she'd refused to go to the cabin. She wanted him in her bed only if he wanted to be there.

When she showed no sign of consciousness, he moved closer and leaned over her, lightly skimming her cheek with one finger.

She opened her eyes to see him wearing—again—nothing but a pair of blue jeans.

"Sorry to wake you," he murmured, as a shiver of excitement crawled slowly down her spine to twist and swirl somewhere in the vicinity of her stomach.

"Is something wrong?" she whispered in deference to the quiet that surrounded them.

"No, I was…" His words fell off, and Delaney waited.

"You were what?"

"I was trying to stay in my own room, but...I didn't want to start out this way."

"What way?"

"Sleeping apart." He straightened, shoved his hands in his pockets and spoke calmly, unemotionally. "I don't think it sets a good precedent."

Precedent? He wanted to sleep with her to create a precedent? "That is a big concern," she said, but couldn't tell if he recognized the sarcasm in her response. His face was inscrutable in the darkness, his eyes shiny dark pools.

He glanced reluctantly at the door. "You'd rather sleep alone, then?"

She considered how she'd feel if he walked away, and how she'd feel if he didn't, and knew she wanted him here. But pride demanded she establish some standards. "Stay only if you want to, not because you think it's best or want to mollify your mother or—"

"I want to," he said, his eyes meeting hers.

Delaney's breath caught as his gaze lowered to her shoulders, fixing on the ivory material of her negligee. "You're wearing it," he breathed. "Can I see?"

She lay perfectly still as he folded back the covers. He looked at her for several seconds, then smiled and ran a hand over the small bulge that was finally providing visual proof of her pregnancy. "Hi, baby," he said, bending down to brush a kiss across her abdomen.

Smiling in spite of herself, Delaney cupped his cheek and held him against their baby for a moment longer. It felt so right to have him close again—at last.

When she let go, his eyes swept over her negligee as one hand outlined the curve of her waist. "You make me crazy, Laney. There isn't any question about that."

Delaney already knew she made him crazy. Any questions she had didn't revolve around that, but she didn't want to think about questions right now. Somehow her need for answers abandoned her the moment Conner's hands started sliding over her skin, caressing her, exploring every sensitive spot he could find while watching the expressions on her face change as she responded to him.

"Pretty," he said, teasing her nipples with his thumbs through the fabric. Then he slid the straps off her shoulders and buried his face in the valley between her breasts, and Delaney felt her body go boneless.

"Come to bed," she murmured, as he lifted his head to kiss her. Unlike the brief kiss he'd given her at the altar, this one held enough promise to curl her toes.

"Careful, Laney. I might actually think you want me," he said.

"I do," she admitted.

Grinning, he stood and stripped off his jeans, and she couldn't help admiring the changes in his body since she'd first seen it. He'd been muscular and firm from the beginning, but he was slightly thinner now and even more defined from the physical nature of his work.

"Somehow it doesn't feel real that we could be married, does it?" she whispered.

He tossed his jeans aside as though he couldn't be less self-conscious, and his teeth flashed in a grin. "It's going to feel very real in a minute," he said. Then he climbed into bed with her and the warmth of his bare skin surrounded her as he drew her into his arms.

Delaney didn't get a moment's sleep all night. Yet she woke feeling more satisfied and refreshed than she'd felt since...Boise.

THE NEXT WEEK PASSED QUICKLY, and for the most part, Delaney's days were no different than they'd been before the wedding. She helped Dottie cook and clean, do the grocery shopping, feed the animals and run errands in town. But once the sun went down and the stars came out, things *were* different. She'd moved into Conner's room the day after the wedding. He always gave her plenty of attention at night, and she did her best to make sure he'd be too tired to work the next morning. But he never was. He always got up early and closed himself in his office or headed outside to ready the horses. She helped make breakfast for Grady, Isaiah, Ben and Roy, who still grinned broadly every time they caught her eye, even though she'd been married a whole week.

"Roy, how long is it going to take before you stop with all the silly smiling?" she said in mock exasperation when she noticed him grinning at her again.

He chuckled. "How's that bun in the oven?"

Delaney wasn't sure, but she thought the flutter she'd been experiencing low in her belly just might be the baby moving. Then again, being around Conner seemed to cause the same sensation, even during the day, when he didn't show any interest in her at all.

"The baby's growing," she said. "I think I can feel it move."

"Did someone say 'baby'?" Dottie asked, and started right in on a retelling of her own granddaughter's birth.

As she rambled on about how marvelous it had been to participate in the process, Delaney let her mind drift—as usual—to Conner. She loved it when he held her and made love to her and slept in her arms. His presence in her life fulfilled her like nothing she'd ever experienced, far more than being a single parent ever could, she thought. Sometimes she'd just sit and daydream about the way he smelled. And the way he moved. And the way his eyes closed and his lips parted when she—

"Earth to Delaney," Isaiah said, interrupting her reverie.

Delaney blinked and looked over at him.

"How long is it going to take before you stop with all the silly smiling?" he asked, and the others laughed.

"I was thinking about the baby," she lied. She stood up to rinse the dishes so she could hide her blush, but Conner came in at that moment and any embarrassment she felt was instantly lost in the hope that today would be the day he acknowledged her outside the bedroom. Just a smile or a meaningful glance or a quick kiss on the temple... Anything to tell her he cared about her, that the relationship developing between them wasn't just sexual.

She dried her hands and made him a plate of scrambled eggs, ham and toast. Her heart was in her throat when she gave it to him. But he didn't even look up. He spoke to Roy about some missing cattle, took a chair at the table and ate. Then he told the cowboys he'd meet them outside and started toward the back door.

"Conner?" Delaney said, catching him before he could leave.

He turned and Delaney felt everyone else's eyes on her, too. She suddenly wished she'd kept her mouth shut. It was stupid to push him for more than he was willing to give. But now that she'd drawn his attention, she had to say something. "I—I have a doctor's appointment later. I thought maybe you'd like to go with me and meet him."

"Sorry," he said with scarcely a pause. "I can't make it today." He went outside and the door banged shut behind him.

Isaiah met Delaney's eyes, his expression one of empathy, and she hated that he understood the hurt Conner had so carelessly inflicted. She wanted to leave and avoid the awkward silence that had settled over the room, but she refused to be that much of a coward. Keeping her back straight and her head high, she accepted each cowboy's dirty plate with a smile and wished them all a good day as they filed out.

But Isaiah didn't go. He lagged behind, and when Dottie—whistling obliviously to herself, probably thinking about her new grandbaby—went into the pantry, he touched her arm.

"He'll come around, Delaney," he said. "Don't worry."

"Sure he will," she responded. But she wasn't so sure. Isaiah didn't know about Boise.

CHAPTER TWENTY-TWO

LIFE AT THE RUNNING Y was peaceful enough during the next few weeks. Conner left before Delaney woke in the mornings, stayed out on the ranch most of the day, then buried himself in his office at night, working until ten, eleven, sometimes twelve o'clock. Delaney tried to get involved in his work so she could relieve some of the pressure. She knew he'd purchased the ranch from his family, understood that he was fighting desperately to save the home he loved. But he insisted everything was fine and wouldn't share his burdens with her. If she asked what was on his mind, he'd say nothing or tell her not to worry. That was it.

So she turned her attention to cleaning blinds and baseboards and organizing closets, since Dottie was back to manage the kitchen and the chickens, dogs and goats. If Conner wasn't going to let her share his load or give her any responsibilities, she'd find some other way to make herself useful.

But soon every nook and cranny in the whole house was sparkling clean, and she had nothing to do but plant a garden. Dottie's knees bothered her; she couldn't bend and weed or plant, so Delaney gratefully took over the small plot of earth just outside the back door and spent a great deal of time reading books about gardening. As the days of June passed and the baby's movements became more obvious, she planted tomatoes, corn and zucchini, peas and carrots, and some bulb flowers she'd found for sale in a magazine—dahlias she'd ordered from Denmark. All the while, she hoped that once Conner grew used to her presence, used to the idea of having a wife, he'd let go of the grudge he held against her.

But he remained as aloof and reserved as the day she'd married him. He was still coming to her at night. He made love to her often and was gentle and kind and generous during those times. But when morning came, he gave the ranch everything he had without sparing so much as a thought for her.

With a sigh, Delaney rocked back on her heels. A strand of hair had fallen from the sloppy knot on top of her head and tickled her face, but her hands were covered with dirt, so she shoved the stand back with a forearm. She'd been planting since just after breakfast, and her garden was growing—but so was her belly, which made it difficult to bend over for long.

"Don't overdo," Dottie called, passing by as she threw last night's table scraps to Champ and Sundance. Delaney had fenced them out of her garden with three-foot wire.

"I'm not," Delaney replied, but she had to pause a little longer to ease the ache in her back.

"Rebecca called," Dottie said. "She told me she's planting watermelons with you today."

Delaney smiled. Rebecca had never planted anything in her life, not even a small garden like the one Delaney had weeded for Aunt Millie and Uncle Ralph when she was a teenager, but she'd thrown herself into Delaney's new love with unexpected enthusiasm. She came out to the ranch often, and together they weeded and planted. Or Delaney met her in town and they went to Boise to buy Rebecca's wedding dress, search for the perfect bridal bouquet or gather ideas for the caterers.

"Did she say if she had to work later?" Delaney asked.

"I'm afraid not. But she said she's found something else for the nursery. You want me to bring you the cordless phone so you can call her back?"

"No, she'll be here soon. But thanks."

The screen door slammed shut and Dottie disappeared, leaving Delaney alone in the mellow midday sun. A butterfly hovered at the end of the row of peas Delaney was planting, and Sundance and Champ barked and growled in the grass not far away, wrestling over the beef bones Dottie had given them. But neither the peacefulness of such a lovely setting nor the knowledge that Rebecca was on her way could lift Delaney's spirits. She had another doctor's appointment at four o'clock and had made a point of asking Conner, once again, to accompany her. He'd mumbled something noncommittal and left the house early, and since she hadn't heard any more, she doubted he planned to join her. Again.

Oh well, she told herself, trying to be positive. Her marriage wasn't perfect, but things could be a lot worse. She'd known when she said "I do" that Conner didn't love her. Had she really expected that to change?

Deep down, she must have, she realized. She'd probably been trying to live the "happily ever after" fairy tale every woman dreams about. But Conner made a poor Prince Charming. He was good in bed, but Delaney was learning that she needed more.

In any case, Rebecca would go to the doctor's with her. And maybe while they were in Boise, they'd find a good price on a car seat at some secondhand store.

Bending over her work, she managed to finish the row she was working on before the screen door swung open again and Rebecca strode into the yard. Sundance and Champ barked and wagged their tails, and Rebecca patted heads and rubbed ears and let the dogs lick her fingers. But when she turned to Delaney, her usual smile was strained, and it struck Delaney that her friend had lost weight.

"Are you feeling okay?" she asked.

"Sure. Why?"

"Something's wrong. What is it?"

"Nothing," she said impatiently, her initial smile replaced by a look of irritation.

"Rebecca—"

"I haven't been sleeping well, that's all." She shrugged.

"Why?"

"Come on, let's plant," Rebecca said. "I brought some watermelon seeds. Late summer isn't anything if there's no watermelon."

Delaney used the shovel at her side to help her stand. "Is it Buddy? Are you two having problems?"

"Not exactly," Rebecca said.

"Then, what *exactly* is it?"

"He wants to postpone the wedding again."

"Why?"

"He said his mother wants to attend. She lives in Georgia and can't come until August."

"But that's a good thing, right?"

"I don't know. I think he's scared."

"Wouldn't he tell you if he was scared? Maybe he just wants his mother there, like he said."

"Maybe." Rebecca pulled a small bag of seeds from her pocket and tore open the top. "Do you really think we can grow these things from scratch? I mean, maybe I should've bought little seedlings we could transplant, so they'd have a better chance of surviving."

Delaney propped her hands on her hips. "The seeds will work just fine. Quit trying to change the subject."

"I don't want to talk about it, okay?" Rebecca snapped.

"You're miserable out here, yet you won't ever talk about that. Why should I spill *my* guts?"

Delaney blinked in surprise. "I'm not miserable. I love the ranch. And I'm excited about the baby."

"That might be true, but something's making you unhappy."

Delaney opened her mouth to deny it, then changed her mind. What was the use? Rebecca knew her too well. "My husband ignores me all day. He's generally polite when I see him—if he acknowledges me. And he's great in bed. But he doesn't care about me enough to seek my opinion on anything. He doesn't trust me enough to let me help him. He never needs me except for a little warmth at night. And he won't take two hours off work to come to the doctor with me. Is that what you want to hear?"

Rebecca's eyes narrowed at this revelation, and she began to scan the surrounding hills, as though she'd take Conner on right now if she could find him. "I'm going to have a talk with him."

"No, you're not. That's precisely why I've kept my feelings to myself. I don't want him to start being solicitous because he feels he isn't measuring up. I think he's busy trying to prove something to himself right now, though I'm not really sure what that is. Anyway, he has pretty big plans for the ranch, and I want to give him the space he needs to succeed. And if he ever comes to care about me, I want him to do it on his own, okay? Love isn't something we can force."

Rebecca tapped her foot, obviously thinking this over, but not making any promises.

"Tell me you'll leave him alone and you won't say anything," Delaney insisted.

"Oh, all right. If that's what you want. For now," she relented.

"That's what I want." Delaney wiped the perspiration from her forehead and let herself out the makeshift gate. Then she pulled Rebecca down next to her on the back steps. "Have you ever thought that maybe you and Buddy aren't really right for each other?" she asked.

"What? We're in love. Of course we're right for each other." She thrust a hand through her hair—hair she'd bleached blond for the summer and cut into a messy style reminiscent of Meg Ryan's. It suited her much better than the red ever did, made her look younger, more carefree, and highlighted the fine bone structure of her face. "I'm out of here in two months."

Delaney gathered the folds of her loose cotton dress around her ankles. "See? You're 'out of here in two months.' That's what has me worried. Is Buddy the man of your dreams, or a ticket out?"

Rebecca scratched Sundance, who immediately laid his large head in her lap and gave a few grateful whines. "He's both."

Delaney tried to read Rebecca's face while fending off Champ. Was she right to push this subject? Maybe it was none of her business. Maybe she needed to let Rebecca make her own choices.

"Well, two months aren't going to make much difference in the long run, then, is it?" she said.

Rebecca lowered her forehead to meet Sundance's. "Just as long as he doesn't put it off again."

CONNER STARED at his sleeping wife. Sometimes she was simply too beautiful to touch. He'd stand in the shadows of the room and watch her sleep, and think about the way she welcomed him into her arms every night, how she'd smile and press his hand to her belly when their child moved, how good she smelled when she cuddled up to him—and he wished he could breach the barrier between them.

But something inside made him hold back, and no matter how hard he tried, he couldn't let go.

Part of it was fear. If he loved Delaney as much as he knew he could, he'd have even more to lose than the ranch, and the voice in his head told him he'd already risked enough. He'd probably fail and she'd leave him, anyway. Why up the ante? And yet, for the first time in Conner's life, happiness seemed so close. If only he could…

He must have made a noise, or perhaps Delaney sensed his presence, because she stirred and opened her eyes. "Conner? What are you doing? Aren't you coming to bed?"

He felt the familiar desire in his gut, was amazed at how badly he always wanted her. "Yeah, I'm coming," he said, and started peeling off his clothes. It was okay, he told himself. He just needed to feel her against him. He wouldn't love her. He wouldn't give any more of his heart.

IN THE LIGHT seeping around the door from the hall, Delaney watched Conner dress for work. He'd made love to her twice last night, passionately, his fervor almost all-consuming, even though she knew he had to be exhausted from the long hours he'd worked. But he wouldn't open up, wouldn't really talk to her or share himself with her, and loneliness settled over Delaney as completely as it had before he'd come to bed.

"Why don't you sleep in once in a while?" she asked. *Or tell me you'd at least like to stay with me.*

He tossed her a sexy grin while stepping into his jeans, but she could tell that his mind was already on something else, something that haunted him. "Didn't you get enough last night?" he teased.

Sex again. It was his out, his way of avoiding anything deeper. "You work too hard," she said, not knowing how to reach him.

"Everything's going well. Josh and I have managed to raise the money we need to fund the resort. We've already signed all the agreements and have had an architect draw up the plans—"

"What about me? Don't I get to see them?"

He shrugged. "Sure, if you want to."

"When will you be breaking ground?"

"By the end of the summer, if we can get our engineering done in time."

"That sounds great." She waited, hoping he'd offer more, but he didn't.

"Have you talked to your uncles lately?" she asked, reluctant to see him walk out the door because she knew she wouldn't have any time with him again until nightfall.

"Not lately."

"Do they know what you're doing?"

"Yeah." He yanked on his boots. "They don't think it'll work."

"Do you?"

"Sure," he said.

But Delaney doubted the smile he flashed at her went much below the surface. And she couldn't help wondering if his confidence reached any deeper.

"HOW'S THAT BABY?" Aunt Millie asked.

Delaney rested the phone between her shoulder and ear so she could finish tying her shoes. "Getting big. I'm feeling like a cow and waddling like a duck. Those are good signs, from what I hear."

"You can't be waddling too much. You haven't gained enough weight."

"My doctor said the bulk of the weight generally goes on between the fifth month and the end, so I should still be okay."

"You are in your fifth month."

"I know. I'm just saying there's still time."

"How's Conner treating you?"

"Very well," Delaney said, keeping up the front she'd established right from the beginning. She didn't want to start the whole town talking about their marital problems. And, in a way, she felt that she deserved whatever she got because of what she'd done to put herself in this situation.

"How's Uncle Ralph?"

"Good. You two coming for dinner on Sunday?"

Delaney thought about the weekends and how Conner worked through every one of them. "Conner might be busy," she said.

"Again?"

"He's trying to build that resort, you know."

"So?"

"That's not an easy thing to do."

"Well, you'll come, won't you? I don't like you staying out there by yourself all the time."

"I'm not by myself. Dottie's here. And I'm busy with my garden."

"Are you missing your job at the library?"

"A little."

"I talked to Dave Small on the city council. He didn't seem to think it'd be a problem for you to return once they open, now that you're married and all."

"I'm pretty settled out here with my garden and helping around the house. I don't think I'll go back until the baby gets a little older."

"I just wanted you to know it's an option."

"Thanks. Can I bring Rebecca to dinner with me?"

Aunt Millie paused, but she didn't say any of the things she would've said only months before. Rebecca had redeemed herself—partially—by doing Millie's hair for the wedding and giving her the kind of set she claimed no one else had ever been able to achieve. Now Rebecca was her regular hairdresser, and the fact that she went to Aunt Millie's place once a week to get the job done had helped soften the old woman's heart even more.

"Fine," she said at last. "Rebecca's not as bad as she used to be."

Rebecca had never been "bad." But her sweeter side was still one of the best-kept secrets in town.

"Rebecca's great," Delaney said, and smiled, thinking of the cradle her friend had painstakingly refinished for her, insisting that in her condition, Delaney couldn't be exposed to the fumes. "See you later."

WHY WASN'T CONNER HOME YET?

Delaney paced in front of the fire, feeling tension knot the muscles in her neck and shoulders. She stretched, trying to work out the kinks, and took another sip of the herbal tea she carried in one hand. But the stiffness wouldn't ease, and neither would her worry. Roy and the others had arrived at the house hours ago. When they'd left to go to the Honky Tonk at eight, they'd assured her Conner was on his way. But he'd never appeared, and she was beginning to wonder if something had happened to him. He put in long days, but he generally spent the hours after dark in his study, not outside on the range.

She wished Dottie were around to reassure her. She liked the stalwart older lady, knew she could trust her advice and her devotion to Conner. But Dottie had headed into town about the same time as the ranch hands, to stay with her son and daughter-in-law for the weekend, as she usually did. Delaney was alone. Even Rebecca wasn't answering her phone; Delaney had tried to reach her several times.

What now? she wondered, glancing nervously at the clock and cringing to see that it was nearly midnight. Should she call the police?

No. What if Conner had simply gone into town without telling her? He didn't exactly give her a detailed rundown of his activities. But she'd checked the vehicles. Those she recognized were still in the drive. Could he have caught a ride with Roy and the others and forgotten to tell her?

She hated the thought that he might have joined the hands at the Honky Tonk instead of spending time with her, hated the thought of him drinking and dancing while she paced a hole in the carpet. But that was the most likely explanation, which meant she shouldn't bother the police.

Pivoting at the end of the Navajo-style rug that covered the hardwood floor, she rubbed her arms to ward off the chill settling deep in her bones and told herself that her husband would come strolling in any second.

But he didn't. The minutes continued to tick by. Finally Delaney called Directory Assistance to get the Honky Tonk's phone number, and dialed the bar.

"'Lo?'' A gruff male voice answered. It had to be Bear, the weekend bartender. Music blared in the background, partially drowned out by raucous laughter and voices.

"Bear?"

"Yeah, who's this?"

"Delaney Armstrong. Is my husband there?"

"Haven't seen him, but hang on, let me check." He covered the receiver, but Delaney could still hear him when he shouted "Conner Armstrong here?"

"Sorry. No one answers to that name," he said after a few seconds.

"Can I talk to Roy, then?"

"Roy White?"

"Yeah."

"Just a minute."

Another music-filled pause and then Roy came on the line.

"Roy? It's Delaney."

"Something wrong?"

"I'm looking for Conner," she said. "He never came home tonight."

"He didn't?"

The surprise in Roy's voice heightened Delaney's anxiety. "I thought maybe he went to the Honky Tonk with you," she said.

"No, we left him near the south pass. He was going to check on some cattle that came up missing. But that shouldn't have taken him more than an hour."

"What do you think happened?"

"I don't know. But I'll be right there."

"Should I call the police?"

"No, I'll take a flashlight and go out and look for him. I'm sure he's fine."

The phone clicked and Roy was gone, leaving Delaney even more worried. The concern in his voice had belied his words. Conner could be hurt. He might need help....

Delaney couldn't bear to waste another second. Scribbling a quick message for Roy, she tacked it on the front door, grabbed a lightweight sweater and slipped out the back. She'd go after Conner herself.

CHAPTER TWENTY-THREE

CONNER WAS EXHAUSTED. Stamping the mud off his boots at the back door, he stepped into the house to find a light burning and his dinner waiting for him in the refrigerator.

"Thank you, Dottie," he murmured, sliding his plate into the microwave. The smell of steak, potatoes, peas and garlic bread soon filled the kitchen and made his stomach growl, but he was almost too anxious to wait for his food to heat. This time of night, Delaney would be asleep, curled up on her side, all soft and womanly with her small round belly, and he couldn't wait to slip into bed with her. Somehow, when he held her in the dark, all the worries that came with the light of day—the frustration, the anxieties, even the past—seemed to disappear....

The telephone rang just as the microwave buzzer went off. Conner grabbed the receiver to keep the noise from waking Delaney, then pressed it to his ear as he retrieved his plate. Who the heck would be calling at nearly one o'clock in the morning? he wondered.

"Hello?"

"Conner?"

"Rebecca?"

"Yeah, it's me. Thank God you're home. When did you get back?"

"Just a few minutes ago. Why?"

"You don't normally come home so late."

"I went up on the mountain to look for a few calves that

were missing. I didn't think it would be difficult to find them, but one had fallen down a gorge and it took me quite a while to get it out.''

"Delaney left five messages on my answering machine while I was out tonight. She was afraid something had happened to you."

"I'm fine."

"That's good. Tell her I'll call her in the morning, then."

"Just a minute," he said, carrying the phone as he hurried along the hall. If Delaney had been upset, had she calmed down enough to sleep? Because she certainly wasn't up and around.

The door to their bedroom stood slightly ajar. Conner pushed it open the rest of the way, hoping he'd find his wife safely asleep. But he didn't even need to turn on the light to know Delaney wasn't there. The same full moon that had been his salvation out on the range illuminated a bed still perfectly made.

"She's not here," he told Rebecca. "Where could she be?"

"What do you mean she's not there? Every message said to call her at the ranch."

Conner kept the phone to his ear but ignored everything Rebecca said as he jogged through the house, calling Delaney's name. He'd thought there might be a chance she'd become frustrated with his tardiness and gone to sleep in her old room or on a couch. But only darkness and silence greeted him.

"Where would she go if she was angry with me? Would she go back to Aunt Millie's?" he asked, but something niggled, telling him he was missing an important detail. Had all the horses been in the barn when he'd put Trigger away? He'd been so tired he hadn't even noticed. Someone, probably Roy, had already put some hay out for Trigger, and he'd simply removed the saddle and bridle and turned the horse into his stall before flipping off the light and heading wearily to the house.

"I don't think she was angry with you," Rebecca was saying. "She was worried. I'm angry with you, but that's a different story."

Conner didn't know what Rebecca was talking about, and right now, he didn't care. "Delaney?" he called again, but every room he checked was empty. He hurried to the front door to see if all the cars were still in the drive, and they were.

Just as he turned around to go and check the barn, he found a yellow piece of crumpled paper lying on the floor. Picking it up, he ironed it out to see his wife's handwriting.

Roy, I couldn't wait. I went after him myself. Don't worry. I'm a good rider, and I'll be back as soon as possible. Laney.

I went after him? Oh God! That meant at least one horse had been gone when he'd put Trigger away. His pregnant wife was out in the mountains in the middle of the night by herself. What if her horse tripped and went down? What if the animal spooked and threw her? What if she lost control? She hadn't ridden since she'd come to the ranch. She didn't know these horses.

"I think I know where she is," he said to Rebecca. "I gotta go."

"Wait! Should I come out there?"

"No, stay put. I'll call you as soon as I find her," he said and hung up.

He ran to the barn and checked the stalls. Two horses were gone.

So Roy was out there, too. Maybe he'd already found her.

THE CIRCLE OF CONNER'S FLASHLIGHT bounced as he urged his horse into a full gallop and headed for the south pass. The moon bathed the open range in mercurial silver, but the evergreen trees towering around him on this hilly section of the Running Y blocked all but the most meager natural light. Cicadas chirped a constant, rhythmic chorus, and small animals, alarmed by the beating of his horse's hooves, scurried away in the underbrush. But Conner's attention was on scanning the landscape on either side of him for his pregnant wife. Delaney was out in the dark alone. He had to find her before something happened.

Problem was, he couldn't be sure he was even looking in the right places. Delaney didn't know the ranch. Not like he did. She wouldn't have known where to search for him, which meant he didn't know where to search for her. With so many miles of raw land surrounding them, she could be anywhere.

And she could be hurt....

Conner felt sick at the thought. What if she lost the baby? Would she give up on him? Leave him?

Just last night when he made love to her, he should've told her how much she'd come to mean to him. He should have gambled it all when he had the chance. But he hadn't. He'd kept the most private part of himself from her, and now it might be too late....

"I'll have another chance," he muttered, hoping the sound of his words would convince him. But he couldn't help imagining the worst, couldn't help wondering what he would do if he lost her for good. Suddenly, all his efforts to keep her at an emotional distance seemed foolish. He couldn't stop himself from caring because he already did. He loved her. He loved her more than anything.

"Delaney?" he yelled, his words whipped away by the wind. He'd been riding for almost an hour and wasn't far now from the south pass, where he'd been looking for those calves—but he didn't know if she was aware of that. And he heard no response. "Delaney?"

He came to the campsites he and Roy had organized, and found a couple of men sleeping in a tent.

"Hey, wake up," he called, not caring who they were or whether he dragged them out of the depths of sleep.

A tall unshaven man finally stumbled to the tent door, dragging a rifle and squinting at his light. "Who is it? What do you want?"

"It's Conner Armstrong. I own this land, and I'm looking for a woman. Have you seen anyone tonight? Heard anything?"

"Haven't seen a woman, but a fella came by 'bout half an hour ago, wanting to know the same thing."

Roy. They were on the same track. Conner used his flashlight to scan the surrounding area, just in case. A creek ran alongside the campsite, gurgling over moss-covered rocks, but everything else remained silent and still.

"Thanks," he said, and started following the creek upstream. But he wasn't so sure he should be heading upstream. Maybe he should go downstream instead. Or to the north or east side of the ranch...

Delaney. He could search all night and never find her. Did she need him? Was she okay?

He rode for another two hours without seeing anything other than a few deer, so exhausted he could hardly remain in his saddle. He was about to head back to the house to see if Roy had found her and planned to gather a search party if not, when someone finally answered his call.

"Delaney?" he cried again, adrenaline chasing away his fatigue.

Nothing.

"Delaney?"

Finally he heard his name. Kicking his horse into a trot, he followed the sound. It led him farther up the mountain, where the forest grew denser and rocks, foliage, fallen limbs and rotting logs made progress difficult. He recognized the voice that answered him. But it wasn't Delaney. It was Roy, and it wasn't difficult to tell that something was terribly wrong.

CONNER'S CHEST constricted until he could scarcely breathe when he saw his wife lying on the ground. Roy was kneeling over her, but he got to his feet when he heard Conner's horse burst through the trees.

"What's wrong with her?" Conner demanded, his voice sounding oddly strangled to his own ears.

"She's having cramps," Roy told him. "Probably from all the riding. Or maybe she's just too tired or cold or...I don't know." He shrugged helplessly.

"Dammit!" Conner cried. "What did she think she was doing coming all the way out here?" Pulling on Trigger's reins, he jumped down before the horse had even stopped moving. "She could've died. She could've lost the baby."

Conner knew she could still lose the baby, but he wasn't willing to face that.

"Conner?" Delaney's eyelids fluttered open when he bent and touched her cheek. "Conner, are you okay?"

God, she was worried about *him?* "I'm okay, babe," he said gently. "Tell me what's going on with these cramps."

She rubbed the lower part of her abdomen. "It's probably nothing. Anyway, they're getting better," she said, but her smile faltered when their eyes met, telling him she was being more optimistic than the situation warranted.

"We've got to get her out of here," he told Roy. "Go get the wagon and bring it as far as you can. I'll get her out of the trees and meet you by the road that leads to the campsites.''

His foreman quickly mounted his own horse and trotted off without a word.

"And hurry,'' Conner called after him.

"I thought maybe you'd been hurt,'' Delaney said when the beating of Roy's horse's hooves died out. "I couldn't stand waiting—''

He pressed a quick kiss to her temple. "Shh, it's okay. I was only saving a stranded calf. I'm fine, and you're going to be fine real soon.''

Please make it true, he prayed, wishing Roy Godspeed. He couldn't bear the thought of losing Delaney or their baby. He wanted to get her to a doctor as soon as possible.

"I didn't mean for anything like this to happen,'' she said, trying to get up.

Conner pressed her back down. "Just rest.''

She relaxed but clung to his arm. "I'm an excellent rider. The horse wasn't the problem. It was just that the baby didn't like the rough ride and I...I couldn't turn back without you.''

"You should never have come,'' he said. He knew his words sounded too gruff, but he couldn't staunch the deep emotion that turned them so harsh.

She glanced away from him. "I'm sorry for all the trouble.''

She'd just risked the child she wanted more than anything in the world—for him—and she didn't know he loved her. She didn't know because he'd never told her. Maybe he hadn't even realized how much a part of him she'd become until this moment. "Laney, it's not the trouble you've caused that upsets me,'' he said. "You could have destroyed my whole world tonight, you know that?''

Confusion flickered on her face. "But you've never been

happy about the baby. You've never wanted it—or me. Not really. I hate that I trapped you into all of this. I was crazy to think you'd eventually love me—''

"Laney, don't talk like that."

"It's true. You've never said anything more meaningful to me than, 'You're beautiful,' or 'I love to touch you,' or 'You make me crazy.' You—''

"I'm saying it now," he said, feeling more vulnerable than ever before in his life. He was frightened of his own revelation, frightened that he could love someone so much, frightened that she'd now realize how much power she held over him.

But somehow *he* didn't matter as much to him as she did. "I love you, Laney. I was stupid not to tell you before." He kissed her forehead, her cheeks, each eyelid. "Nothing means more to me than you do."

Tears filled her eyes. "Does that mean you forgive me?"

"For what? For coming out here?"

"For Boise."

"Are you kidding? There's nothing to forgive. You've made me the happiest man on earth."

She shook her head. "No, I don't deserve your love, Conner, not after what I did."

"I don't deserve you, either, Laney," he said. "And that's the truth. But we're together, and we're going to stay together, okay?" He smiled down at her. "I'm just glad," he whispered, "that mercy is as much a part of the world as justice."

"YOU'RE *WHERE?*" Rebecca asked.

Delaney propped up the phone and snuggled closer to Conner, even though it was nearly three o'clock in the afternoon.

"In bed," she said.

"With your workaholic husband?"

"Last I checked, it wasn't the telephone man."

"How are you feeling? Has the cramping gone away?"

Conner had called Rebecca last night when they'd finally reached the ranch to tell her Dr. Hatcher was meeting them at his office, and she'd shown up there, too.

"Yeah, the muscle relaxants he gave me are doing the job. The baby and I are going to be fine."

"You're sure?"

Delaney had donned Conner's T-shirt a few minutes earlier to go to the kitchen and bring them both some orange juice, but his hand had already found its way beneath the fabric to caress her belly. "Better than I've ever been."

"You sound good. Now you know why I'm mad at Buddy for postponing our wedding."

"Is it still going to happen in August?"

"Yeah."

"Then, it'll happen soon enough. Sure you don't want to wait until after the baby's born?"

"I'll come back."

"Okay."

"Delaney?"

"Yeah?"

"You can tell Conner I'm not mad at him anymore."

"I'll pass on the good news," Delaney said. Then Conner kissed her, and she couldn't remember later if she'd even said goodbye before she hung up the phone.

CONNER HAD A DIFFICULT TIME keeping his attention on his dinner. "Say it now," he said, nudging Isaiah under the table with his knee.

Isaiah looked up at Delaney, who was busy frosting the cake she'd made them for dessert. "Laney, did you remember to feed the bunny today?"

"The what?" she said, sounding preoccupied.

"The bunny."

She stopped with the frosting. "What bunny?"

"Haven't you seen it?"

Delaney frowned. "I don't know what you're talking about."

"It's back here." Isaiah jerked his head toward the door. "Come see."

Delaney sent Conner a curious glance, but he shrugged as though he didn't know what was going on, and Dottie and the others did the same.

"What's this all about?" she asked. Her face showing a trace of suspicion, she followed Isaiah into the backyard, and Conner slipped out behind her so he wouldn't miss her reaction.

"Oh, my gosh!" she said at her first sight of the fluffy white bunny nibbling a carrot inside the cage that now stood next to the chicken coop. "This is the cutest bunny I've ever seen."

"It's for you," Isaiah said. "It's a late wedding present."

Roy, Grady, Ben and Dottie crowded behind Conner on the back stoop as they all watched Delaney unlatch the door, scoop the little bunny into her hands and rub its soft fur against her cheek. "Isaiah, it's just what I wanted. How did you know?"

He grinned. "I didn't. It's from Conner. He wouldn't even let me help him build the cage."

Delaney turned and gave Conner a brilliant smile, and he felt his heart melt. She did that to him, unexpectedly. Sometimes he'd look at her, and his spirit would just soar. She was so beautiful, so pregnant, so...*his*.

"I love you, Conner Armstrong," she said, loudly enough for everyone to hear.

Conner crossed the lawn, put an arm around her and, even with Grady, Ben, Isaiah, Dottie and Roy looking on, lifted her chin with one finger. "I love you, too," he said, and gave her a kiss.

"Now beat it," he growled to the others, who had started to clap.

EPILOGUE

CONNER SAT ON HIS HORSE, partway up the mountain, and watched the tractors in the valley below start to grade and level the dirt where the lodge would soon stand. He could hardly believe it was happening. The ground-breaking was a little later than he'd scheduled—he'd run into problems with the engineering of the golf course—but construction was now under way, and if everything went according to plan, they'd have their grand opening in May of the following year.

He thought about Stephen, Dwight and Jonathan, and grinned. They'd been so skeptical at first, so sure he'd never get this far. They pretended not to care that he was even trying, but he heard bits and pieces of what they said through his mother, and he knew it was driving them crazy that he'd figured out a way to save the ranch. Not only to save it but to make it pay off with such potentially high returns.

Or maybe it wasn't the money that bothered them. They had plenty of money. Maybe it was the words of praise his grandfather lavished on his efforts. Either way, Conner didn't really care. Somehow his uncles and even his past seemed like such a small part of his life now. He had other things to think about, bigger things, like his wife, his baby, his dreams.

He heard the QuadRunner he'd bought for Delaney—to keep her off a horse until after she had the baby—and turned to see his wife slowly driving up the hill. She was coming to join him for the big moment. It was something they wanted to share.

"Don't tell me they've already started," she said, her voice tinged with disappointment as she cut the engine.

Conner got down from his horse and held out a hand to help her off the squat, four-wheeled motorcycle, admiring the healthy glow the dawn light lent her skin and the bright smile that never failed to reach inside him and tell him the world was good.

"They just started a few minutes ago," he said.

"So I missed it?"

"You haven't missed anything. Come see."

He took her hand and led her to a better vantage point and together they watched the machinery and men below.

"It's going to be great, isn't it," she said.

Conner shifted to stand behind her, slipped his arms around her and locked his hands beneath the bulge of her belly so she could lean against him. "It's going to be better than great."

"Your mother called. She caught me just as I was leaving the house. She wanted to congratulate us on the big day."

His mother. She'd been so happy since he'd turned his life around. "Grandpa mentioned she was seeing someone, when I talked to him on the phone last night. Did she say anything about it?"

Delaney shook her head. "She told me about a trip she's taking to the Coast, and I doubt she's going alone, but she didn't say anything about who might be going with her."

"I guess she'll tell us about him when she's ready. Grandpa really likes him, so I'm sure he's a good guy."

"She deserves to find love."

"Now that she feels I'm on the right course, maybe she will."

They stood in silence for several minutes as Conner thought about his mother marrying and living a fuller life. Then he imagined the land before him in its finished state, the lodge filled with vacationers, the golf course buzzing with white golf carts. It was going to be so perfect—

"Conner?" Delaney said, breaking into his daydream.

"Hmm?"

"What if all this doesn't work out? What if, in five years, we lose everything?"

"Then, we start over someplace else," he said.

"You're sure? You won't take it too hard? It's just land and buildings and money, you know. Those aren't the things we need to be happy."

He nuzzled her ear. "I know, babe. Don't worry. I can never lose everything as long as I've got you." He kissed her, only to be interrupted by Roy and Josh.

"We come all the way out here to enjoy the ground-breaking, and what do we find? The two of you necking like a couple of teenagers." Roy clicked his tongue and shook his head, but even in the shadow of their hats, Delaney had no trouble making out their smiles.

*   *   *   *   *

Watch for Rebecca's story in
A Husband of Her Own,
coming in 2003.

This is the family reunion you've been waiting for!

TRUEBLOOD
Christmas

JASMINE CRESSWELL
TARA TAYLOR QUINN
& KATE HOFFMANN

deliver three brand new Trueblood, Texas stories.

After many years, Major Brad Henderson is released from prison, exonerated after almost thirty years for a crime he didn't commit. His mission: to be reunited with his three daughters. How to find them? Contact Dylan Garrett of the Finders Keepers Detective Agency!

Look for it in November 2002.

HARLEQUIN®
Makes any time special ®

A
BETTY
NEELS
Christmas

What better way to celebrate the joyous
holiday season than with this special
anthology that celebrates the talent of
beloved author Betty Neels? Bringing to
readers two of Betty's trademark
tender romances, this volume will
make the perfect gift for
all romance readers.

*Available in October 2002
wherever paperbacks are sold.*

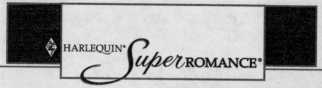

International bestselling author

SANDRA MARTON

invites you to attend the

WEDDING *of the* YEAR

Glitz and glamour prevail in this volume
containing a trio of stories in which
three couples meet at a
high society wedding—and
soon find themselves
walking down the aisle!

Look for it in November 2002.

HARLEQUIN®
Makes any time special®

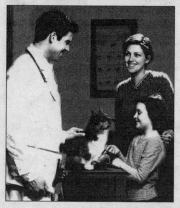

Princes...Princesses...
London Castles...New York Mansions...
To live the life of a royal!

In 2002, Harlequin Books lets you escape to a world of royalty with these royally themed titles:

Celebrate a year of royalty with Harlequin Books!

Available at your favorite retail outlet.

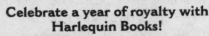

HARLEQUIN®
Makes any time special®

Visit us at www.eHarlequin.com

HSROY02